Praise for *The Girl from the Garden*

"This elegant debut focuses on a family of wealthy Iranian Jews and the inheritance crisis that nearly tears them apart. Told from the viewpoint of the daughter, who's left her homeland to live in Los Angeles, it's a riveting portrait of family strife in a troubled land—and the fallout when a woman's fertility determines her worth."
                                                                —*People*

"[A] powerful and moving debut. . . . In short, this is a riveting, finely wrought novel by an author who joins the ranks of other young cross-cultural writers who tell their stories through the lens of gender. In that tradition, it will not be easily forgotten."
                                                —*New York Journal of Books*

"Coolly lush. . . . The slender book is brimful of sensual detail: of food; of flowers; of an Iranian garden's honeysuckle scent; of fascinating, intricate ritual. . . . It's a rich portrait of a society in which men held the power and fertility was destiny. . . . Ultimately, *The Girl from the Garden* is about how telling stories helps us to hold our past in our hands—and about how a flowering yard 'teeming with life' in far-off Los Angeles can movingly become, for one wandering storyteller, a home."
                                                                —*Seattle Times*

"In this stunning first novel, Foroutan draws on her own family history to integrate the lore and traditions of old Iran. Suspenseful and haunting, this riveting story of jealousy, sacrifice, and betrayal and the intimately drawn characters within will not be easily forgotten."
                                        —*Booklist* (starred review)

"Foroutan's lyrical debut offers a mosaic of stories evoking life within a wealthy Jewish home in Kermanshah, Iran. . . . Deftly structured, this novel traces those complications to their core, exposing the pain, oppressive forces, and difficult allegiances within and without the estate, while lending grace through the delicacy of its observation. . . . There's little joy to be found in this tale of a doomed family, flavored with myth and fairy tale, yet the poetic narration overlays the suffering with surprising beauty." —*Kirkus Reviews* (starred review)

"Parnaz Foroutan's scorching debut novel, *The Girl from the Garden,* takes us to Iran, where a couple's inability to conceive pits a young wife against her tyrannical husband, who will stop at nothing to secure an heir." —W Magazine (online)

"What's gripping in *The Girl from the Garden* are the layers of menace in these women's lives. They are at the mercy of their husbands and of an Islamic country growing increasingly hostile. Foroutan's characters grapple, often vainly, for control against larger forces—a God who doesn't answer prayers, a state that doesn't recognize their humanity, and people who cannot be made to bend to their needs, no matter how badly they love them." —*St. Louis Post-Dispatch*

"Inspired by her own family history, Foroutan's fluid narrative successfully paints an immersive tale of the inner strength of women living in a time and within a culture when their personal thoughts and opinions were unwelcomed by men and meant to be kept to themselves." —*Library Journal*

"Spellbinding. . . . Readers will not easily forget Mahboubeh, this motherless child whom Foroutan describes poetically as a woman forced to live her entire life with 'a palpable sensation . . . the presence of an absence.' Nor will they forget Foroutan's perceptive prose that is laced with a pained aliveness that cuts deep and penetrates." —*Jerusalem Post*

"Eden is rife with thorns in Parnaz Foroutan's *The Girl from the Garden*, a lush debut novel about the pangs and triumphs of an Iranian family. Foroutan is a modern-day Scheherazade, weaving her tale through the entire 20th century, from an aging woman in her L.A. garden to the brothers whose determination to spawn heirs tortured the harem she was raised in."

—*Willamette Week*

"Drawing on her own family history, in *The Girl from the Garden,* debut novelist Parnaz Foroutan offers an evocative portrait of Iranian Jewish culture, and the experience of being a woman who felt that both her family, and her body—which dictated her worth—had betrayed her." —Bustle

"Despite their suffering, Foroutan's characters experience moments of beauty, too—a lovely girl gathering apples in a fountain, a pomegranate tree in California grown from a cutting taken from the family courtyard in Iran on the eve of the revolution. Filled with lingering sorrow, broken hearts and cold revenge, this walk down a sometimes-darkened memory lane is not for those seeking a light-hearted read, but fans of well-paced dramas will find much to adore." —Shelf Awareness

"Though the reader gets a taste of what the Iranian Jewish community was like, this is really a novel about the culture of women, from the ritual baths and other religious traditions to the gardens and distinctly gendered spaces of the home. The novel mimics cinematic techniques in which one scene dissolves into another, shifting seamlessly across decades and continents. We never learn Mahboubeh's own story, but the sense of a personality forged by the sacrifice, betrayal and restrictions of the women who came before her will remain with the reader long after the book is over." —*BookPage*

"A powerful and moving novel about the devastating choices women face when their worth is tied to their wombs but not themselves. Parnaz Foroutan takes the timeless themes of love, honor, sacrifice, and betrayal and makes them new."

—Gloria Steinem

"*The Girl from the Garden* is a spectacular novel—a riveting, finely wrought portrait of loss, longing, and passion in the intimate lives of an extended family in Iran. Foroutan is a writer of astounding talent, and her tale is moving and unforgettable."

—Carolina De Robertis, author of *The Invisible Mountain*

"Set against the tumultuous backdrop of early twentieth-century Iran, *The Girl from the Garden* is an evocative tale of loss, betrayal and family ties. Parnaz Foroutan is a stunning new literary talent, and her debut novel is a gift to readers everywhere."

—Amy Greene, author of *Bloodroot*

"In her debut novel, Parnaz Foroutan has written an incantatory tale of love, sacrifice, and an unquenchable yearning for paradise. By threading together the silvered remembrances of an elderly woman among stories of a family, generations past, in the Iranian town of Kermanshah, Foroutan unfurls a sensuous, poetic tapestry of gardens and seasons, of women enshrouded and silenced by culture, of men made intractable by honor, religious tradition, and filial loyalty."

—Melissa Pritchard, author of *Palmerino* and *A Solemn Pleasure*

"Some novels open the door to historical worlds you've never seen before, worlds that contain unforgivable cruelty and spectacular grace. Parnaz Foroutan's *The Girl from the Garden* is just such a novel, a powerful story about the contorted lives of women in an ancient patriarchy, radiantly told."

—Robert Eversz, author of *Zero to the Bone*

The

Girl

from the

Garden

The
Girl
from the
Garden

Parnaz Foroutan

ecco
An Imprint of HarperCollinsPublishers

THE GIRL FROM THE GARDEN. Copyright © 2015 by Parnaz Foroutan. All rights reserved. Printed in the United States of America. No part of this book may be used or reproduced in any manner whatsoever without written permission except in the case of brief quotations embodied in critical articles and reviews. For information address HarperCollins Publishers, 195 Broadway, New York, NY 10007.

HarperCollins books may be purchased for educational, business, or sales promotional use. For information please e-mail the Special Markets Department at SPsales@harpercollins.com.

A hardcover edition of this book was published in 2015 by Ecco, an imprint of HarperCollins Publishers.

FIRST ECCO PAPERBACK EDITION PUBLISHED 2016.

Designed by Suet Yee Chong

Library of Congress Cataloging-in-Publication Data has been applied for.

ISBN 978-0-06-238839-1

16 17 18 19 20   OV/RRD   10 9 8 7 6 5 4 3 2 1

For Mahboubeh,
and for my daughters

The

Girl

from the

Garden

Prologue

⚜

There are two stories as to how our family arrived in Kermanshah from Tehran. The first story is this, that once upon a time, your great-great-great-grand-father worked in the royal court of Fat'h Ali Shah as an expert goldsmith. The Qajar king was so pleased with this Jewish goldsmith's re-creation of His Highness's own radiant countenance on a gold coin, that he granted the goldsmith permission to create the coin currency of his kingdom. And so, night and day, if you were to walk through the *tang'e tarik* alleyways of the *mahalleh* and pass the goldsmith's shop, you'd hear the *chinkchinkchink* of his industrious hammer, and if you were to peer through the crack of the door, you'd see his back bent in the dim light, pounding out the details of His Majesty's face, coin after coin after coin.

Now it just happened that this Jewish man had a most beautiful young daughter. Hair like a field of golden wheat. Eyes deep blue. His Highness, Fat'h Ali Shah, earned a certain notoriety for his collection of beautiful young girls. Indeed, the official count of the Royal Harem numbered 158 wives, from the Afshar lineage of princesses to the Zand, all of whom had certain unique traits that made them worthy of the king's interest. Despite the richness of his stock, Fat'h Ali Shah employed his most trusted eunuchs to continue scouring the cities and villages in search of his next *sogoli*. And it must have happened this way, that one of these eunuchs, in the sullen blue of the evening, passed the goldsmith's shop and saw in the golden glow of the lantern not only the man bent over his toil, but also a most exquisite young Jewess, her hair capturing the warm light, her skin the translucent pink of Darya-e Noor. And the eunuch hurried off back to the palace to report to The Crown, who listened, mesmerized by the descriptions of the child, and he raised his arm from the bejeweled rest of the Peacock Throne and with a subtle motion of his ruby laden fingers, ordered the eunuch to procure the girl at once.

When news of the Shah's intentions reached the ears of the goldsmith, he put down his hammer and looked up from his work to see the eunuch's face waiting expectantly behind the pile of coins. For a young girl to become a wife of the king, such honor bestowed upon a Jew, no less, and the financial and personal gain it allowed the family. . . . The eunuch smiled and nodded at what he thought was gratitude brimming over in the old man's eyes. The goldsmith mumbled that the king's wish was his command and with that, the eunuch turned and left.

That night, the goldsmith gathered all his possessions, his pots and pans, his clothes and blankets, his tools, his kettle, his rugs, his goat and rooster, and he loaded up his sad, old donkey with many bulging burlap bags and when the night watchman's snores sounded through the silent sleeping streets, he slowly opened the door of his home and shooed out his wife, his sons and his beautiful daughter, the goat and burden-laden donkey, into the alley and began walking with great haste in the direction of Baghdad. They walked all the way to the city of Kermanshah and when the old man felt he was far enough from the Qajar Court, he laid down his load and built a new home in the Jewish mahalleh of that city.

That is the official story of why your great-great-great-grandfather left Tehran for Kermanshah. The second story is this, that the Jewish goldsmith was appointed coin-maker for the king, and that he made coin after coin after coin. Then, in the still of one night, without taking official leave from the king's court, he left Tehran with many bulging burlap bags and arrived in Kermanshah a very, very rich man.

One

⚜

In the outskirts of Los Angeles, in the
sprawl of suburban homes that sit in the
lap of dry, gold hills, there is a garden.
In the warmth of late summer evenings, the per-
fumes of honeysuckles and jasmines in this garden are maddening. Earthen pots of cosmos and
geraniums surround the yard. Near the back wall
grows a pomegranate tree. A fig tree fruits in the
late summer, the grape arbor hides her clusters
in among the leaves, the boughs of the apple tree
nearly touch the soil in autumn, and the orange
tree, soaking beneath the Southern California sun,
provides year-round. Mint vines creep to cover

the grounds, and nasturtiums explode in blossom. This garden belongs to an elderly woman. Her name is Mahboubeh Malacouti. Her first name means "the most beloved." Her last name means "of the heavenly."

Mahboubeh tends to the trees and flowers of her garden, dirt in the creases of her hand. She pats the trunks of her trees, and speaks to them softly. "This you must learn," she says to them, "that the word *paradise* is a Farsi word. It means 'the space within enclosed walls, a cultivated place set apart from the vast wilderness.'" She talks to her roses, holds up a thorned stem and says, "First, I grate the end of your stalk." She rubs a small knife against the stem. "Then bind you to the stalk of another rose." She wraps string about the two sticks and pushes them into the soil of a small pot. She waters the bare sticks, and waits silently for the water to be absorbed. Then, after a long while, she says, "You will take root, and once you have roots, you can grow in the soil of any garden." Her garden brims with blooming roses, yellow, pink, loose-leafed, petals in candy-stripe of red and white, pungent and scentless, long stemmed and short bushes. Each year she grafts more and more, searching for a rose with the color and the perfume of the one she remembers from another garden.

Mahboubeh carries with her stories. They pour out of her and fill the spaces she inhabits, like so many hungry ghosts, begging to exist. Sometimes she forgets the parameters of that space, the dictations of time, and she slips into the past of her stories. The urgent horn of a car in the street outside her home sounds, and in her mind, Mahboubeh hurries through the crowded streets of Tehran a young woman again, with her books clutched against her chest, her heels *click clicking* against the sidewalk, her eyes focused on the end of the block, the turn that follows, to the gate of Danesh Saraye Alee. She greets the schoolmaster who waits outside to ensure the safe passage of his charges. She enters the school, walks up the stairs, against the marble of the hallway to the classroom, with its scent of chalk, its wooden desks, the chatter of girls, laughing and talking. An instructor walks in and the girls rise immediately and, in unison, greet him, *salaam Agha Mohebi,* and he responds *Be seated, class,* before he picks up the chalk and begins writing on the board. Mahboubeh copies furiously in her notebook, page after page, and at the end of the year, again, and again, and again, she is recognized as the best, the brightest among the students. The schoolmaster announces her name, and she hears applause until a neighbor shouts in English, "I'm coming, give me a minute." Then, Mahboubeh looks about her as though she is waking from a dream.

She remembers the garden from her childhood. A tall brick wall separated it from the streets of the Jewish mahalleh in Kermanshah. Within those walls, the garden grew secretive and lush, teeming with flowers and fruiting trees. It encircled the family estate, and in the middle of those buildings sat a courtyard, surrounded on all four sides by the family home. A large fountain gurgled in the middle of that courtyard.

There is a photograph of Mahboubeh standing before that fountain as a young woman, already married, returning to visit Rakhel on the day the family estate in Kermanshah is sold. The remaining members, Yousseff's widow and all her children, will move to Tehran, trailing an old, embittered Rakhel behind them, who cursed and damned fate and G-d and every member of the family on the whole of the journey there, and for the rest of her days, which she spent in the attic of the new mansion on Shah Reza Street, yelling from an open window so that all those passing below could hear how she was cheated out of her fortune.

On that last visit, Mahboubeh asked Rakhel again, "How did my mother die?"

And the old woman sat there, quietly, pensively, reflecting. Then she looked up at Mahboubeh and answered, "I've told you a thousand times, a thousand times. *Degh marg shod.* She died from sorrow."

That usually ended the conversation between them, but Mahboubeh knew that this might be the last chance she'd have at getting an answer from Rakhel and so she summoned her courage, looked the old woman in the eyes, and asked, "What sorrow?"

"*Degh. Degh.* The kind that chokes you. That one that clenches at your throat. *Degh,*" Rakhel said, holding her own throat with a bony hand. "All that anger and all that grief welling up inside you, and no voice to scream it out beneath the sky, so that you have to swallow it. Until it turns into a poison inside and eats your heart."

"What was the source of sorrow?" Mahboubeh asked.

"What do I know? Why do you ask me?"

"Because you were there."

Rakhel looked out of the window, at the gardens. It was late summer. The leaves were green, dusty. The air carried the chill of an impending autumn.

"I was there," she said.

"And you saw."

"Yes. I saw," Rakhel said. She looked at Mahboubeh for a moment, nodding her head. Then she turned to look out of the window again and said, "Do you think I could have done anything? I had as much choice as she. I swallowed my share of grief, too. But she was frailer than me."

"What did you see? Tell me what you saw."

"Leave me be," Rakhel said. "Here I am, my own home sold from underneath me, with nothing more than this head scarf on my head to call my own, with that thief selling whatever she can get her hands on, selling the wealth I built, and me, a beggar now when I was once a queen. . . . And you come here with your questions to steal the last bit of peace left me?"

Mahboubeh got up, quietly, and looked at the old woman glaring at her. "I'm leaving," she said.

"Go. To hell with the rest of them. Go and don't ever come to see me!"

Mahboubeh did see Rakhel again, in Tehran, but always in a crowd of relatives and family, which didn't afford an opportunity for them to speak privately. When Rakhel became too old to attend the gatherings, Mahboubeh would see her peering out of the attic window, from behind the curtains, each time she rang the doorbell of the house on Shah Reza Street. Sometimes Rakhel only looked down at her, then withdrew into the dark room. Other times, she leaned out of the open window and yelled obscenities. But by then, everyone in the neighborhood knew of the old woman in that attic, and they either chuckled or quickened their pace when passing. When Rakhel died, she did so with a single breath. The doctor emerged from the room and said, "She was just a shell. So old. Nothing left in her, but that last breath."

That was the summer of 1977, before the students took to the streets. By 1978, nothing remained for Mahboubeh in Tehran. Everyone she knew was either dead, or leaving. So Mahboubeh packed her one suitcase, lined her coat with money, and hid her jewels in jars of powders and creams. And she remembers thinking, as that airplane lifted her away, that she had finally escaped history.

Mahboubeh walks into the kitchen from her garden to search in the album on her table for that photograph of herself standing in the courtyard of the old family estate. She remembers preparing for that day. She painted her mouth red and wore a tailored black dress with black heels that strapped around her stockinged ankles. She cannot remember who took the picture, but she remembers turning afterward to look behind her, to where the fountain glistened beneath the noon sun. And behind that fountain to where

Uncle Asher's home stood, stately and tall. And somewhere, in one of the many rooms of that home, she knew that Ra-khel sat waiting.

Instead of the photograph, Mahboubeh finds a picture she clipped from the pages of a travel magazine some years ago. It is of a hammam designated for Jewish women in Kermanshah. A large, empty room, save for a single at-tendant, an old woman in a dark floral print chador stand-ing beside the pipe that must have fed the baths with hot water. Mahboubeh stares at this image for a long while. She remembers the proprietor of that hammam, waiting beside the door.

She sits at her table, holding the picture and remem-bering, and somewhere in the incremental spaces between the shifting of the morning shadows, Mahboubeh imagines Rakhel as a girl of fifteen, perhaps half a century before the time this photograph must have been taken, looking up to the ceiling of that same hammam, where a mosaic of mirrors reflects fragments of the bodies in the room below. Buttocks and thighs on the green tile work, legs stretched out over the edges of the large central pool, arms raised overhead, straight backs and curved backs and large hips, slender hips and sagging breasts, and breasts like apples, and flat girl chests, the wild hair below navels, stomachs round and protruding and flat and ribs beneath the skin.

The old attendant scrubs Rakhel's shoulders with a coarse mitt, moving her body violently back and forth. Ash-colored flakes of dead skin fall from her arms onto the marble floor. Rakhel's sister-in-law Khorsheed sits naked beside her and worries over the skin of her heel with a pumice stone. Her black abundant hair covers her shoulders and breasts, and her thighs and the plump flesh of her arms shake and jiggle with each move. She stops, turns to Rakhel and says, "I don't want my feet to become like yours, Dada. Rough-skinned like some shoeless peasant's." Khorsheed nudges Rakhel with her elbow to get her attention. "See how dainty and white they are? Soft, too, like I've walked on rugs of silk my whole life." She holds up her foot beneath Rakhel's nose and wriggles her toes. Rakhel pushes her foot away. Their mother-in-law, Zolekhah, looks up at them in warning, then continues to apply indigo and henna to turn her own white hair a raven black.

The steam rises and rolls thick into the air and carries the scents of rosewater and soap. Suddenly, the door bursts open, pushed by a crowd of women that fills the room. The women throw their heads back and their tongues rapidly hit the roofs of their mouths. The sound *klilililili* rings through the vaults of the large room, crashes against the stone and tiled walls, echoes in the corridors announcing the arrival of a soon-to-be bride. Servants balance on top of their heads wide silver trays laden with fruits and sweetmeats, they carry rugs and pillows as they walk through the hammam to the dressing room to arrange for the feast that follows the ceremonial bath. The eldest hammam attendant begins clapping a rhythm. She walks around the room, motioning with exaggerated gesture for the women to join her, until all the women in the hammam are clapping to her beat. She stands in the middle of the room and sings, "Lips press lips . . . "

"Lips press lips," the women chorus.

"Navel presses navel . . ."

"Navel presses navel."

"An aleph straightens into *qaf's* round ladle."

"Vah, vah, Khadijeh Khanum! Where did you hear that one?" An elderly woman says and the rest of the women laugh.

"Here's one more polite for your taste," she says. "Dum dum dadee dum dum . . . " The attendant waggles her head, snaps her fingers and moves her large hips to the rhythm of the women's clapping.

Rakhel turns to watch the young bride, still standing hesitantly in the doorway. Her breasts are tiny swollen buds, her nipples small and pink, her straight body without hips, yet, the beginning of soft brown hair between her legs. The girl blushes and holds back until the mother of her betrothed finally takes hold of her shoulders and pushes her forward into the room. The bride's own mother walks closely behind her and burns seeds of wild rue in a small plate, the smoke to ward off glances of envy.

Amidst the singing and the blessings, the family of the young bride and groom take her to a far corner of the hammam and sit her on a chair. They close in around her, part slightly to allow in Naneh Adeh, the old midwife, and a sudden hush falls upon the room. The older woman approaches the young bride, kneels before her, takes her face, looks her in the eyes and asks if she has known a man. The young girl shakes her head frantically, her eyes wide and round. The woman places her wrinkled hands on the girl's thighs, pulls them open, holds the outer folds of her vagina with the dry fingers of one hand and explores the hidden folds with the fingers of the other. All the women hold their breath and wait. No one moves. The silence is suddenly broken by the old woman's confirmation that the girl is untouched. The singing and dancing resume and they lead the girl to another corner of the room to remove the down of her arms and legs and to pluck and shape her eyebrows.

Rakhel turns to see her mother-in-law studying her back, her forehead wrinkled with concern. "Rakhel, is Asher happy with you?" Zolekhah asks.

Khorsheed turns quickly to glance at Rakhel, who meets her look with alarm, then drops her gaze to the floor.

"Does he send you to the *miqveh* each month?"

"Dada went to the miqveh earlier this week, Naneh Zolekhah," Khorsheed says.

"I am speaking with Rakhel, child. Rakhel, does my son have frequent husband–wife relations with you?"

"Yes."

"Khorsheed has been with my Ibrahim for less than a year and she is already pregnant."

Rakhel is silent. In the hollowness of the hammam's vaults, she hears the accusation amplified and feels a hundred eyes on her skin. Her body feels cold. The attendant pauses a moment in her task, still holding Rakhel's arm, and squeezes the girl's hand in reassurance.

"Perhaps Rakhel Khanum is not eating well enough," the attendant suggests.

"She eats well," Zolekhah responds.

"Does she eat enough red meat?" asks a woman from across the hammam.

"She eats well."

"Have you tried camel rennet?" asks another woman.

"It only works if she doesn't know she's taking it."

"My cousin went to Mashhad and walked beneath the city gates past the stone lion. She bore a son nine months following."

"Did it look like the lion?"

"Efat's eldest daughter, too."

"That was the Pearl Cannon in Tehran she walked beneath."

"No, it was the stone lion at the gate of Mashhad, everyone knows . . ."

"She's too thin, she needs girth. Put sheep fat in her meals."

"Do you get up too quickly after he is done?" another woman chimes in.

"No." Rakhel's voice barely a whisper, she shakes her head no, no, no. She keeps her eyes on the floor, studies the dark green veins of the marble as the women shout all around her.

"Don't rise after he is done."

"No, stay very still . . ."

"For an hour."

"For more than an hour."

"Stay on your back and raise your hips to the ceiling."

"Yes, that's the way to do it, but move your hips back and forth."

"Like this!"

Rakhel does not look up.

The women laugh, clapping a rhythm to match the woman's undulations. "Yes, yes!" They laugh and clap. "Shake it just like that."

An old woman's voice breaks in, grave and steady. "Daughter, you should never run or jump, or make any sudden moves of any sort." The room is silent once more.

"Yes," the crackling voice of another old woman chimes in. "You must remain calm, always remain calm. Never raise your voice. Never disagree too wholeheartedly, swallow your anger quietly."

"A peaceful woman makes for a peaceful womb."

"And he will love you more the less you speak!"

Laughter again. Laughter rings through the vaults, ripples the humid air, waves of it break against Rakhel's body. Her eyes burn with tears. She keeps her gaze to the floor.

That night, Rakhel presses Asher to herself more frantically, wraps her legs tighter against his waist, raises her back off of the bed cloth, pushes her hips against him, pulls him into herself. The muscles inside her hold him as she heaves and pants in her effort to take him in. She grunts, her body damp with sweat as her fingers clutch at his back and her fists pound against his shoulders. And he holds her arms down and says *be still* as she struggles. *Be still,* he commands, and she feels the spasms of his body, the slap of his thighs against her flesh. When his breathing evens and she hears the soft, regular snore start in his throat, she turns onto her back, raises her hips and gently sways from side to side, weeping.

The gate in a neighboring yard slams. For a moment, Mahboubeh can't place the sound. She looks down at her hands, resting on the lace tablecloth. She can see the blue of her veins. And her fingers, knobbed like the limbs of an old walnut tree. She holds her hands up to the light, then drops them to her lap and looks through the open window. Her garden. Los Angeles. Perhaps noon, a weekday. Photographs from her album lie strewn across the table. She picks them up, one by one, and wonders how they fell from their pages.

She finds among them a photograph of herself as a young woman, standing beside her father, Ibrahim. Her hand, fine fingers, smooth skin, rests on his shoulder. Her brother Yousseff also sits beside their father, and Yousseff's young wife stands beside him. Yousseff's children crowd behind them. They move too much. The photographer peaks his head out from the black cloth and tells them that they will blur in the image. Yousseff's youngest boy sticks out his tongue.

"Your face will remain like that, like an ape, forever,"

Mahboubeh says. Yousseff smiles, but their father Ibrahim's face remains unchanged.

Mahboubeh grew up an orphan in that home in Kermanshah, despite Ibrahim's presence, who spent his days reading poetry, lost in thought. As a child, whenever she asked him what became of her mother, he'd respond with silence, or else he'd say, "She died from the complications of womanhood."

Ibrahim's gaze seems distant in the photograph, and Mahboubeh feels a sharp pain in her breast. She hurriedly places the picture back in the album before a distinct memory from her lonely childhood can take shape in her mind. She picks up another picture. Family and relatives crowd in the portrait. An engagement party in Tehran. Children sit at their parents' feet, young women fret with their hair, mouths open midsentence, old men stare with eyes agape. Some faces are caught in surprise, some in exasperation, some in dreams, perhaps, of the past, or the future, the photographer capturing the image one instant too soon, before the subjects have adequate time to compose themselves. In the corner of the photograph, at the far edge of the group, Rakhel stands, her white hair covered by a modest head scarf.

Mahboubeh recalls watching a reel of film from another party, a wedding of a niece. For a few brief frames, Rakhel stood still amidst a dancing crowd. She looked about her, then looked directly at the camera, one second, two seconds, three seconds. In the film, Rakhel appeared diminutive, vulnerable, bent with age. She hardly reached the shoulders of those she stood among. Mahboubeh had looked at that flickering image of Rakhel on the screen, and even then, in a room certainly too distant in both time and space to allow for Rakhel's reach, Mahboubeh felt a clenching at her throat.

She shakes her head, closes the album, and listens to the empty silence of the deserted streets outside her home. The children at school, their parents at work, only the mailman, the gardeners interrupt the lull. She closes her eyes and thinks about the quiet afternoons of the old Jewish mahalleh in Kermanshah, when the men abandoned the streets for a few hours and the women emerged, softly shutting the heavy doors of their homes behind them, and walked briskly to their destinations, their shadows passing now on the other side of the towering walls that enclosed the inner courtyards where they lived out their days. Rakhel would have left for the miqveh to do her ritual cleansing in the silence of those afternoons.

Mahboubeh imagines Rakhel as a girl, waiting by the women's entrance to the synagogue, around the corner from the main door where the men enter, in the clutch of the narrow alley. She sees Rakhel peering carefully around the wall, searching for the old midwife. The afternoon sun is languid, the streets empty, save for the hammam proprietor, sleeping on a chair propped against the wall, and the brown and yellow leaves that scatter at his feet with the passing of a breeze. The man coughs and stirs in his sleep. Rakhel hides quickly behind the wall. After a few moments, she peers from behind the wall again. The man's chin rests on his chest, his limp hands dangle to the ground. She watches the street for the midwife and worries that the old woman won't recognize her beneath her *hijab*. She reaches up and unfastens the *ruband* that covers her face. The air carries a subtle coolness. She closes her eyes and touches her own damp forehead. Autumn, she thinks, another harvest. And still.

Rakhel has seen Naneh Adeh many times, in the hammam, in the miqveh. Once at the bedside of her own dying mother, though there was nothing even the old midwife could have done then. The women of the mahalleh call Naneh Adeh for births, but also for the grim maladies of the female body. The old midwife enters their households to apply leeches for the cleansing of bad blood and hot glass cups to draw out malevolent spirits. They ask her in whispers about how to apply fresh leaves of the date palm for the ending of a pregnancy. They buy from her the little bundles of *chasm-e khorus* and *taranjabin*, which they secretly sprinkle on their husbands' meals to reawaken baser appetites.

Three days earlier at the miqveh, Rakhel had stood naked at the top of the stairs that led into the pool of rainwater below when the old woman spoke to her. "No fire in the hearth, yet?" Naneh Adeh had asked her. Rakhel shrugged and shook her head no.

"How old are you?"

"I'm in my fifteenth year," Rakhel said.

Naneh Adah looked at Rakhel with narrowed eyes. She leaned in and sniffed the air near Rakhel's shoulder, then took a step back to look at her again. Rakhel wrapped her arms over her abdomen and breasts. "There is nothing you need to hide from me, child. I can see into the workings of your body." Rakhel hugged herself tighter and looked down at her feet. "How many years have you been a wife?"

"Three."

Naneh Adah raised her leathery hand, nudged away Rakhel's arms and placed her palm on the tight flesh of Rakhel's stomach. Rakhel sucked in her breath. The old woman rubbed her dry palm in circles on Rakhel's belly, closed her eyes, and tilted her head to the side, as if she were listening for a sound far away. She opened her eyes and pronounced, "Nothing good, child, nothing good." Rakhel jumped back from the old woman and bent her body slightly forward, wrapping her arms across her middle again. "Don't be afraid, daughter," Naneh Adah said. "There may be a remedy."

"A remedy?"

"Ah, yes, child, if G-d sees fit, there is a cure to your problem. Sometimes when a woman wants a child too badly and cannot conceive, it is because the djinn Al has settled deep inside her body."

"Al?"

"Yes, child, sometimes Al takes the form of a beautiful woman, and enters the dreams of men to collect their spilt seeds. Or she comes as a demon, the body of a goat, the head of an old woman, and snatches newborns from their mothers' breasts. Inside the womb, she takes the form of a fish, swims in your belly, and eats the baby before it even has a heartbeat."

"Can you help me?" Rakhel said. "Can you get her out of me?"

"I'll see what I can do, child." Naneh Adeh stared at the mosaic on the wall for a few moments, nodding her head. Then she turned to Rakhel and said, "Meet me in three days after the noon *azan,* by the women's entrance to the synagogue. Go, now, cleanse your body in the rainwater below, and empty your heart, too, of its longing, so that you can begin your month in a state of purity."

Rakhel clasped the old woman's hands in her own.

"The want of the heart is a powerful force, child," the old woman said and patted Rakhel's hand before motioning with her head for Rakhel to go.

Rakhel turned to descend the stone steps to the dark waters of the pool beneath the ground. Naneh Adeh reached out and touched Rakhel's shoulder. "Though sometimes, daughter, no amount of desire, no potions or prayers or am- ulets, however strong, can change one's *qesmat.* I will try to help you, but the rest is the will of G-d."

The stone steps were cold and damp. Rakhel placed one foot down, searched with her toes for the ledge, then brought down the other foot, stood firmly with both feet beside each other, her hands clutching the walls on either side of the stairwell, before her foot ventured out again in search of the next step down. The miqveh was dimly lit, and the farther she descended, the harder she strained her eyes to make out the shape of the hole in the earth filled with dark rainwater. *There are no djinns in a holy place,* she reminded herself. *No djinns waiting in the shadows to pull me under the water and hold me down.* When she reached the pool's edge, she hesitated. Her skin became her eyes, the tiny hairs of her thin arms and back rose, she felt the air for motion, for a slight change in the temperature, she listened to the drip, drip of water, her own heart pounding in her ears. Then, she lifted her foot and touched the dark surface of the pool with her toe as she whispered the prayer for purification, *Baruch atah Hashem,* allowed her foot to find the submerged step, placed one foot down firmly, there were no more walls to hold on to, her arms stretched out for balance, *Elokeinu Melech Ha'Olam,* she brought down her other foot and her ankles now below the surface *asher kidshanu,* her knees now below the surface *b'mitzvotav,* her thighs, her slender hips *v'tzivanu,* she folded in her arms to hold her small breasts, her nipples taut, the water to her neck *al ha-tevila* and then, darkness, no breath.

She emerged with a gasp, water streaming from her face and hair. She hurried out of the pool, knelt beside it, the skin of her knees against the smooth stone. "Lord, grant me a child," she whispered to the dark water. "Please, grant me a child. A son, Lord. If only a son, so that my husband will be pleased with me. So that I, too, can have a place in his home. Please, Lord, I must have a baby." Rakhel sat on the ground, clutched her knees to her chest, and raised her eyes to the darkness above. "If You are there, if You can hear me . . . "

Her voice a hoarse whisper, commanding now rather than pleading, she rose to her knees again, her body erect, moving back and forth. "Grant me a son. Like the miracles they say You perform. It is all I ask. It is all I will ever ask of You."

"Rakhel Khanum, who are you speaking with down there?" Naneh Adeh's voice rang down the stairwell and filled the empty space between the walls. "Hurry, there are other women waiting for their turn."

"No one, Naneh Adah, I'm just praying. I'm on my way up." She cupped water in her hands, splashed her face, and quickly clamored up the stairs toward the light.

Three nights passed after her meeting with Naneh Adeh and each of those nights, Rakhel lay awake beside her sleeping husband, her breath short with the anticipation of the miracle, her palms on her abdomen. She imagined the face of the son she would bear. The dark curls of his hair, the fingers of his hands, the curve of his delicate ears. On the third day she asked Asher's permission to visit the miqveh, told her mother-in-law about the necessity for further cleansing, and set out for the synagogue during the noon azan, the hour the town settles for their rest. Once the heavy door of her home closed behind her, she clutched her chador tightly below her throat and stared at the abandoned street through the mesh of the black ruband that covered her face. When she saw that there was no one in sight, she ran in the direction of the synagogue. She turned the corner into the side alley and bent over to catch her breath.

Now, waiting in the empty alley, Rakhel begins to

worry that Naneh Adah might not come. Just as she peers from the corner of the building to look into the street once more, she feels the midwife's strong fingers clutch her shoulder. She turns around quickly and Naneh Adah pulls aside the ruband covering her own face. "Did anyone see you, child?"

"No, I was careful."

"Take this." The old woman passes a piece of folded paper into the girl's hand. "It is writing from The Book, the passage when G-d plants Yousseff in Rakhel's womb so that she wins favor with her husband. Dissolve this piece of paper in water and drink the water. The next morning, bathe yourself and perfume your body, but don't allow your husband to sleep with you. Just stay close to him so that he can smell you. Hover about him like a moth to a candle flame. For a night. Cat and mouse. You understand?" Rakhel nods her head yes. "After that, make certain he lays with you each night, for a week's time. He is young, do what you know to lure him." Rakhel looks down at her feet, blushing. Naneh Adeh takes her chin and raises Rakhel's head so that she is looking into the girl's eyes. "Come, daughter, you are no longer a child, you have been a wife for a few years now. No shame in any of this, forget that nonsense and think of it as a grave task, one that you must master, for your own sake. But follow my instructions as I've said them, so that your endeavors are met with success." Rakhel takes the old woman's hands in her own and brings them to her lips. "Enough, child. It is not I, but G-d who helps you," Naneh Adah says as she turns the girl by the shoulders and pushes her back out into the main street. "And may I not see you at the miqveh for nine months."

Rakhel turns back to say good-bye, but the old woman already hobbles with haste down the alleyway, her black chador taking the wind so that it billows out behind her. Rakhel watches her for a moment, then walks into the empty streets toward home. The hammam proprietor still sleeps in his chair. A fly hovers close to his mouth, and settles on his chin. Rakhel passes him slowly. She does not need to hurry. The town men retire, still, in the curtained rooms of their homes, or in comfortable corners of their shops, or beneath some shade to rest through the heat of the afternoon. She listens to the hollow sound of her own footsteps against the cobblestones. She clasps the folded paper in one hand and traces with her finger the cracks along the high walls that enclose the mahalleh homes. Then she stops to look at the buildings crowding the narrow street. She feels the breeze on her cheeks and realizes that she forgot to cover her face, but no one is there to see her, to ask her what business a young woman has to be walking at this hour of the day, un- chaperoned, with her face revealed. She closes her eyes and turns her face to the sun. She hears the chatter of children, their laughter rising from the *andaruni* of one of the homes. A woman quietly sings a folk love song from some hidden garden. Rakhel listens to the sound of caged birds, the coo of doves, finches chirping, a yellow canary, mad with song, longing for flight.

Two

꤂

The finches clamor in the yard, darting in and out of a rosebush. Mahboubeh rises from the table and looks out of the window. It must be late afternoon, now. The scattered leaves in the grass mean autumn. She has lost something. Something has been misplaced. She turns and begins opening the kitchen drawers. Spoons, forks, matches. She opens cabinets. She looks behind boxes of dried goods, bags of rice. A silver tray. Perhaps. This silver tray. She reaches for it and holds it in her hands. She looks at it for a while, until the dusk settles, and the crickets begin, and the hum of the refrigerator lulls her into a wakeful dream, where she finds herself sitting in the corner of her father's room again, a child of no more than five. Ibrahim finishes his dinner and nods at her. Mahboubeh takes his silver tray, removes the dishes, sits on the floor, and cleans the tray with her skirt. He rises heavily from his place and leaves the room wordlessly. The refrigerator clicks off and the silence places Mahboubeh back in the kitchen once more, though it is dark now. Her hands, oblivious to the passage of time, hold the hem of her skirt and polish the silver tray. She switches on the light.

The reflection of her face in the tray, that has changed. But the tray itself . . . It is a substantial thing, certain in its weight, concrete in its form. She served her father tea, warm bread in this tray. It held the glass, the crumbs, it carried the print of his thumb. She holds this in her hands. She looks again at her reflection. *Nothing remains,* she thinks, *nothing is left behind.*

She carries so much within her, the streets of her childhood, the garden of that andaruni, the sycamore trees, the shallow pool and its goldfish, the street peddlers' songs, the bazaars, the caged birds, the beggars, the shahs, the revolution, the fear, the hope, and now the crowding of this other place, Los Angeles.

She remembers that other garden, in that home, in Kermanshah. Mahboubeh looks out of the window at the shadows in her garden. This is her home, now. It has been home for years. She turns off the kitchen lights and walks to her bedroom.

Mahboubeh lies in bed, in the cold darkness, and re-members a story she read in college, of Odysseus, lost at sea. He chances upon an island, and the goddess of that island entices him, and holds him while season after season passes, save that there are no changes, no shifts in the arc of the sun or the color of the leaves, so that Odysseus forgets time, and the ocean, and the beckoning of that land he left somewhere behind him, and the one that calls him to her shores, that place where in the recesses of his mind he knows as home, but cannot remember anything more of than a few scattered memories, the scent of her earth, a certain tree. And one sunny day, after another, after another, that other place, the one ascribed home, becomes more and more distant, until he forgets all about it save on a dawn here or there, when he awakens in proximity to his dream as a dog yaps outside his window and he hears, distinctly, from the warmth of his bed, the tired shuffle of a servant's feet as she comes in with the kindling and a pail of water. But as soon as he tries to hold, for a moment, the sensation so that he can say *yes, I re-call that place, it is also who I have been, other than who I am now,* it dissipates and he loses all traces of the past. And this loss is so shocking, the pain of it so acute, that he allows himself to forget again, and he rises from his bed and looks at the sun, as he knows it, and the cloudless skies, and the strange blos-soms, no longer spectacular, as they know no death.

This place is a loneliness named Los Angeles, Mahboubeh thinks. *Los Angeles is not home. It is the place that erases all memory of the past.* Though home itself is no longer anything more than a brief outline for her, a sketch done by the hand of a child. A certain tree. The unlikely orange of dusk. The proportions of the self too large in relation to the house in the background, the birds, black marks in a white sky, undecipherable pigeons or sparrows or crows, the rest a blank space.

Mahboubeh remembers that garden, in that other home, in Kermanshah. It belonged to two brothers . . . She closes her eyes and falls asleep.

Rakhel pulls back the curtains of the window facing the garden to look at the dark sky from the warmth of her bed. Her ankles rest on the windowsill, her toes press against the cool glass. A rooster crows, then another. The sky above is still dark when the first note of the muezzin's song rises from the minarets to announce the morning. *Allah hu Akbar.*

She imagines the town awakening. The silent motions of believers, kneeling in prayer. The rustle of bedclothes as children stir in their sleep, the pouring of water into iron kettles, the crackling of fires, the tired shuffle of the feet of women walking across kitchen floors. The muezzin's song ends. *La ilaha illallah* ripples the air, the rings growing wider and more distant and then a moment bereft of sound, until the silence is finally punctuated by birdsong.

She hears the approach of a street peddler, his song about the salt he sells growing louder and louder, *"namakee, ai, namakee . . . "* until he must be right outside of their estate, behind the high walls in the narrow cobblestoned street. He stops singing and Rakhel imagines him standing in the middle of the mahalleh, placing his heavy burlap bag down, wiping the sweat off his brow with the sleeve of his torn *qaba,* considering the closed doors surrounding him, sighing and picking up his burden and his song once more.

Soon the men will open the creaking doors of their homes, Rakhel thinks. She imagines them stepping into the street, securely closing the doors behind them, straightening their shoulders and taking the first public step of their day. And soon, the stillness of the morning will give way to the ca-cophony of exchanged greetings, news of the day, the trans-actions of business. The streets will be full of men and pack animals, braying and yelling. From the andaruni she will hear these sounds rise into the air and merge, now and then pierced by a whistle or a voice raised in anger, or another passing street peddler, singing of the salt he sells, or of his metal pots, or of his coal, or his needles, his pins, his thread.

When she wakes again, it is near noon. Someone knocks at her bedroom door. Rakhel does not respond. She watches the door, then the crack of light as Khorsheed pushes it ajar with her foot. Khorsheed balances a silver tray with both hands, walks in the room, and nudges the door closed with her hips. Rakhel turns to face the wall and pulls the blanket over her head. "Dada?" Khorsheed calls softly. Rakhel does not respond. "Dada?" she calls again. Khor-sheed walks to the bed, places the tray down on the floor beside it, then jumps on the bed and reaches to pull the cover off of Rakhel. "Have you gone hard of hearing?" she asks.

"You shouldn't jump. Everyone knows it's not good for a pregnant woman to jump," Rakhel says. She keeps her face to the wall and continues to look through the black strands of her hair at the tiny cracks in the plaster.

"It's your woman's time again, isn't it?" Khorsheed grabs Rakhel's shoulders and struggles to turn her so that she could see her face. Rakhel resists silently. She is stronger than the younger girl. Khorsheed reaches under the covers, finds the softness of Rakhel's belly, plunges her fingers into the flesh.

"Stop." Rakhel wriggles and tries not to laugh. "I'm impure to your touch. Stop it. You'll get hurt, stop. Stop!" she yells. Khorsheed pulls her hands away and caresses Rakhel's face.

"Your eyes are so swollen," Khorsheed says as she brushes the hair away from Rakhel's face. "Crying really makes you very ugly. Naneh Zolekhah has been asking about you. I told her it was probably your woman's time." Rakhel continues to stare at the wall. "Have you eaten at all today? Come sit down and eat with me. I'm famished. Can't eat enough." Khorsheed edges her way off the bed and sits cross-legged on the rug. She takes a piece of rock sugar and strains to break a piece. "Come break this for me, your rough peasant hands are much stronger than my delicate ones." Rakhel grunts a response. "Hands like a Kurdish woman," Khorsheed continues, "hands made to milk goats." Rakhel sits up slowly. She throws the covers back and looks at her own bare feet, then she studies her hands resting on her shins. She turns and slides off of the bed onto the rug beside Khorsheed and clutches her knees to her chest. "Here." Khorsheed holds out the chunk of gold sugar candy. "Use that *pahlivan* strength of yours to break me a piece." Rakhel takes the sugar and without much effort, breaks it into five pieces. "Rostam," Khorsheed laughs, "do you caress your husband with those big, strong hands?" Rakhel hurls the sugar pieces at the wall. They shatter and fall to the rug. Khorsheed gets up heavily, sighs, and gathers the pieces. Rakhel watches her back, the curves of Khorsheed's wide hips beneath her *shaliteh*.

Khorsheed blows on the sugar pieces to remove the dirt and places them back into the bowl. "I was trying to make you laugh." She drops one in her own chai. "Shall I put one in your cup?" She places another piece in her mouth. "Do you want a little cheese and bread?" Khorsheed asks.

Rakhel looks at Khorsheed's face, her full cheeks and bright eyes, like the women in all those songs, eyes big like saucers, lips small like blossoms. Rakhel's face begins to move without her consent. Her chin trembles. She fails to keep her lips from contorting. Finally, her face twists and breaks. "Why?" She pushes the word out with a sob. She shakes her head from side to side with her eyes closed. "Why, why, why?" She places her open palms over her face and rocks back and forth. Khorsheed tries to catch Rakhel in the embrace of her arms, but the minute she touches her shoulder, Rakhel screams, throws her head back and stares wildly at the ceiling, then falls forward, pounding her fists against the rug and hitting her forehead repeatedly against the floor. "He will get rid of me," Rakhel says.

"No. No, he won't. Please don't hurt yourself, Dada, please. Dada, please. He won't, he won't get rid of you."

"Yes. He'll divorce me. He'll send me back. And who will take me then, my mother dead, my father an old man? Or will I be pushed into the corners of this house. Like a servant? A burden to him? Grateful for each crumb of bread I eat?"

"Dada, please, please stop crying." Khorsheed clutches and wrings her hands in anguish. "Please, Dada, please. He won't send you away, please. You'll get pregnant soon, you'll see. Sometimes it takes time, sometimes it takes a long time."

When she is sad, she is no longer so pretty, Rakhel thinks. In fact, she looks like that toothless old woman that comes around selling little bundles of herbs she grows in her garden. Rakhel laughs, a short burst that sounds like a choked sob. She looks at Khorsheed's face again and breaks into uncontrollable laughter. Khorsheed stares back in bewilderment. After a moment, Khorsheed starts laughing herself, and the two girls laugh until they lose their breaths, their faces still wet with tears.

The heat of the afternoon pushes against the windows, the light filtering through the green leaves, their shadows dancing against the walls. The girls lie on the rug, their languid limbs and black hair spread across the blue patterns, their smooth cheeks pressed against their folded arms. They are both exhausted and in the opiate of the warm afternoon, they drowse to sleep. "Khorsheed?" Rakhel whispers, her eyelids heavy.

"What is it, Dada?"

"Khorsheed . . . Naneh Adeh says I may be possessed by a djinn."

"A djinn?" Khorsheed asks.

"Yes. Do you think I am possessed by a djinn?"

"Why, have you seen it?" Khorsheed asks.

"Sometimes, at night, when I am asleep beside Asher, I think I feel her."

"You feel her?"

"I feel something deep inside me, and a weight on top of my body, like Asher, except she holds every part of me and when I move, she melts my flesh."

"Your flesh melts?"

"It starts in the middle of my body, like waves, moves out, and I become a river, rushing out to the sea, then I rise like vapor and pour down like a summer rain."

"How do you know it's a djinn?"

"What else can it be but a djinn?" Rakhel asks. "When I feel her steal into my sleep, I know. And I could wake up, if I wanted to, but I don't."

Outside it rains. Shepherd boys huddle with their sheep. Cats run underneath fences, crouch low to enter stables where mules snort and toss their heads, their eyes rolling in their faces. Old women run to gather white sheets that blow on the lines. Men rush toward the shelter of shops and homes.

The rain patters on the roof of the house and against the windowpanes. Mahboubeh wakes with a start. She listens to the sound of water running through the rain gutters of her home. She closes her eyes and remembers the water in the open channels alongside the streets in the old mahalleh. For a brief moment, she sees clearly twigs and leaves caught in the currents of an open channel. A red ribbon from a girl's braid snakes in and out of the eddies.

Mahboubeh is late for school. Dada did not let her sleep last night until she cleared the dinner plates, washed the silver, swept the floor of the kitchen. Mahboubeh stands in the street outside the closed gate of her school and stares at the rushing water. She holds an orange sycamore leaf in her hand, speckled gold, brown, the edges remembering green. She drops it into the channel and watches it catch in a current, swirl, disappear beneath the water, reappear and float fast away. At this hour, the math teacher is delivering her lesson. She will ask Mahboubeh to stand before the class, and recite the times table. If Mahboubeh makes an error, or forgets, the teacher will shame her, perhaps even switch the palms of her hands. "But I never forget," she says to soothe herself. A car drives down the street. Mahboubeh opens her eyes. The nightstand. The clock. The electric green of numbers, 6:37 in the morning. The minute changes. She closes her eyes again. She is not a schoolgirl, anymore. She is an old woman.

She remembers the day she went to Rakhel and asked her permission to attend school. Rakhel responded, "What does a girl need school for? You don't need to know how to read to wipe a baby's ass." But Mahboubeh saw that her cousins Efat and Ismat studied, and read books, and could do mathematics, and she knew she was falling behind on something important. So she'd do little tasks around the house, clean and fetch things for her uncle Asher and for her father, Ibrahim, in return for coins.

Of her few personal possessions, Mahboubeh owned a little *gholak*. She dropped each coin she earned into it and hid that gholak on a shelf behind some books in her father's room. Then came the day she broke it. She stood with a stone in her hand and with one blow, the coins spilled onto the rug. Mahboubeh piled them into a single small, shining mountain. She stared at it for a moment, then worried that Rakhel might come looking for her. Quietly, quickly, she filled her pockets, found her shoes, and stole through the andaruni, and when she made certain that no one missed her, she opened the heavy wooden door and slipped into the street.

Mahboubeh sees herself standing in the headmaster's office. She must be no more than nine years old. He sits behind his large desk, looking at her from above the rim of his gold spectacles. He waits for her to speak.

"I want to enroll," she says.

"You must come back with your father."

"My father is on a trip."

"Then come back with your mother."

"My mother is dead." She reaches into her pockets and takes out all the money, two fistfuls of shiny coins. She does not know if it is a considerable sum, just that it fills both hands. She places her earnings on the headmaster's desk.

He looks at her for a long time, then asks her, "What grade are you in?" Mahboubeh has never been in school. She doesn't know her aleph'beh or how to count, but she responds that she is in the third grade because her cousin Efat is in the third grade and they are the same age. She follows the headmaster down the hall to the third grade class and enters.

Mahboubeh opens her eyes. The clock reads 6:40. The rain has stopped. A garage door opens. A car backs out into the street, the tires slick on the wet asphalt. Someone calls from a window. A man's voice responds. The car drives away. The clock reads 6:41. A transient sunlight floods her room. In a moment, the birds will begin singing.

The voices of men fill the garden. Their *ya Allah, ya Allah* drowns out the birdsong, the gurgle of the fountain, the silence of the women. The women of the household don't have much time to prepare for the arrival of the Kurds. Though they know the time for harvest and though they know that each harvest, the Kurdish farmers arrive unannounced with the landlord's share of the crop, they are still startled to find their inner yard full of a dozen men carrying bundles of wheat, unloading sacks of tobacco leaves twisted into ropes, burlap bags full of *katira,* milked from the *gavan-e shireh* plant of the high mountains, pails full of comb and honey.

The men lead braying mules to the stalls, fill the troughs with water from the well, wash their own hands and faces in the central pool. They keep their eyes averted, looking to the dirt or at each other, their heads bent in respect for the women in the house, to give the women time to retreat to the hidden parts of the home, or to pull their scarves over their hair and to fasten the cloth of the ruband over their faces.

The women peer into the andaruni from the cracks of doors, from behind drawn curtains, to see their inner yard full of unknown men, dressed in a billow of black pants wide in the legs, tight around the ankles. The men wear colorful scarves in bold patterns wound about their waists, held in place by belts, which secure their knives. From hidden posts, the women notice the dark proud eyes alive beneath heavy eyebrows, thick mustaches that hide youthful or toothless mouths, the loose sleeves of white shirts that reveal hard, veined, calloused hands, cracked nails, hands that know the feel of the earth, that goad and beg from her, that draw from her the abundance now spread in the inner and outer yards of their own home.

Flustered and excited to have the monotony of their

daily lives interrupted, the women rush from their hidden posts to cover their heads and faces, then steal into the kitchen to prepare the samovar and boil water in copper pots. They pour cups of rice into the boiling pots, then grind saffron in sugar with mortar and pestle. They fill silver trays with figs, and load bowls with crisp apples. They make a hurried dish of fried eggplants and tomatoes to fill the platters for this unexpected feast.

When the Kurdish farmers arrive from the villages with the harvest, Asher pushes Rakhel and Khorsheed into the cellar. The girls are frightened by the urgency in Asher's demands, but more so, they are disappointed that they can't sit quietly in some corner and hear stories about the world outside of the heavy wooden door, or at least go to and from the sitting room like the maids, bearing trays of fruits and tea, catching bits of sentences about life in the villages, or the adventures of nomads on horses, or the retreat of the Russian soldiers, who take the cattle of peasants, pillage bazaars, tear down homes, and burn the wood for heat along their way.

Inside the cellar, lined against the walls, rest large earthen pots, taller than a man, full of wheat and grains, wicker baskets full of beans, and large cylindrical mud jars full of rice. Bushels of grapes hang from the beams of the ceiling, strings of onions and garlic, pomegranates, baskets of apples, sacks of dried fruits and nuts pile on the floor, watermelons lay buried beneath straw, to stay fresh for the long winter nights. Shelves cut in earthen walls are filled with jars of pickled vegetables, preserved jars of quinces, pears, and apricots. The air always dry and crisp, the walls cold. The girls stand on the stone steps, their arms around each other, pleading behind the closed door.

Zolekhah waits beside Asher as he locks the door and whispers *hush hush* to the muffled voices of the girls. He places the key in his breast pocket, and looks heavenward, either to beseech G-d for the safety of the young girls or to express his exasperation. Zolekhah pats his shoulder and follows him to the yard. She unobtrusively counts the mouths to feed as Asher walks among the dozen farmers, with Ibrahim beside him, their hands placed on the small of their backs, their chests thrust forth. Asher appraises the harvest of wheat and questions the farmers as they finish unloading. The old khan, strong and straight of back like one of the sculpted men Zolekhah has seen in the rocks of Bisotun, walks toward Asher and says, "May Allah give you strength." He then nods at Ibrahim, who returns the greeting with a slight bow of his head.

"May G-d preserve you, may he keep tiredness from your hands. Please come inside and join us for a piece of bread and some tea to ease the fatigue of your journey," Asher says.

Zolekhah has known the old khan since her sons' childhood, when Asher stood beside his father, and Ibrahim hid his face in the folds of his father's qaba. He has watched her boys grow into manhood, taught them about the seasons and how the earth can give, and how she can take. He stood beside them when they buried their own father and helped them learn to become the owner of the lands.

"We will not burden you," the old khan says.

"It is no burden, a piece of bread and tea, the men must be tired, please honor us with your presence," Ibrahim replies.

As children, Ibrahim and Asher rode to the villages astride two mules that trotted alongside their father's horse. During the ride, Asher debated with his father about the best seeds to sow, whether the white, or the red and yellow, or the *kuleh* seed, which sprouted a large, hard grain. Ibrahim, however, rode in silence, lost to the seduction of the soil, the undulations of a field of wheat stalks in the breeze. "Asher listens closely to the farmers talk about irrigation and rotation," Rebbe Yousseff would tell Zolekhah when he returned from the lands, "but Ibrahim only listens closely to the snorting and whining of the mule."

Zolekhah looks at her sons, now proud men, walking steadily amidst the Kurds. She closes her eyes to hold, for a moment, the image of her sons as boys, running back into her arms upon their return from their journey to the villages. She strains to hear the sound of their voices calling her, but that is lost to her. Instead, she remembers her husband's funeral, and how Asher stood stoic beside the open grave. Ibrahim wept beside him, holding tightly to his brother's mourning coat.

"We still have many hours to ride back to the village," the old khan says.

"And so it would be wise to allow the men some rest.

It would honor our family if you would accept our invitation," Asher says. Zolekhah watches the old khan pause at the threshold of the open doors of the guest hall, place his palm against his heart and bow his head. Asher returns the gesture with a deeper bow of his head.

Zolekhah enters the kitchen to find the old family servant Fatimeh and the two younger maids engaged in a storm of motion and words, an orchestrated cacophony accompanied by the clang and clatter of teacups, then the sudden commotion of an overturned box of silver spoons against the stone floor. "Is the chai ready?" Zolekhah asks.

Fatimeh stops in the middle of the kitchen and raises her hands to the ceiling. "I've had enough of these girls, Zolekhah Khanum, you would think they had never seen Kurdish farmers, Allah forgive them. Be' Zainab, I have to do everything they have done once more over," she says. She adjusts her head scarf to cover the few strands of hair that slip out, then slaps Sadiqeh's ample thigh with the back of her hand and motions for the girl to cover her thick black braids with the scarf that hangs behind her head. Sadiqeh takes the end of one braid and places it between her teeth, then gives Fatimeh a coy smile. Zahra walks between them, holding a copper pot full of rice. Her rolled-up sleeves reveal long, white arms, delicate wrists adorned with a few gold bangles, and fingers hennaed red. Fatimeh steps in front of her and unrolls Zahra's sleeves to cover her arms, almost causing the girl to drop the pot of rice on the floor.

"You see, Zolekhah Khanum, I must protect their honor

and see that they don't spoil the food, besides," Fatimeh says.

"It's not me, Zolekhah Khanum," Sadiqeh says. "It's Zahra's honor in question. She fancies the young Kurd with the long mustache and clear eyes."

"I said he reminded me of my cousin Ghollum. Fatimeh, didn't I say he reminded me of my cousin?"

"A married woman mustn't look in the direction of another man, child, not even a cousin. It is haram by The Book."

"Her husband is so old, Fatimeh, she could sit in that peasant's lap fondling his mustache in the middle of her home and the old man wouldn't notice."

"Sadiqeh, hush up before you start trouble for me."

"It's true. You've seen him, no, Fatimeh? When he hobbles here to fetch her in the evenings?"

"Hassan Khan is a righteous man, not a blemish to his name."

"Better old than a simpleton like your husband. Fatimeh, if you tell her husband that a man is a eunuch, he asks how many children does he have."

"It's true, Fatimeh. I tell him it's a stone, he tells me it is cheese."

"Zolekhah Khanum, these girls will drive me to the mortician's bath with their antics."

"Zahra, is the chai ready?"

"Yes, Zolekhah Khanum."

"Don't tarry any longer, the guests are waiting."

"Yes, Zolekhah Khanum."

Zolekhah returns to the sitting room, followed by

Zahra, the girl unidentifiable beneath the black fabric of her hijab, balancing the tray full of glass teacups and saucers, her white braceleted wrists revealed each time she stretches out her hands. Zolekhah stands beside the door and watches the girl as she moves underneath the sway of her long full hem, steps, kneels, places saucer and glass in the outstretched hands. The men, tired from the ride from the village, accept the hot chai and offer gratitude and blessings in return. They keep themselves from noticing the soft touch of the hennaed fingertips that brush their own calloused hands in the passing, they look away from the small toes hennaed red, pressed against the wool of the rug near their own feet.

The old khan takes his tea and a piece of rock sugar. He places the sugar in the corner of his cheek and pours some tea into his saucer, then sips. His men wait for him to take this first sip before they begin drinking their own tea. The room remains silent until he begins to speak. "They burned wheat fields," he says. "Wheat fields. Before the harvest. We saw some of those farmers. Men walking with no direction. Hollowed eyes. They had watched their women raped, seen their children killed, and in the wake of that horror, those savages burned their wheat fields."

"The Russians have no honor," Asher says. "They don't follow any rules in their war. Nor the British. In the streets of Tehran, the people wait for hours outside the bakeries and walk away empty-handed. The British purchase the wheat from the shah's granaries above the market price. No bread comes of it for the peasants. They buy it for their own use.

And they come here with their treaties, speaking of friendship, of building this country. Upon the bones of its children?"

"Still, it is our shah who chooses to sell to them, son," the old khan says. He shakes his head and places his cup and saucer before him. "There was a moment, when your father was still alive, may he rest in peace, when we held the reins of our own country, disposed of the Qajar king, created a Majlis of representative, when we fought for our right to be men," he says.

"Neither the Russians, nor the British, would ever allow us that. To be men. Mules, at best, to carry the burden of their greed," Ibrahim says. "But never men."

Asher snorts. "Even if the foreigners allowed it, brother, do you think the clergy of our own country would allow you and I, two Jews, to ever be fully human?"

A silence falls upon the room. The old khan sips his tea and looks at Asher for some time. Then, he says, "Your father was a man among men, Asher. In the beginning, many refused to buy his wheat, for fear that it was *najis,* sullied by the touch of his hand. But soon he proved that he was a man of honor. A fair and just man."

Zolekhah leaves the room quietly. She stops before entering the kitchen and leans against the wall. She breathes in deeply, once, then straightens her shoulders and walks in, picks up the cloth *sofre* and motions for the maids to follow her with the steaming platters of rice and mutton. She enters the guest hall, lays the sofre on the floor, and steps back to allow the women to set down the warm sheets of flat bread, and the mounds of fresh herbs and soaked walnuts.

"Please, welcome, eat," Zolekhah says.

"You have humbled us with the trouble we have put you and your household through," the old khan says.

"The food we eat is grown by your hands," Ibrahim says. Zolekhah watches as the men rise to sit at the edge of the sofre and begin to eat. Silently, she leaves the room, followed by the maids.

In the cellar, Khorsheed buries her face in Rakhel's shoulder. The younger girl fears the shadows and the darkness behind the large earthen pots that tower over her, but Rakhel prefers this room to any other room in the large estate. In the heat of the afternoons, when Zolekhah is fast asleep, Rakhel steals her heavy ring of keys and unlocks the cellar door, runs to place the keys back beside the sleeping woman, and returns to the cellar. Sometimes she sweeps the stone floor, sometimes she checks the grains to make sure that pests haven't spoiled the food. Often, she just sits in the dim light of the lantern and gazes at the stock. She knows the amount of everything in the storage room, feels the approach of a new season by the decrease in the quantity of a certain fruit, less of the dried spring plums means that the season of the pomegranates approaches, and persimmons, too. Sometimes Khorsheed cracks the door of the cellar open and hears Rakhel talking.

"Who are you speaking to?" Khorsheed asks.

"I wasn't speaking to anyone."

"I heard you."

"I was measuring."

"Measuring?"

"The amount of animal fat left in the barrel, so I can tell Naneh Zolekhah how much more we need for winter."

"Come up out of there."

"Why?"

"It's dark."

"I have a lantern." And Rakhel would hold up the lantern to her face and grimace, which always sent Khorsheed running with a yelp before concern led her back, again, to the top of the cellar door.

That afternoon, while they wait behind the locked door for the Kurdish farmers to leave, Khorsheed lifts her face from Rakhel's shoulder and says, "Dada, I'm pretty sure I'm having a boy. Yesterday I found a pin on the floor of the bedroom and last night, to be sure, I placed a knife to the left of my pillow and scissors to the right, and this morning, I awoke looking at the knife. Imagine if it should be a boy. The first son of the family. Ibrahim would be so happy with me."

"What if it's a girl?"

"Khasveh shalom."

"What if it is?"

"Don't ruin my luck with your envy."

"But what if it is a girl?" Rakhel asks.

"Then the next one will be a boy."

"Are you scared, Khorsheed?"

"Scared?"

"Of the djinn Al. She kills pregnant women and eats the liver of newborns."

"Rakhel."

"You should be cautious."

"Are you scared?"

"I'm not pregnant."

"Of other djinns?"

"I'm protected against them," Rakhel says. "You never know where one might be lurking. In the mirror, in the passing glance of a stranger. In this dark cellar. I know for certain one lives at the bottom of our well." Rakhel listens to the silence and imagines that she can hear a thousand little eyes open and close.

"How are you protected, Dada?"

"I have this iron key." Rakhel lifts her shirt and points to a small key, tied around her waist by red yarn. "They won't come close to you if you have iron against your skin, especially an iron key. It belonged to my mother. She wore it as protection, too. Before she died she put it in the palm of my hand, blew on it three times, and promised that it would always keep me safe."

"But what about that djinn Naneh Adeh said lives inside you?"

Rakhel hears the whisper of movement, as light as the footfall of ants. From the corner of her eyes, she notices the shadows draw closer to the foot of the stairs, crawl on their hands and knees, lift their heads to sniff the cold air for the acrid smell of metal against human flesh. "She lied," Rakhel says. "No djinn lives inside me."

"So why haven't you gotten pregnant yet?"

Rakhel feels the shadows move in the darkness and settle back into corners to imagine the baby growing in Khorsheed's belly. She shrugs her shoulders in response. The cellar is full of a waiting silence.

"How much longer before the farmers leave, Dada, I need to eat for my strength."

"I don't know, another hour maybe. Do you want to play a game?"

"What game?"

"I'll hide and you find me."

"No, Rakhel!"

"It will be fun."

Khorsheed grabs frantically onto Rakhel's clothes. "No, Dada, this is no fun."

Rakhel pushes Khorsheed's arms away and runs down the stairs into the darkness. "Come find me," she says.

"Dada, come back, please."

There is only silence. Rakhel watches the shadows crawl back up the stairs. The sound of their breath grows louder and louder.

"Dada?"

Rakhel sees them reach out the tips of their fingers, like the flickering of snake tongues, to taste the warmth of the air around Khorsheed's feet.

"Dada, I don't want to play. It's not good for my condition." There is panic in Khorsheed's voice. She moves down one step. "Rakhel! Stop!" Khorsheed bends to pick up the lantern. A thousand shadows dance on the walls. "Rakhel, come back, I don't have any iron and the djinn . . . "

Rakhel waits quietly as the hands stretch out in the darkness, hovering close to Khorsheed's skin. She watches Khorsheed hurry down the stairs. Before it happens, Rakhel knows that Khorsheed's foot will miss the last step. She watches Khorsheed fall to the stone floor. The lantern crashes and breaks, the light burns out. Khorsheed screams. Rakhel puts her hand across Khorsheed's mouth to muffle her screams. Khorsheed thrashes her arms and legs.

"It's me, it's me, Khorsheed, it's me. It's me, Rakhel, it's me, be quiet." Rakhel feels the girl's body suddenly fall limp. "Khorsheed!"

The door clanks open and light fills the cellar. Rakhel looks up from the foot of the stairs. Khorsheed lays in her arms, a pool of blood at her feet.

"What happened?" Zolekhah asks. She runs down the stairs.

Fatimeh hurries down the steps behind her. "Ya Abolfazl," she cries. "By the pure blood of Imam Hossien, what catastrophe is this? What has happened here?"

Zolekhah slaps Khorsheed's cheeks. "Khorsheed." The girl's eyes flutter. "Fatimeh, rosewater and sugar, quick. She's bleeding. She may have lost the child."

Khorsheed moans in Rakhel's arms. Zolekhah holds the girl's chin and calls her name. Khorsheed finally opens her eyes. Fatimeh returns with a glass in one hand, the other holding on to the wall as she steps down the stairs heavily, huffing with the effort of her haste.

"Drink this," Fatimeh says and brings the sugar water

to Khorsheed's lips while fanning her face with the fold of her chador.

"If a girl loses her first child, Fatimeh, all her others are doomed. This one, too, unable to have a child? G-d spare my sons this curse."

Fatimeh pulls up the hem of Khorsheed's tumban to inspect her legs. "Allah is merciful, it is only her foot. The blood is only from her foot, Zolekhah Khanum," she says. "There is no blood on her legs."

"What were the two of you doing?"

"Playing," Khorsheed whispers.

"Stupid girl, you're at the beginning of your pregnancy. You may lose the baby, G-d forbid. You are not a child to be playing."

"Sorry, Naneh Zolekhah," Khorsheed says. "We were bored."

Fatimeh gets up heavily to fetch another lantern from the kitchen. She returns and, in the dim light, studies the girl's foot for shards of glass. Rakhel doesn't speak. She waits to hear Khorsheed say that it was her fault, that she had scared her, made her fall. Rakhel tries to think of a defense in response, but all she can remember is the strange pleasure she felt as she watched the terror in Khorsheed's lamplit face at the top of the steps while the shadows drew nearer and nearer. Khorsheed cries silently in her arms. Rakhel looks at her chest rise and fall with the sobs.

Khorsheed repeats, in choked whispers, "I don't want

my baby to die, Naneh Zolekhah. Oh G-d, please, I'm sorry. I don't want my baby to die."

"You are pregnant with the first child of this family. And what if you lose the baby for your games? What will you say to your husband then?" Zolekhah says.

Ibrahim appears at the top of the stairs.

"No, no, no," Khorsheed says. She bites her hands, shaking her head back and forth.

"What happened?" Ibrahim asks, walking down the steps.

"She fell down the steps. They were playing in the dark," Zolekhah says.

"How G-d can entrust women with the miracle of life is one of His greater mysteries," Ibrahim says. He shakes his head as he gathers the girl in his arms and carries her up the stairs.

Zolekhah rises off the ground and offers Fatimeh her hand. "We'll have to sacrifice a lamb, Fatimeh, to be sure. Sprinkle the blood on these steps, give the meat to the poor."

"May the All-Merciful accept the offering, Zolekhah Khanum," Fatimeh says, rising with effort. "Where I am from, they say that a pregnant woman is like a sack of setting yogurt, she should not be shaken at all." The two women ascend the stairs, muttering, then disappear into the light.

Rakhel sits on the cold stone floor. She feels a rustling behind her and turns to look, but the cellar is full of light. She hears Asher's voice above, full of concern for a baby that is not his. Zolekhah complains about the immaturity of her sons' brides. The servant girls join the conversation, shrill with concern.

"Brother, you need to be more strict with her, she does not know the value of what she carries," Asher says.

"All that is left for me to do is to forbid her to walk," Ibrahim says.

"A great danger, G-d willing, has passed us," Zolekhah says.

"Best not speak of it yet, Zolekhah Khanum," Fatimeh says.

"Tie a white cord about her belly," Sadiqeh says.

"It can be white or of two colors," Zahra says.

"Fatimeh, can you recite the Ya Sin Sura?" Sadiqeh asks. "You must recite that particular sura seven times while she ties seven knots in the cord. My older sister had a terrible scare when she was pregnant. We tied a padlock to the cord, blessed by mullah Sayyed Khan, the one from Qom. Her boy was born without a flaw. I can ask her for the padlock."

"Zolekhah Khanum, perhaps someone has looked at the child with an evil eye?"

"We'll burn some wild rue to protect against it."

"Blow three times, Khorsheed."

"We mustn't praise her progress anymore, we must say *Masha 'Allah*, praise G-d instead."

Rakhel listens to the voices. She waits for someone to remember her.

Three

❦

Dada, Dada, Dada. Mahboubeh remembers how even the mention of Rakhel's name made the women and the children of the household nervous. She was all everyone ever talked about. The only authority. Mahboubeh walks into her garden with a length of rope in her hand. The rain fell for a long while, for days and days, with fierce winds. Mahboubeh's feet sink into the mud. She walks slowly. Should she fall, who knows how long before someone comes. The fig tree leans dangerously to one side. Mahboubeh wraps the rope around its trunk several times, then walks to the line of conifers growing behind the fig tree. "Which one of you shall bear the burden?" The tree tops sway. Beaded drops of rain sit on their needles. Mahboubeh raises a trembling finger and takes a drop. "Such diamonds," she says. "For my eyes only?" She chooses the middle tree and wraps the end of the rope around its trunk. "Hold her, for now, until I can hire a man to build her a crutch." She pulls on the end of the rope, then knots it. She walks back to the fig tree and plucks a dried fig from its branch. She remembers how the other children ran to their mothers whenever Rakhel caught them picking fruit from the garden trees. Rakhel chased them, cursing and yelling that she'd summon a djinn to visit them in their sleep and choke them for their thievery. Mahboubeh had no one to run to, no one to protect her from Rakhel's anger and spite.

Mahboubeh knew that if she asked her father, Ibrahim, how her mother died, he'd respond with silence, or else he'd repeat what he always said, "She died as most women died in her time, from the complications of womanhood." So she stopped asking him.

When she finally summoned the courage to ask Rakhel, Rakhel replied, "Your father killed her."

Mahboubeh walks slowly to the single pomegranate tree in her yard. The garden in Kermanshah boasted several pomegranate trees, raised from the graftings of the pomegranate trees that grew in the garden where Mahboubeh's grandfather Rebbe Yousseff spent his own childhood. She remembers a game she used to play as a child, walking through the garden in Kermanshah. Mahboubeh would see a rose, then she'd think about her mother smelling a rose, and Mahboubeh would lean in, close her eyes, and breathe in its perfume. *My mother loved this scent above all else,* she'd tell herself. Or she'd sit beneath a tree and say to herself, *my mother sat beneath this very tree, and what she saw then, I see, now.* This way, she felt her mother's presence, felt as though she shared that garden with her.

When Mahboubeh escaped from Iran after the revolution, after everyone she knew had either left or died, she placed a scion from a pomegranate tree in her suitcase, thinking, *no need to hide this, though it is more valuable than anything I have sewn in the lining of my coat.* Now, with each autumn that passes, the tree grafted with that scion fruits for her. *And when I am gone,* she thinks, *someone will buy this house and this pomegranate tree will fruit for them, and they will not know who cared for it, who pruned it and watered it and buried fish heads near its roots, and who spoke to it stories about its distant relatives, from a place this tree must know of, somewhere in its memory, in the kernel of its ruby-coated seeds, in the fiber of its wood, the tapestry of its leaves.*

Mahboubeh touches the delicate, supple branches of the tree. She can't remember when its leaves turned yellow. Amidst those yellow leaves, the scarlet fruits hang. The topmost ones are hollowed combs. Mahboubeh notices a crow watching her from the branches. "Thank you for leaving me my share." She reaches up and plucks a pomegranate, wipes it dry with her sleeve, and drops it in the pocket of her coat.

The crow flies off the branch, calling out. "Tell the dead to wait for me," Mahboubeh calls after it. She looks at the clouds, gray and swift. A drop of rain falls on her forehead. She closes her eyes and imagines her mother.

"What did my mother look like?" she had asked Rakhel once.

"Nothing like you. She was beautiful. Had thick, black hair. Wore it long and hung little golden trinkets in it. Real gold. Vain about her hair and all else, too."

"Her face, what did her face look like?"

"Like any face, two eyes, a nose, a mouth. Big like yours. Stupid girl with your stupid questions. Go on. There must be something you can do to make yourself useful. Lazy just like your mother was. Do nothing but eat and sleep and talk nonsense all day."

Mahboubeh listens to the wind and watches the shower of dry, yellow leaves before her. She imagines Khorsheed's abundant hair, loose, black sheened like a crow, adorned with gold. She pictures Khorsheed's face, round and radiant like the sun, eyes full of kindness. She must have smiled easily. And her arms, always welcoming. Mahboubeh sees Khorsheed as she must have sat beneath the pomegranate tree, pregnant, young, staring absently at the exposed earth brick beneath the white plaster of the garden wall, and twisting a strand of her long hair with one hand, while dipping her fingers into the loose earth with the other.

Khorsheed looks down at the hand holding the brown soil and studies the blue web of veins that are now visible beneath her skin. Her breasts feel tender to the touch. The skin on her stomach itches. Her appetites are ferocious, and unpredictable. She listens to the birds sing madly from the treetops, the sound of the fountain from the andaruni, the constant gurgle, interrupted by the occasional splash of a fish coming to the surface to feed. The street and the household settle deep into the slumber of afternoon.

Khorsheed looks at the shiny brown earth in her hand. In an instant, she sees the dissolution of her form into a thousand forms, decomposing, growing, nourishing. She imagines her body wedded to worms, crawling with ants. She sees pieces of herself clamped by tiny, powerful jaws, dispersed, fed to a thousand hungry larvae, little by little, her flesh moving away from her bones, until she crawls the glistening earth, becomes food for birds, then flies all over the whole wide land. She smells the earth in the palm of her hand, then allows it to slip between her fingers. She hesitates for a moment to look behind her, then clutches another handful.

Not so long ago, she played with dolls in the courtyard of her father's home. Then, one day, Zolekhah came from a town some distance from Khorsheed's village to visit with her mother. She turned to Khorsheed and said something to her about her beauty. A few days later, her father's sitting room filled with men and Khorsheed's mother whispered urgent instructions to her about how to serve the tea and how to keep her eyes on the rug. One of her aunts pulled her aside and pointed to Ibrahim, who stared intently at her.

"That one will be your husband," her aunt had said. And Khorsheed remembers accepting it, as easily as if someone had pointed to a chair and said, "That is where you shall sit."

After the men came and went, she continued to play with her dolls, but her aunts paid closer attention to her. They told her how, soon enough, she would have real babies to play with, and when they told her this, she thought how wonderful it would be if her dolls called her maman and cried for her. Then came the day they dressed her in fine clothes, and painted her cheeks. They celebrated with much ceremony and food. On the seventh night, she lay nervously beneath the blanket of a different bed, waiting for this stranger she had wed, this person now called husband, to enter this unfamiliar room in a new home that replaced the old. She remembers the following day. She stood weeping in the courtyard, pleading to go back to her mother and her dolls. She smiles to herself. It was a period of brief sorrow. She quickly learned to cling to her husband, to win his favor and his affection.

She places her hand on her stomach, and feels for the tiny flutter that suggests the other exists. "I'm here," Khorsheed says out loud. She hopes that the baby inside can hear her voice, or at least feel the reassurance of her palm against the tightness of her skin. She hums a song from her past. Who sang it to her? She closes her eyes and hums, trying to remember. Darkness. All she feels is the hum itself, the tremor of its chords and the vibration of her own flesh in response. In that darkness, she tries to make out the face of the child growing inside her, the curve of the lips, the rise of the flesh of the cheeks, the softness of lashes.

Instead, she imagines a young boy. Long-limbed. Black curls. He walks the street outside of their home, from the direction of the synagogue, a book in his hands, a bounce in his steps. The merchants in the streets pause a moment as he passes them and the boy greets each of the merchants by name. He stops before the barber to ask something, and Khorsheed waits to hear the barber pronounce the boy's name, this beautiful child with his rosy cheeks. She listens closely, but instead she hears the unfamiliar rattle of something metallic, a horn, shouted oaths. The sounds fade, the sunlight becomes brighter, and she sees the shadow of the boy's body turn toward the house, step to knock against the door. In her mind's eye, it is Rakhel who lets him in.

Khorsheed opens her eyes and notices that the day has turned ashen and the air cold. Perhaps the vision means that Rakhel will soon have a son, Khorsheed reasons. She senses that she is being watched and turns to look behind her again, but sees no one. A breeze passes.

The pomegranate tree sheds more leaves. The rattle of something metallic again, a horn, shouted oaths. Mahboubeh can't remember how long she has been standing outside, but her legs feel numb and her hands tremble when she holds them before her face. She studies the blue veins, now visible beneath the thin parchment of her skin. *Winter ap-*

proaches, she thinks, looking at the gray skies. But she cannot remember the passing of any season in this land. Only the periods of fire and the times of flood.

Mahboubeh places her hands on the small of her back and begins to walk slowly toward her home. She thinks about brewing tea. Her socks feel damp. A blanket. She remembers the snow in Kermanshah. She passes the fig tree and tests the rope she wrapped around its trunk. "A blanket of snow would have covered your branches, settled upon you, allowed you to sleep deeply, and dream of blossoms, humming bees," she says as she pats the trunk of the tree and continues to the kitchen. "Here there is no rest," she says, "just this partial wakefulness." She walks into her kitchen and to the stove. She lifts the kettle and fills it with water from the sink. She turns on the stove. The hiss, the blue flame. She sits at the table in her darkened kitchen and watches through the window as the shadows conquer her garden.

"Hurry," Rakhel says. She pushes the door open only halfway so that it does not creak on its hinges.

"What about our shoes, Dada?" Khorsheed says.

"We'll go barefoot, go."

"You go first." And Rakhel, impatient with the need to breathe fresh air, slides out of the door and runs through the breezeway, beneath the fresco of Moses parting the Red Sea, down the marble steps, across the empty courtyard toward the outer gardens, with Khorsheed at her heels. The wind catches the fabric of the girls' chadors, whips it off their heads so that they clutch it at their waists as their hair trails behind them. Their feet fall into the soft earth, the mud splatters against their bare calves, their tumbans rolled up to their knees. Once they round the corner of the house, they stop to breathe. Their cheeks are flushed with the excitement of their escape. Khorsheed bends over her protruding stomach and rests her hands on her knees, breathing heavily. "Ibrahim forbids me to run, Rakhel."

"We didn't run so much."

"Yes, but if he finds out. Or worse, if Zolekhah sees us out here, barefoot in the mud?"

"We'll be quick, and wash our feet in the pool before returning to the house." Rakhel looks down at her feet and curls her toes into the earth to feel the cold, smooth mud squeeze between them.

"I told you to ask the maids to pick some for us, Rakhel. I can't play with you like this anymore, I need to be much more cautious."

"It's different if we do it."

"There is no difference, you're just being childish."

"If we do it, the blessing would be a gift from our hands."

The pomegranate trees are heavy with fruit that have skin like worn leather, some already cracked into a smile of ruby teeth, some almost half empty of their seeds, the white combs left hollow by the black crows or the squirrels that dangle from the limbs, stuffing their fat cheeks. Rakhel takes her chador from around her waist, holds two corners, and watches the cloth ripple out into the wind as she lowers it to the wet grass. She stands on the tips of her toes and reaches her arms up to the nearest branch. She clutches the fruit with one hand and pulls the branch lower until there is a snap and the branch bounces back, leaving her holding the pomegranate, surprised by the sudden drops of water that fall from the wet leaves onto her face. She tosses the pomegranate into her chador, the fruit bounces and rolls like a red ball. Khorsheed reaches both her arms to lower a branch so Rakhel can pick more fruit. After Rakhel's arms are full, Khorsheed releases the branch suddenly and the tree rains down on them. Each time, the girls turn their faces up to the drops of water falling from the leaves that land on their eyelids, their lips, their cheeks.

"My feet are cold, Dada, I'll get sick."

Rakhel looks at Khorsheed, her cheeks red, her jaw trembling, her face damp, strands of her wet, black hair against her forehead, painted across the white of her neck. Khorsheed's breasts are full and Rakhel notices the insisting bulge of her belly beneath her shirt. Fat drops of rain fall from the gray clouds against their foreheads and arms.

"Come on," Rakhel says, gathering the corners of her chador and throwing the bundle over her shoulder, her back bent slightly under the weight of the fruit. They walk across the garden, then peer from the corner of the wall to see if anyone is in the courtyard. "I'll take the bundle and leave them by the kitchen, you start washing your feet," Rakhel says and quickly crosses the courtyard.

Khorsheed walks to the central pool and sits on the

ledge with her feet up, cups water from the pool and washes her ankles, rubs between her toes with her fingers. Rakhel returns, rolls the bottom of her tumban farther up, and steps her thin legs into the cold pool, scattering the goldfish this way and that, the water up to her knees. She walks around the pool, making waves, clutching her shaliteh high up around her waist, shivering. The water flows over the edge of the pool. Khorsheed jumps up, turns, and with a swoop of her hand against the surface of the water, splashes Rakhel, drenching the front of the girl's shirt. Rakhel bends and cupping water with both her hands, throws it out toward Khorsheed, who runs from the pool's edge, her feet slipping in the mud, her arms out for balance. The rain becomes steadier. The girls' eyelashes are wet, water streams from their faces, their clothes stick against their bodies.

"Khorsheed, come back and wash your feet, we have to go back inside before Zolekhah finds us."

"Promise you won't splash me."

"You are a pregnant woman, you must be treated with great care. Petted and fed and pampered like an exotic bird from Hindustan. Now come back."

"Promise," Khorsheed says, standing in the rain. "Or I'll tell Zolekhah you dragged me out here against my will." She walks back, puts her foot gingerly on the edge of the pool, and bends forward.

Rakhel grabs a handful of Khorsheed's hair and with her other hand, splashes water into her face. "Your nose is dirty," Rakhel says. "Let me clean it for you."

Khorsheed clutches Rakhel's wrist with both hands. "Dada, you're hurting me."

Rakhel laughs and releases Khorsheed, who spits out water and begins coughing violently. The rain comes down hard now, sheets of it break against the surface of the earth, against the water of the pool. Rakhel steps out of the pool, her tumban wet and sagging, drops of water falling from her fingertips. Khorsheed takes the hem of her short ruffled sha-liteh and twists it with her hands, squeezing out the water. The two girls walk back to the sitting room, the door blown wide open by the wind. Rakhel closes the door behind them and they stand soaking the edge of the thick red rug.

"Take your clothes off, quickly," Rakhel says when she sees that Khorsheed's lips are blue from the cold. She helps Khorsheed pull off her clothes, then removes her own. She drops the wet clothes in a pile and shakes her head back and forth. She walks across the room to the small brazier, takes a match and lights the coals inside it with trembling fingers, kneels on her bare haunches to blow so that the fire catches. Once the fire starts blazing, she closes the metal door, places a short-legged table on top of it, and drapes a blanket over the top of the table. Khorsheed walks across the rug on the tips of her toes, both hands clutching the small curve of her belly. She lays down beneath the blanket and Rakhel pulls it up to their chins. As the heat spreads from their feet, over their thighs, toward their hearts, the two girls fall fast asleep.

That's how Fatimeh finds them, asleep in each other's arms, naked under the *korsi*. She recognizes the wet chador stained red and bulging with pomegranates. She follows the muddy footprints up the stairs and across the marble of the breezeway, pushes open the door into the sitting room against the mound of wet clothes, sees the two girls asleep on the rug, Khorsheed snoring gently.

Fatimeh picks up the soaked pile of clothes and shuts the door softly behind her. She walks to the kitchen to pour more water into the samovar for the chai. She was much younger than Khorsheed when she herself married and bore her first child, born with its face clenched up and clutching at the cord wrapped like a black snake around its throat. Rakhel's age when she bled out her second child, two months before it was due. Both had been girls. By then, her husband was already old, working as a servant in the governor's office in the plaza of the city. "Should the Lord have seen them fit to live, my daughters would have married by now," she says out loud. "They would have had children of their own." She wrings out the water from the girls' clothes and imagines holding the warm, fat bodies of her grandchildren, imagines kissing the soft pink flesh of their arms and legs. She might have lived with her daughters, in the house of their husbands, raising those children. She shuffles to the hearth to tend to a pot.

"G-d is great," she says beneath her breath. She begins hanging the clothes from a rope drawn from one kitchen wall to the other. "G-d is great," she repeats, wiping her eyes with the hem of her chador. "G-d is great, G-d is great."

Snow covers the ground. And in the snow, footprints this way and that. The men's footprints lead toward the stables, the horses' footprints toward the gate, the women's footprints back and forth to the central pool, the kitchen, to the steps leading into the cellar. The sun travels a low arc in the sky and, not too long after making its appearance, it sets. In the kitchen, the girls work fast, their fingers stained a deep purple, their black chadors wrapped around their bodies to protect their clothes. Rakhel sits on the ground and Khorsheed squats, her belly resting between her thighs. Cracked and whole pomegranates form a mountain between them, beside which stands a bucket of the red skins with empty white combs and a crystal bowl full of the glistening, ruby seeds. Fast, their fingers remove the seeds into the bowl. Red juice pools beneath their hands, splatters onto their arms.

Zolekhah stands by the doorway of the kitchen, waiting for Fatimeh to return from the cellar with the fruit stored in the late summer for this very night. Sadiqeh and Zahra silently scrub cooking pots by the fountain, their breaths visible. Fatimeh returns, carrying a large watermelon. She sets it on the ground and poises the knife on the tip of the melon's tight green skin. One move and the whole melon cracks open, the flesh crisp and jagged, the heart red, surrounded by black teeth. She removes the rind and cuts the

flesh into square pieces, then arranges the pieces on a silver tray. Fatimeh leaves and returns from the cellar again,
this time with a basket of persimmons. She moves her legs
briskly up and down for warmth, her arms clenched to her
body. She shakes her shoulders and heads back into the cold
afternoon to tell one of the girls to wash the fruit in the
nearly frozen pool.

The women work silently, the dim light of the day
having made them somber and lethargic, though the cold
keeps them moving. When the women are finished arrang-
ing the fruits, they shuffle across the snow toward the five
doors of the sitting room. They place the trays on the tables
while Fatimeh pokes at the coals in the small brazier, places
the low table over it, and drapes the blanket over the table.
The girls push the chairs out of the way and gather the large
pillows to spread around the blanket. Wordlessly, they leave
the room. Sadiqeh and Zahra nod good-bye to the others
and walk to the gate, where their husbands await to escort
them home. Fatimeh retires to her room for the evening, to
say her prayers, eat her dinner, and drift to sleep. The rest of
the women leave for their private bedrooms, to prepare for
the evening. All that is left of the sun is a streak of orange
against the horizon.

Rakhel peers through her window in time to see Asher
leading his horse back across the courtyard toward the stables. Ibrahim follows silently behind him. When they return to the courtyard, they both stop near the pool, and she
watches them hold council, as is their custom each night,

before they part. Asher speaks at length and Ibrahim listens, nodding in agreement. Then Asher takes his leave, and Ibrahim walks toward his bedroom where Khorsheed sits brushing her hair by the lit window.

Asher walks past Rakhel's room toward his private study, his gaze down, his hands clasped behind his back. Rakhel waits a moment, then steals quietly down the breezeway toward the study. Through the window, she watches Asher light a lantern and walk to the gramophone. He turns the crank, carefully sets the needle down, and, after a few moments, closes his eyes.

Rakhel knocks softly on the door. He must be listening to his music, the *records* he orders from merchants he knows in faraway places like Austria and France. Places where men play instruments and catch the music on flat, black plates, music which sounds different from what she hears played by musicians at weddings and bar mitzvahs.

"Asher?" Rakhel calls from behind the door. "Asher, may I come in?" He does not respond. She cracks the door wider and calls his name again. He keeps his back to the door, and looks out of the window at the snow-covered courtyard.

She walks to him and places her hand on his back. He turns quickly and catches her wrist. He looks her in the eyes for a few moments, then brings her open hand to his lips and kisses her palm. Rakhel, unaccustomed to such tenderness from him, trembles at his touch. He pulls her into his chest, lowers his face into her hair, and breathes in. Then he holds her an arm's length away to look at her. The record stops. It is silent in the room, save for Asher's heavy breathing. Rakhel drops her eyes in shame. Asher takes her chin in his fingers and lifts her face until he is looking into her eyes again. He brushes his fingers across her cheek, traces a line down her neck, then he draws her to him and places his large hand under her shirt against the tight skin of her stomach. He moves his hands up the warmth of her flesh to where it rises into the small mounds of her breast, her nipples hard against his palm. Hastily, without warning, he pulls her jacket off of her arms, lifts her shirt over her head until she stands before him in the soft lamplight, looking down at her own thin arms, her small taut breasts, her tight abdomen. She raises her arms to cover her chest and he pushes them back down.

"I want to look at you," he says. She keeps her head down, biting her lower lip to keep her teeth from chattering with cold and fear. "Look at me," he says. She raises her eyes to meet his. "When will you give me a child?" he asks. She shudders and he draws her roughly back into his chest, lifts her chin with his fingers again to look into her eyes. "When?" he asks.

Now, she trembles violently against his body. With his other hand, Asher unties the waistband of her tumban, it falls to the floor and Rakhel stands with the skirt of her shaliteh covering her navel, the upper part of her thighs. He reaches his hand and pulls the shaliteh down her legs. She stands naked in the lamplight, her arms straight by her side, and looks at her feet. Her skin is raised in gooseflesh, the soft hairs standing, her legs pressed tight against each other. She bends slightly forward as if readying herself to take a blow from his clenched fist. He looks at her, then pulls her down onto the rug.

"I want a child," he whispers harshly into her ear as he struggles above her to push his own clothes out of the way. "I am tired of this waste," he says. "I want a child and I will give you until spring."

After dinner, Rakhel sits silently beside Khorsheed, who rests her legs under the heated blanket and eats spoon after spoon of pomegranate seeds. Rakhel keeps her eyes on the trays and platters that wait in a pile on the sofre, with the remains of food and pools of oil gathered in them. The conversation, as customary when there are no guests, is between Asher, Ibrahim, and Zolekhah. Khorsheed tried whispering with Rakhel at the beginning of the meal, but found Rakhel unresponsive and thus, busied herself with the task of eating. Rakhel tried to eat, too, but the food repulsed her.

Rakhel tries to look everywhere but at her husband. She imagines the servants washing the trays and the plates. She listens to Khorsheed hum to herself while she chews. When Rakhel does catch a glimpse of Asher sitting at the head of the sofre, a weakness takes hold of her arms and legs, and a strange dizziness clouds her eyes. Her mind begins to drift, but each time Asher begins to speak, the sound of his voice slaps her back to rigid attentiveness.

"I have decided what to do about the goyim bread

maker Haydaree's demand for a *jazieh*. The tax for being Jewish has been abolished since Nasir al-Din Shah, and these ruffians still think they can strong-arm money from us," Asher says. He turns to address his mother. "He says either we sell our wheat to him half price, or else he'll go to the authorities and complain about the proximity of Jews doing business beside Muslim merchants at the caravansary." Asher takes a handful of sunflower seeds from a bowl. He places a seed between his teeth, cracks and spits the shell to the floor, and chews the meat.

Ibrahim leans over and takes a handful, too. "He suffers, brother, like everyone else with the rise in the price of grains," he says. "Perhaps it might be wise to pay him, a mitzvah, and forget the whole ordeal?"

Asher continues cracking, spitting, chewing for a few moments, then turns to his brother and says, "So that every other bastard can come along and demand their own price? We have already kept our prices low. All that is left is for us to give the wheat away for free. I will send a couple of Kurdish farmers to respond to his proposal. We are men, even if the laws insist otherwise. It is time to set an example and Haydaree is the perfect opportunity. It happens thus, time to time, when we need to respond with a measured violence, to prove that we are not as vulnerable as they think. There comes a time when a man must act as a man."

Ibrahim still holds a seed in the palm of his hand and looks at it, before he finally cracks it between his teeth. "Perhaps you are right, brother," he says. "Though I spoke to the rabbi this very afternoon about this topic, at length. He said that compassion, even for one's enemies, is a necessity for spiritual growth."

Asher brushes off his hands, leans forward and says, "Speaking of compassion, did you ask the rabbi about Kokab's situation?"

"Briefly. Like everyone else, he wanted to leave early for Yalda," Ibrahim says.

"Kokab, your cousin Eliyahoo's wife?" Zolekhah asks.

"Nullified yesterday," Asher says. "Eliyahoo divorced her officially and took her back to her brothers' home."

"There's been talk among the women for months. Rumor says she bared her arms before a gardener or some such nonsense?" Zolekhah asks.

"Our cousin has always been a lazy man, a brute and a drunk," Asher says. "I am certain that Eliyahoo found it too difficult to keep a wife and has fabricated this story to hide his own shame."

"His sisters say that he plans to keep their young daughter and will refuse to allow Kokab to see her, even from a distance, for fear that the girl will learn from her mother's lewd nature," Zolekhah says.

"The poor wretched woman, to bring such calamity and shame upon her family," Ibrahim says.

"Yes, but from loss one can still profit," Asher says. He clears his throat. "Ibrahim and I have discussed this matter at length, with the rabbi. I plan to ask Kokab's brothers for her hand in marriage, as a second wife."

A heaviness settles in the room, the way a fog some-times comes in at night, rapidly. It is a tangible thickness Ra-khel can feel. It muffles the rest of the words Asher speaks. It makes breathing arduous. Zolekhah stares at Asher, then looks at her. From a tremendous distance, Rakhel hears Asher say, "If by spring, Rakhel has not conceived . . ."

"It is a mitzvah, this decision, an act of compassion," Ibrahim says.

"Yes," Asher says. "Kokab will be rescued from shame, her brothers will be free of their burden, and I may have children through her still, if G-d sees it fit."

Rakhel stands up in alarm and looks about the room. The door. She must reach the door, open it to the cold night air, before this heaviness buries her beneath its weight. She walks slowly in that direction, reaches the latch, pushes the door open. Rakhel watches herself as though she is not within herself, but standing somewhere, a witness to her own escape. There is Rakhel, stepping out into the night, and there she walks, barefoot, against the ice-cold marble, down the steps, through the snow toward her dark room.

Rakhel enters the stillness of her bedroom, and walks to the mirror. She sees the reflection of her embroidered head scarf, her black hair, but she can't make out the features of her own face. No eyes, no lips, no nose. She looks down at her feet and searches her memory to see if her face exists somewhere in the recesses of her mind. Her eyes are brown, yes, her nose has a slight bump, but it is not unattractive. She sees these parts as fragments, separate from each other, but she can't fit together the pieces to recall the whole they create. She puts her hands on the frame of the mirror, brings her face closer to the silver surface, and meets her own eyes. When she can see the reflection of her eyes, she takes a step back to look at the whole of her face. The girl looking back at her smiles. Rakhel shudders, turns away from the mirror, and covers her face with her hands.

In the sitting room, Khorsheed weeps. Zolekhah pats her hand repeatedly and says, "No, child, you mustn't allow yourself to cry. Consider the poor lamb in your womb. You must be calm for your baby."

"Khorsheed," Ibrahim says. Khorsheed stops sobbing and looks at him. "Enough." Khorsheed whimpers and wipes her eyes with the back of her hand. "Go to your room." Khorsheed begins to cry, again, silently. "No more crying. Go to bed." Khorsheed rises to leave.

Once she is gone, Zolekhah turns to Asher and says, "Perhaps you should have discussed it with me, first, son."

"It was not a matter for discussing," Asher says.

"Of course it is a topic for discussion. Look how upset you have made everybody. You are bringing another person into this family, somebody we all must live with."

"Mother, it is not a matter for discussing."

"There are ways of doing things, Asher. Proper ways of doing things."

"Nothing has been done, yet. I have not gone to her brothers, I haven't spoken to anybody. This was the private announcement of my intentions, that's all."

"You should have discussed it with me first. Then, I could have instructed you on how to tell Rakhel, first, rather than shaming her in front of all of us. There are certain words a man should say to his wife . . . "

"Wife? What sort of *wife* is she to me if she cannot do her sole task?"

"She is human, nonetheless. There would have been a better way to tell her."

"What better way, Mother? What better way to tell her that I will marry again, that she will have a *havoo*?" Asher leans toward his mother, his fists clenched against his side and hisses, "And what business of hers is it, besides? A girl to decide my fate? A girl who cannot do what even a stupid cow can do with ease?" Asher picks up the bowl of pomegranate seeds and throws it against the wall across the room.

"Brother, please," Ibrahim says and places a hand on Asher's arm.

Zolekhah stares at her son steadily. Asher looks back at her, red with rage. "For what reason must I waste everything I have built? For what reason? For her, Mother? For a worthless girl?" Asher clenches his jaw, pushes Ibrahim's hand away and stands to leave. "A man who has no son, Mother, is no man at all."

In her room, Rakhel turns to look back at the reflection in the mirror. The girl in the mirror watches her, too. She studies the outline of Rakhel's body. Too lean. Her breasts too small. Her stomach caves in, her limbs are too hard, her arms too long, her legs too long, her feet too big, her skin too dark.

"Why did You choose me to curse?" Rakhel asks. She throws herself at the mirror with her fists clenched, but the surface only bounces back slightly. She hits her forehead against it, hits her clenched fists against it, again and again and again, not noticing the small veins that cracked in the surface of the glass where she pounds, or the walls shaking. She hears a distant screaming, though it is her own voice. Then, the clear sound of shattering glass.

Four

❦

Outside it is night. There will be frost in the morning, the concrete treacherous, the grass white, the rooftops, too. The kettle whistles. Mahboubeh rises from the table and measures out tea leaves. She remembers the last time she saw her uncle Asher. He sat in the courtyard, in the snow, looking at the pool and fountain. He must have been returning from the caravansary, because he wore a heavy wool coat over his clothes. He walked into the courtyard, but rather than heading to his private study to place a record on the gramophone, which was his custom, he stopped and sat on the steps beneath the fresco and looked at the fountain for a long, long time. A few days later, he died. Mahboubeh remembers that she was asleep in her room when Rakhel walked in and sat beside her bed and said, very calmly, "Asher is dead."

By then, Rakhel already had her son, Asher's sole heir. Her position in the household was firm. So when she announced Asher Malacouti's death, Rakhel's voice was clear of the panic that should have followed such a statement. And clear of sentiment, too. She spoke as though discussing a settlement of accounts. "Asher is dead," she said, then rose and left.

Mahboubeh pours herself a cup of tea and wonders what her uncle sat reckoning that cold, late afternoon as he gazed at the fountain. He was not a man to give to idle thought. Perhaps in that moment, whether he knew of his encroaching final hour or not, he stopped to consider the value of his life. Certainly he had earned respect, built an empire, but what about love? Did he love, was he loved in return? Nothing in Rakhel's voice hinted at a loss of love when she announced his death, though in those days, love was not a factor to determine any marriage.

Before Rakhel became Asher Malacouti's wife, she was just a bread maker's daughter. Rebbe Youseff, Asher's father, had already rested in the earth for many years before Asher came to the age when it was time for him to take a wife. By then, he had already multiplied his father's inheritance exponentially, and everyone spoke of Asher Malacouti's ability to turn even mule dung into a brick of gold. When Asher's beard came in fully, he was the richest Jew in Kermanshah, and men much older than he, Jew and Muslim alike, who had been investing and selling and buying for years and years, came to him for advice. At home, he ran the household and took on the role of father for his younger brother, Ibrahim, advising him and tutoring him, even chastising him about the necessity of being more shrewd, more zealous in the pursuit of building wealth. Zolekhah watched her eldest son with great pride, and sometimes with a bit of fear. When one of the women at the hammam commented about her son playing the man without ever bedding a girl, she knew it was time to find Asher a wife.

One day, when Zolekhah went visiting the sister of the widowed bread maker in the andaruni of their home, she saw the bread maker's daughter helping with the dough, kneading it with her hands, flattening it paper thin, slapping it against the wall of the *tanoor* in their yard. "This one," Zolekhah told Asher when she returned home, "this one is intelligent and not lazy." She went to the hammam the following day, knowing that Rakhel and her aunts were attending, and she watched the girl from a distance. The girl had no deformities, her skin was healthy. "Yes, this one will be a good match for you," Zolekhah told Asher later, and he agreed that she should approach the bread maker's sister to speak her intentions.

Once the women had the preliminary dialogue, it became the men's business. The men entered the bread maker's home and sat on the rug, against the cushions that lined the walls of the small room. Asher's eldest uncle sat to his right, and Ibrahim to his left, directly across the room from the bread maker. Asher leaned back onto the cushion to survey the room, then quickly thought his posture suggested laziness, or indolence, and sat upright. The windows were open, and the breeze that passed through the dancing lace curtains felt cool against his perspiring forehead.

"Are you nervous?" Ibrahim whispered.

"I carry the better half of this deal," Asher said. He wasn't nervous. But the room. The room was stifling, with all those men gathered, and the excited whispers of the hidden women that peaked from behind the tattered cloth that separated this room from the only other room in the home. Asher felt the women's searching eyes on his skin. They watched his every gesture, considered his height, measured the width of his shoulders, decided whether the tilt of his chin suggested strength or too much pride masking weakness, perhaps even laughed at the way he sat. Asher relaxed his shoulders and arranged the cushions behind him so that he could lean against the wall with his back straight. He looked at his own hands clutched in his lap and instead decided to hold each knee of his folded legs. Once he felt that his posture was correct and that his visage commanded respect, he turned his attention to the bread maker, without looking directly at him but focusing on the roses in a vase in the alcove of the wall above the bread maker's head. The bread maker talked to the man beside him, his brother, a merchant of spices Asher recognized from the caravansary. The bread maker fingered the beads of the *tasbih* he held in one hand and patted his knee absentmindedly with the other. The brother spoke to him in low urgent tones, stopping to smile at someone on Asher's side of the room, to bow his head in greeting a couple of times, before resuming his whispered counsel.

"He is probably telling the old man to demand a higher dowry than the one we suggest," Asher whispered to Ibrahim.

"Allow Uncle Moshe to do the talking, out of respect," Ibrahim said.

Asher looked at his aged uncle sitting beside him. It should have been his father. It should have been his father, beside him, these many years. How proud Rebbe Yousseff would have been to see the way the men at the caravansary address Asher, how proud he would have been to see the loyalty of the Kurds. The two of them might have worked alongside each other, building this future together. And when his father would have grown too old, he'd leave the business in his son's capable hands, and rest, surrounded by the joy of his grandchildren, Asher's sons and daughters, who'd dote on him and give him living proof that there was some meaning to all that toil, that his life wasn't a life lived in vain.

Asher felt a heaviness in his chest, and turned his attention to the sound of a group of boys playing in the streets. A passing street peddler interrupted their play with his song, *lima beans, lima beans, the greenest, freshest lima beans.* The children took up the peddler's song, their voices taunting, adding their own vulgar refrains until the peddler's loud curses were followed by the sound of running feet. The other men in the room stopped their conversation to listen to the commotion in the street, and the silence that ensued hung heavy in the room.

"Boy children," Asher's eldest uncle said, "a blessing, the devils." The men in the room laughed.

"Yes, a blessing. If they do not turn every hair on your head white with their antics," the bread maker said. "Now a daughter, a true blessing, a comfort, a balm for the aching heart in old age." The room resumed a grave silence for a moment, and then came the jingle of teacups on a tray. A hand reached out and pulled aside the curtain, and a woman in a chador, an elder aunt perhaps, stepped through and into the room amidst the men. She walked to Asher's eldest uncle first, offered him chai and dates with a reserved smile on her lips. She whispered welcome, welcome, then served each man until she reached the bread maker last, who took his glass and saucer without looking at her. He held the glass delicately and tipped the chai with one hand into the saucer he held in the palm of the other. He blew noisily on the saucer, then sipped from it. The woman glanced around the room once, her gaze resting on Asher a moment longer than the rest, then bowed her head slightly and disappeared behind the curtain.

"Your hospitality is commendable," Asher's uncle said.

"For a guest of such great honor, it is nothing."

"No, truly, the honor is ours."

"No, no the honor mine, you have graced my home with your presence."

"We have come with intentions we hope worthy of you and your home. We have come to ask for your daughter as a bride."

"Ah, she is more than a daughter, more than a girl to me. So intelligent, she is, so hardworking. Worth twelve sons, that one."

"Asher is a jewel of a son, had I one like him, myself, though he is like my own." The uncle nodded his head toward Asher. "This young man is one of the richest merchants of the caravansary, goyim and Jew alike. My brother's wealth, *zichrono livracha,* grows like weeds beneath Asher's hands. He owns three villages, and land in several others . . . "

"Yes, yes, a praiseworthy young man," said the bread maker. "Alas, how material wealth leaves the heart empty, though."

"Yes," the uncle said, "but the belly full," and he patted his own protruding stomach. The men laughed quietly and sipped their chai. The bread maker smiled and nodded his head. He placed his tea glass and saucer down, and picked up his tasbih once more.

Fingering the beads, he said, "Rakhel is a gem. Unlike girls raised to sleep and gossip all day. She is a rare, rare gem. And since having lost my poor wife, I cannot bear the thought of losing her, too." The bread maker shook his head.

"I have yet to see a girl like her. I'm sorry, but I will have to say no to your admirable offer." A silence settled on the room once more. Asher knew it was a ritual, but he couldn't help feeling slighted. He cleared his throat, and his uncle touched his arm.

"Well, we must be on our way, we have put your household through enough trouble," his uncle said and he rose with difficulty. The rest of the men in the room stood. After much procedure, of bowing of the head and praise of the host, Asher found himself in the street once more. He stood in the late afternoon sun, blinking.

"The requirements of custom are cumbersome, son," his uncle said, patting Asher's back.

"Everyone in the room knows the fortune that has be-fallen the bread maker," Ibrahim said.

"Yes, but he must refuse in order to save face. It is important to do so," the uncle said. "For Asher, as much as himself. We do not want people to say that Asher's bride was thrown at him."

Asher smiled at his uncle. "When will we return?" he asked.

"In a week's time."

"And will I see her, then?"

"I'm sure you will," his uncle had said. "He cannot af-ford to lose your interest."

After being turned away, Asher and his uncles waited a week, then returned to meet again with the bread maker and the men of his family. Once they settled on the rug and leaned back on the cushions propped against the walls, there came a hushed commotion from behind the curtain. Then, pushed forth from the other room behind the tattered cloth, Rakhel stood before them. A swell in the cloth discreetly nudged her farther into the room. Rakhel took a halting step forward with the heavy tray, stopped, looked around until her gaze reached Asher, then looked down quickly. A moment, she waited, then raised her head firmly back up, a look of stone resolve in her eyes and she marched across the rug, balancing the tray in her hands with stoic grace. She lowered the tray before Asher's uncle first and said, "Welcome."

Asher's uncle took his saucer and glass of chai, then hesitated in his choice of pastry, his extended finger hovering over the *beheshti,* faltering before the baklava, until he selected a square of *sohan* and said, "Thank you, daughter. Surely sweetness offered from your hands is an omen of sweet days to follow." Rakhel's cheeks turned crimson and she looked back, for a brief moment, in the direction of the curtain. Asher studied her profile. A delicate face. Fine cheekbones. She took a step in his direction and he smiled to himself. She extended the tray, the amber liquid in the cups moving perceptibly, the silver spoons attesting to her uneasiness.

"Welcome," she whispered. She kept her eyes on the chai, the pastries on the tray. Asher looked at her neck and her defined collarbone. There was a certain grace to her body, despite how thin she was. He glanced at her hands.

Her skin seemed so soft. She was a bit too thin, but then, after the first child, her hips would certainly widen. He realized his survey exceeded the accepted time allotted for choosing a pastry, and he quickly picked one before the host might presume his too-slow assessment of either his daughter or his baked goods an insult.

Rakhel moved to serve Ibrahim, and Asher poured chai from his glass into the saucer and blew on it, the steam rising, swirling into the filtered sunlight of the room. The lace curtains cast rose-patterned shadows on the floor. He noticed Rakhel's bare feet from the corner of his eyes. Despite her measured movements, her hennaed toes nervously clenched and unclenched the red wool of the rug.

Yes, he thought to himself. *She will do.*

Asher nodded at Ibrahim. Ibrahim smiled in response and shrugged his shoulders. Then Asher looked at his uncle, and the old man looked back without blinking, waiting for Asher to reveal his decision about the match. Asher nodded his head slightly and closed his eyes briefly to convey his approval. His uncle smiled and leaned over to pat Asher's knee with his hand. Then, he cleared his throat. The bread maker looked directly at the uncle, who smiled again and nodded once. Rakhel had worked her way around the room and approached her father with the final glass of tea remaining on the tray. The bread maker took his glass and saucer and said something beneath his breath to the girl standing before him. She turned slightly so that she might see Asher from the corner of her eyes, and then disappeared behind the curtains once more. When women's whispering in the other room ceased, the men proceeded to discuss the dowry items.

The preparations for a wedding were a celebration in themselves. Mahboubeh remembers those days as the happier ones of her childhood. The house full of women laughing and gossiping, eating and preparing for the feasts. The children, caught up in the merriment, stole from the abundance of sweetmeats and delicacies, a conspiracy overlooked by the adults. So much noise in the gardens, in the rooms, for a moment Mahboubeh felt a sense of belonging.

She looks about her darkened kitchen. A coyote yelps outside in the distant hills. Its brothers begin laughing in response. She imagines the rabbit they must be chasing, the pursuit, the frantic flight, the joy of the chase. Her house is cold. She picks up her cup of tea, but that has cooled, too. She closes her eyes and remembers when the women gathered, even to celebrate little things, in hope of dispelling the monotony of their days. They came together for the plucking of a bride's eyebrows, the sixth night of a daughter's birth, the first meal of a baby, the spilt blood after the first night of being a wife. And they gathered to celebrate holy days, too, and for the preparation of feasts for those sanctified days, and for Sabbath dinners. And sometimes, they entered each other's homes just to bring news, to share the joy or spread the shame, to help with an ailing mother, to mourn, to console, to counsel, to tell stories, to eavesdrop, to bring a talisman against miscarriage, a remedy to win back a straying husband, to bring news about the misconduct of potential grooms, to gossip about the shamelessness of potential brides, to return borrowed china, to apologize, to pray, to forgive.

They knocked on the heavy wooden door, the knocker to the right, a different pitch of iron against iron, to let the women of the household know that it was another woman at the door, a sister, a friend, a seamstress. If a man knocked, the knocker to the left sounded a deeper tone. Then, the woman answering put a finger in her mouth, in the corner of her cheek, to mask her voice before asking who called and for what business, so that the sweetness of her voice might not lead the man behind the door to sinful thought, rouse him to break open that very door and drag her down in shame. Rarely did a woman open the door for an unknown man, unless it was a peddler, selling needle and thread, or one of these men who did small tasks for coins, scouring pots, fetching pails from the bottom of wells, sharpening knives. But if it was a woman who knocked, then the women let in the cloaked figure, and if no men were home, then the woman entering through the threshold removed her ruband, her chador, her head scarf, let loose her hair, took off her shoes, rolled up her sleeve, entered the andaruni, laughing out loud, hitched up her skirt to wash her feet in the pool, splashed water on her face if it was a hot day, accepted the mint sherbet or the chai, and sat down to a feast of words.

Mahboubeh remembers when, a year after Asher's death, news spread throughout the Jewish mahalleh that Rakhel was searching for a bride for Yousseff, the sole heir to the Malacouti estate. All day the knocker announced the arrival of another potential girl, her aunts and mother in attendance, stopping by to pay their respects to Rakhel, on their way from here to there. Mahboubeh sat in her room studying for an exam when one of the servants came running to fetch her. Rakhel insisted that Mahboubeh keep the girl company while she entertained the women.

Mahboubeh reluctantly earmarked the page in her book, closed it, and rose with a sigh. For an hour or so, Mahboubeh sat in the guest hall, sipping her chai and trying to speak with the girl so that she could report back to Rakhel whether the candidate was suitable or not. Sometimes, however, the girl was reluctant to speak. Often, though, the girl knew the opportunity this meeting afforded her, and so she went out of her way to chat with Mahboubeh. Usually, those girls did not attend school, or if they did, they were not too serious about their studies, so that the conversations between Mahboubeh and the potential bride hit walls of silence. Mahboubeh would look to Rakhel, who glared back at her until she attempted another avenue of dialogue. When the visitors left, Rakhel began the questioning. *Does she read too much?* Rakhel asked. *Is she very interested in gold and trinkets? Does she seem docile? Vain? Lazy? Did you sense in her a harlot? A girl who'd demand this and that from her husband?*

Then, one day, a young girl arrived with her mother and aunts. Beautiful. Shy. She held a doll to her chest and sat quietly, listening to the women talk. When Mahboubeh sat beside her, she looked up at Mahboubeh and asked, "Would you like to hold my baby?"

Speechless, Mahboubeh took the doll from the girl and held it cradled in her arms. "What's her name?" Mahboubeh finally asked.

"Hannah," the girl said.

Mahboubeh handed the doll back. "She is very well behaved," she said. "You must be a wonderful mother." The girl smiled, and for the rest of the visit, she tended to her baby.

When the girl and the women who accompanied her left, Rakhel looked at Mahboubeh and said, "That one reminds me of Khorsheed." They sat in silence for several moments. Mahboubeh wondered *does she have her face,* or *her mannerisms, is it the way she loved her baby,* but Rakhel rose to leave before Mahboubeh could find the voice to ask.

"Tell the servants a decision has been made," Rakhel said without looking back. "Tell them to send the rest away."

Mahboubeh sits in her kitchen, in silence. She cannot hear the coyotes in the hills any longer. She considers turning on the lights, but outside her window, she can see her garden silver in the moonlight. *Loneliness is a palpable sensation,* she thinks to herself, *the presence of an absence.* She closes her eyes to shut out the darkness of her kitchen and the quiet of the night, when she hears the sound of women chattering.

She sees Zolekhah, a week before Asher's wedding, standing amidst them like a captain at the helm of a ship. Everyone around her engages in some industry, cooking or baking or washing. They come early in the morning and work well into the afternoon, until they leave for their own homes, where they make dinners for their husbands and brothers before those men return from the work of their day. The merrier the women are, the better the outlook for the match. And so the women laugh easily, and sing often.

On one of those frenzied days before the wedding celebration, Asher decided to send Ibrahim ahead to run the business of the caravansary, while he remained behind to work out the mathematics of yields and taxes. All day he tried to drown out the incessant noise of the women's talk and laughter by closing his study's windows and turning on the gramophone, but by noon he realized that his chances of thinking straight were better in the hubbub of the marketplace than in his own home.

Asher peeked his head out of the door and looked down the breezeway in both directions to see if a wayward aunt might trap him with an offer of advice, or a cousin might entangle him in an hour's worth of synagogue gossip about so-and-so's daughter, but it was after lunch and all the women had retired to the five-doored sitting room to rest during the afternoon heat. He stepped gingerly out of his study and quietly closed the door.

Asher walked across the courtyard to the stables, lost in his own thoughts, when he heard a voice singing and

looked up to see the colors of the afternoon a brighter orange. He felt the depth of the August heat, and the scent of
the dying roses permeated the air. His cousin's new bride,
Kokab, stood in the pool of the fountain, the water around
her a more magnificent blue than he remembered. Her skirt
was tied up in a knot above her knees, her calves glistening
wet in the shallow water. Red apples floated in that pool,
bobbed in the small ripples of her motion, collected around
her, floated away from her grasp. She stood up to rewrap
her chador around her waist and when she bent over again
to wash the apples, the tips of her thick, black hair touched
the water.

She sang and his eyes followed the sound to the
smooth, white skin of her throat, to the rise and fall into
the white valley between her breasts. He saw her, and her
beauty burned into his flesh a yearning deeper than anything he had ever felt before. In this pause in eternity, Asher
felt at once the promise of his own death and the beckoning of his desire. Within that moment, Kokab looked up to
meet his gaze. Asher could not move. He stared at her in
that fountain, trapped in the simple notes of her solitude,
and knew that he would give it all, the wealth, the future of
his progeny, the honor of his name, to hold this woman he
could not touch. He stood thus, frozen in the wake of that
afternoon when his eyes were opened and he perceived with
terror his vulnerability to desire. She looked at him with her
black animal eyes, tilted her head slightly, then went back
to her task, as though it had only been a sparrow she had

witnessed, a dust-covered sparrow hopping in the dirt of the yard. He turned and walked quickly to the stables, his body hot, now with shame.

Though later he forgot how he managed the horse or led it past Kokab and into the streets, Asher soon found himself riding at the foothills of the mountain. A cloud of dust rose behind him. His body rose and fell, the sun beat down on him, his muscles taut. His ears heard nothing but the sound of her voice singing, his eyes saw nothing but the indifference in her eyes, and no matter how hard he rode that horse, his thoughts stayed trapped in that moment in the courtyard, where he imagined how he should have walked toward the fountain, pushed her down into the water, grabbed her bared shoulder, pulled her hair, forced her to turn those black animal eyes away from him with something more than just indifference. He buried his heels into the side of the horse and thought of the soft of her flesh bruised, the white of her skin revealing the evidence of his hurt pride, the spreading deep purple of his shame across her cheeks, and when in the cool of the evening he was spent in his rage, he trotted home slowly and dreamed of the apologies of his lips against the lobe of her ear as they sat, hidden deep in the recesses of that garden.

He did not see her again until the week of the wedding celebrations. That Monday, all the members of his family, his distant cousins, his childhood friends, arrived with musicians who plucked the strings of the *kamancheh* and *tar,* wailed of love through the *ney,* beat deep rhythms with *dafs* raised over their heads. He sang and danced with the guests. He drank glasses of wine and spoke to his cousins and uncles about the future.

Standing to accept the blessings of an old aunt, Asher saw Kokab across the courtyard, leaning against the trunk of a poplar tree, distant from the crowd, gazing at the last brilliant streak of red against the dusk blue skies. Suddenly, the blood in Asher's veins turned to fire and crept into his hands, up toward his face, and he feared that the old woman clutching his hand and talking about his future joy and the merits of his young bride might feel the change in his body and know his shame. He wrestled his hand from hers, smiled and thanked her profusely for her kindness, then stole away. He stood hidden amidst the crowd, among a hundred faces that talked and laughed.

The entirety of a courtyard stretched between himself and Kokab, but Asher felt as though he were close enough to feel her breath faintly on his skin. He turned away, for fear of being caught in such shameful circumstances, at his own engagement party, staring at a woman belonging to another man. His cousin Eliyahoo lurked somewhere in that garden lit by lanterns, his disembodied head floating through Asher's mind, a large, round face with fleshy lips, an insolent nose red with wine, teeth already yellowed by tobacco. Asher remembered seeing him undressed at the hammam. *How a man with arms like a woman thinks himself worthy of holding such a wife,* Asher wondered.

Asher looked up again and in that moment, Kokab

turned in his direction. She met his eyes and held him there, terrified and exhilarated, in her gaze. A circle of dancing women came between them and she continued to look at him. Asher looked at her, too, and the whole world spun madly about them, the garden, the voices, the music, the dusk-darkened treetops overhead, the first few stars appearing in the night skies. From above the heads of the dancing women, Asher watched Kokab's stillness, this woman who stood alone in contemplation first of the setting sun, and now him, this woman who remained untouched by the joy and frenzy of all the other guests.

Then, Kokab was gone. She disappeared into the crowd and he looked for her until darkness descended completely and the lanterns betrayed too many shadows. He could no longer discern one face from another. He mumbled formalities in response to blessings, then found himself carried by the crowd toward the door leading into the tight streets, pushed along by words of encouragement and hands slapping his back. He walked behind his mother, who held a tray of jewels, gifts for the bride, over her head as the procession poured through the door of their home, loud with song, and turned in the direction of the bread maker's home. A few times, he glanced over his shoulder as if to turn back, but the hands were quick to hold his elbows and a chorus of promises to respond that this marked the beginning of a joyous life. Before he knew it, he stepped through the narrow doorway of the bread maker's home and there sat Rakhel in a chair placed in the center of the room, surrounded by women who burst into loud ululations and men who whistled and musicians who took up their tune.

Asher stood frozen before Rakhel, staring at her as though she were a stranger. She looked up to see his expression, her own gaze full of panic, before she looked down to her hands clasped in her lap. With her head tilted down, she glanced up again and he nodded his head, but before he could smile to reassure her that he recognized her, a group of women surrounded her and began adorning her with the gifts from his family, a gold-threaded shawl on her shoulders, gold bangles from her wrists to her elbows, emerald rings for her fingers, heavy gold trinkets for her hair, and gold coins, one after another, *clink, clink, clinking* in time to the music, dropped into a bowl placed in her lap.

Morning came. The men came for him, Ibrahim, his bachelor cousins and boyhood friends. They slapped his face until he opened his eyes and they made him drink hot chai. They laughed and boasted as he groaned with the weight of the previous night still heavy in the pit of his stomach. They rose from the sofre, pulled him up from the floor, and carried him, like a man wounded in battle, to the hammam. In the hammam the men sang loudly and told bawdy jokes and laughed heartily. Asher, too, sang and laughed, but only a part of him sat there in the steam of that afternoon among those young men.

Another night passed and another day. The crowd of people filled his sitting room, spilled into the courtyard, wandered to the outer gardens. Family and relatives surrounded him with much commotion until the dusk of that Thursday. Asher stole away from the guests and retreated to his study. He sat behind his desk, his books and abacus before him, the gramophone caught repeating the same three notes of Beethoven's *Moonlight Sonata*. His eldest uncle entered his study, stood before his desk and asked, "You are hiding?"

Asher could not find the words to speak. His uncle patted him on the back and said, "Come, son, there is nothing to fear. Tonight is a night for joy, and tomorrow night, for an even greater joy." Asher stood absently and allowed the old man to lead him by the hand. They came to a room where Rakhel stood, a window behind her and the setting sun so bright that Asher could see only the eclipse of light behind her darkened body. They led him to her and he stood before her. Without looking at her face, he drew the veil over her eyes, and behind it, in the mesh embroidered with gold thread, she might have been Kokab.

Soon there will be the prayer, Asher thought. *There will be the wine, the ring, the breaking of glass, there will be witnesses and the signing of contracts and the consummation, and tomorrow night, Rakhel's naked body in my arms and she will be mine and it is not the other, not the one who held my soul in her gaze, who left me trembling.* He turned and left the room, walked past the old bread maker, past his uncles, past the singing and clapping guests to the old rabbi who waited beneath the bridal chuppah.

From beneath the canopy of the chuppah, Asher watched

Rakhel's approach. The women's ululations pierced the air. The reverberations of their sound weakened his knees. They clapped and sang as Rakhel walked toward him, faceless beneath the veil, one hand held by her widowed aunt, one held by Zolekhah. The two women released their hold. Asher noticed his own rapid breathing. He closed his eyes. Rakhel circled him once and he felt her nearness. Twice, and he smelled the scent of her flesh and of rosewater. She circled him a third time, and he imagined the glance of black animal eyes. A fourth time, and he searched his mind for the recollection of his bride's eyes, for the eyes of this girl who walked around him. A fifth time and he could not remember the face of the veiled girl at all, not anything of her face. A sixth and he felt overwhelmed with fear. If he could stop the moments from advancing, silence the guests, the rabbi, his own breath, and steal quietly into the night. If he could reach his horse, and lead it softly to the street, into the open fields, over the mountains. If he could just hold this moment, perhaps cast everything into a deep slumber so that he might escape this inescapable dream. He opened his eyes to see Rakhel circle him for the seventh time. Then she stood beside him and someone placed her hands in his own lifeless hands and he felt no heat from either his own flesh, or hers. Nothing burned between them and his body became suddenly drenched with cold sweat and he thought, *this, this is my death* and he heard words and sipped wine and heard his own voice promise *Haray aht m'kudeshet li b'taba'at zo k'dat Moshe v'Yisrael* in response and saw his own hand, trembling, place a gold ring on her extended finger and nothing seemed more impossible than what his body had already done, the betrayal of his hands, the betrayal of his voice. Asher heard the rabbi read the ketuba, and then instruct him to drink again and Asher raised a glass of dark wine to his lips and he understood, then, with great awe and terror, that he had deceived himself, and that this treason lurked within his own heart, a thief in the dark night of his own making, the one that will, soon, very soon, raise the sharp blade of his dagger and rend his very soul. That wine burned his throat, and he felt it spread to his heart and to his arms and to his hands, to his fingers and suddenly he felt Rakhel's hand in his own. He breathed in her scent, this bride who was not the other, and his body betrayed him a third time. He brought down his foot with fury upon the glass, and with the clear sound of its shattering, he felt an intense desire for the veiled girl before him, felt it in his flesh and knew that, this time, there would be a quenching of thirst. Beneath the canopy of the chuppah, made of his father's tallith, the prayer shawl that held the weight of his father's hopes and fears and dreams, Asher remembered that the color of the eyes of his new bride was the shade of honey.

Five

❧

The day is a uniform gray. The sky
still. Mahboubeh sits at the dining
table and looks at the naked branches
of the trees through the living room window. *August is an immeasurable distance from now,* she thinks.
She rises heavily from the table and walks to the
cold fireplace. She takes a book from the mantel
and blows the dust from its cover. She returns to
the table, sits and closes her eyes, the book resting
in her lap. Then she opens the book to a random
page and begins reading out loud. "Like Yakov, I
am crying, for the beautiful face of Yousseff is my

desire. Without you, the city is my prison. Wandering, the mountain and desert are my desire."

Mahboubeh closes the book and remembers her father, Ibrahim, reciting these poems, his eyes closed, tears streaming down his face. As a child, she'd steal into his room, hide in a corner and listen to him, the book open in his lap, his head thrust back, reciting, almost singing poetry. When she became older, she learned the poems, too, by heart and wondered if it was the loss of her mother that inebriated her father with such sorrow that he sang from dawn to dusk, lost to the world before him.

Before her mother's death, her father was a religious man. Each day, on his way to the caravansary, Ibrahim walked first to the synagogue to bind his arms and place The Word upon his flesh in hope that the light that filtered in through the windows, in that instant, in the next, might illuminate a path. And in the afternoons, after the azan sounded from the minarets, when the other men took their rest either at home, or in the caravansary, their bellies full, tired from the work of the morning, Ibrahim hurried back to the synagogue to find the old rabbi and study with him, argue with him, demand answers for all the questions that harried him night and day.

And each of those afternoons, on his way back to the caravansary from the synagogue, Ibrahim passed the same dervish, bare chested, hair unkept, who sat shoeless in the shade of a mulberry tree and laughed, spoke to birds, to the tree, to anyone passing, and sang beneath the skies, sang from dawn to dusk and into the night. Ibrahim asked the dervish one day, "What inspires you to sing all day?" The dervish stopped singing and smiled. He held open his empty hands and said, "Wouldn't you sing, too, if you held all the wealth of this world in the palms of your hands?"

Ibrahim envied the dervish. Often, he stopped to watch him from behind a wall for a moment and imagined himself as that man, wanting nothing, needing nothing, free of the cumbersome possessions of this world, and free, too, of the yoke of custom, propriety, expectations. But that moment couldn't have been long, as his older brother waited, frowning because Ibrahim tarried too long with holy men who got fat from the hard work of real men and did nothing all day but fill the heads of the feeble-minded with fantasies.

Coins and the counting and the goods and the lands and the trades kept Ibrahim busy. Merchants came in from the deserts with their camels, tired and dust covered, and these men led the exhausted animals to water, then drank themselves and came to speak to Ibrahim about their journeys before buying bundles of tobacco and wheat before heading back out, again, into the nothing. *Even they,* Ibrahim thought to himself, *even they are on a path, a meditation in the repetition of the road they travel, learning mirages from reality, disciplined by their thirst and the tiredness in their bones.*

At the end of each day, Ibrahim walked back to his home, its high walls, its large gardens, the rooms of valuable antiques, his beautiful young wife who spoke like a little bird. Then dinner and weekly Sabbaths, weddings, celebrations for the births of sons, or the wild mourning for the dead, or holy days and their circumscribed procedures, which he followed for a while, until that one day when he buried his young wife, and renounced everything.

Ibrahim did not leave behind much. A crowd of motherless children. A handful of photographs. And this book he gave to Mahboubeh before he died. She holds it in her hands, the binding undone, the pages browned, brittled. She touches the green leather cover, traces the engraving on the leather with her finger, the gold of the title long gone. It is a collection of the poems of Jalāl ad-Dīn Muḥammad Rūmī. Mahboubeh closes her eyes and sees Ibrahim sitting, in his old age, in the corner of his room. He sways gently to the rhythm of his recitation.

"What did you gain for your sacrifice?" she asks him, but he does not answer her. He keeps his eyes closed, and weeps and sings until he falls into sleep, slumped on a cushion Mahboubeh places for him against the wall.

Ibrahim awakens in the fraction of the moment before Khorsheed screams. He turns to find his wife's moonlit face contorted in pain, her body drenched with sweat. He stumbles in the dark to find the matches. She moans. Ibrahim's fingers shake so violently that the matches fall unlit, one by one, to the dark floor.

"Hold on, hold on," he says. Again and again, his hands are like hands in a dream, incapable of steady movement, until, suddenly, the gold spark, the blue hiss and light. He places the candle beside the bed and pulls the blankets off his wife.

Khorsheed clutches her abdomen with both hands, and rocks side to side on the soaked bedclothes. Ibrahim feels the room pulsate. The walls move perceptibly in toward him, then out again. The ground softens, giving. He kneels beside her bed. "What should I do?" he asks. Khorsheed screams again and grabs the bedclothes with her hands, the muscles of her body tightening. Ibrahim's whole being halts in this moment, in the stretch of his wife's open mouth, in the quivering of her thighs, in the arch of her back, the bulging veins of her fists. In this instant, he no longer inhabits his own body but feels the great urgency of her body.

"Khorsheed?"

He hears a pounding at the door. It might have been his own chest, or the natural sound of the room, itself, the heartbeat of the sun-baked bricks beneath the skin of white plaster and the wooden-beam bones. He hears his mother and Fatimeh behind him, then feels his mother's hand on his back.

"Ibrahim, stand up, son," Zolekhah says. "Stand up, let me see the girl." He stands, his head spinning. He holds on to his mother's shoulders with both hands.

"Mother?"

"Come, come, agha Ibrahim," Fatimeh says as she ushers him out. "We need a man to fetch Naneh Adeh at this hour."

She gives him a gentle push and closes the door abruptly behind him.

The night air feels cold against Ibrahim's face. In the darkness, he notices the black of the fountain and swaying shadows that might be trees. From behind the door, he hears Khorsheed scream again, and his knees give out beneath him.

"Brother, what are you doing sitting on the cold earth at this hour?"

Ibrahim looks up to see Asher standing over him. "I need to go get the midwife," Ibrahim says. "The child is coming."

"You need to stand up, first. Come to the pool and splash some water on your face so that you return to your senses."

Ibrahim stands with effort and follows Asher to the fountain. The fish are still. He sees the reflection of the round, white moon, black clouds, the thousand stars on the surface of the water. He cups the cool water in his hands and splashes his face, over and over. He blinks his eyes several times and looks about the courtyard. The trees stretch their naked limbs in supplication to the night sky.

"Sit down and wait here, in case the women need you," Asher says. "Though I don't know of what use you can be in your state. I'll go fetch the midwife. Nothing to fear, brother, fortune smiles upon you tonight." Asher then turns to walk to the stables.

Ibrahim watches him leave. He listens to the click of

the heavy metal lock of the stable door, the latch, the creak of the hinges, the scrape of the door against the ground, the *clackclack* of the horse's hooves across the courtyard, into the cobblestoned streets, and he imagines Asher alone, riding atop that horse, full of longing for a son. Ibrahim's heart floods with a tremendous sorrow and he turns his face to the night sky and says, "How do You choose whom to bless and whom to keep bereft of Your blessings?"

Fatimeh emerges from the room wringing her hands and runs to the kitchen. "Ya Abolfazl, ya Allah," she says. Ibrahim listens to her remove the iron grille of the stove. He hears the crackle of twigs broken by the old woman's hands. After a few moments, the faint glow of the fire in the stove illuminates the doorway of the kitchen. Fatimeh bustles out of the kitchen with a heavy copper pot. "Agha Asher, is that you sitting in the shadows?" She asks.

"Asher left to fetch the midwife."

"Agha Ibrahim, you don't mind filling this pot with water from the well and bringing it back to the kitchen for old Fatimeh? I'm afraid age will slow the process." Ibrahim takes the pot from her wordlessly and walks toward the well. The ground, though not covered in snow any longer, still feels frozen against his bare heels. He stops at the low stone wall of the well beneath the hanging branches of the willow tree. The branches sway in the gentle night breeze. They move in a unity of motion, each branch curving in the same supple angle, dancing to the left, bending to the right. He lowers the bucket into the well, listens to the squeak of the pulley, the handle a burning cold to his touch. The bucket hits the surface of the water and there is the lag in the rope. He pulls the lever, the weight of the water awakening the muscles of his arms. He inhales the crisp night air, the scent of smoke in it, and perhaps a faint promise of blossoms. He pulls the rope until the bucket is within his reach. He tips the bucket and fills the copper pot. He bends to pick it up and walks back to the kitchen where Fatimeh waits nervously in the doorway.

Fatimeh takes the pot hurriedly from him and puts it on the stove. She rushes past him back toward the room where Khorsheed lays. Ibrahim stands in the kitchen and stares at the round belly of the stove, the fire blazing inside, the orange of it visible through the grille. He hears Khorsheed scream again and steadies himself against the wall. To take his mind off of her, he imagines Asher in the tangle of the passageways, making this journey to the midwife's home in the cold of the night.

The sun rises to find Ibrahim still sitting beside the pool. Khorsheed's screams fill the courtyard, drown the tiny passages of the mahalleh, echo through the halls of the synagogue to unsettle the rabbis, carry to the merchants in the bazaars, reach barbers in their shops and schoolboys hurrying along. Ibrahim tries to remember if he heard the roosters crow at all. He is certain that Khorsheed's hollering reaches the caravansary on the outskirts of the town, that camels, in

their stride across landscape, turn their heads in the direction of her cries, that men, amidst their business, shudder to
feel the ripple of the air that carries the waves of her pain. In
between, in the periods of her heavy breathing, the horses
in the stalls keep still, the birds keep still, the chickens in
the yard cock their heads, blink, their claws motionless in
the dirt, and when the ripping begins in her body again, she
wails so loud, the skies seem to rend open.

In the room, Rakhel sits pensively on the edge of the
bed and watches Fatimeh and Naneh Adeh hold Khorsheed's
arms as she squats in the middle of a blanket spread out
on the floor. Zolekhah presses wet rags against Khorsheed's
back, her neck, the back of her knees. Sadiqeh and Zahra
wait by the wall.

"You have to push, daughter, with all your strength,"
Naneh Adeh says.

"Khorsheed Khanum, listen to Adeh Khanum. A
woman in the village I grew up in took so long to push
out her baby, the girl was born with a head shaped like a
honeydew melon, and not much smarter than one, either,"
Sadiqeh says.

"G-d forbid, girl. What a time to talk like this," Fatimeh says.

"The All-Merciful as my witness, I wouldn't say it if
it wasn't true. That was her nickname. We called her Honeydew." Zahra nudges Sadiqeh, and the girl stops talking.

Khorsheed moans. She is drenched in sweat. Her long
hair sticks to her skin, her stomach descends between her

thighs, the skin of it tight like a drum. She clenches her fists. The veins in her forearms and calves rise blue and bulge. Her face reddens. She shuts her eyes tightly and screams.

"I can't . . . I can't anymore . . . "

"Do you want to keep this one, child?" Naneh Adeh says.

"Khorsheed joon, child, you're not the first woman to do this," Zolekhah says.

"I've seen the poor soul's head twenty times already and all he needs is one good *zoor* to slide out," Naneh Adeh says. "Lord knows, the Bakhtiari women just stop behind their tribe, squat, and not a sound they make. Alone in the middle of some wilderness. Clean the babe up and run to catch up with the group." Naneh Adeh turns to Zahra and Sadiqeh. "One of you girls go fetch more boiling water from the kitchen hearth. She's taken so long, the last pot's cooled again."

"I'll go," Rakhel says. The women turn to look at her.

"I almost forgot you were here, child," Naneh Adeh says. "So quiet you've been."

Rakhel looks away from the old woman and rises to leave. She steps out of the dim room and into the blinding sunlight. She sees a blurred figure stop and turn expectantly toward her. She squints her eyes until she makes out Ibrahim's face, his eyebrow raised, his eyes wide open, his hands clutched behind his back. She steps out and shuts the door behind her and stands before him. He waits for her to speak, to explain something about what happens in that secret place, what meaning there might be in the mystery of his wife's screams, if the suffering is much too much to endure. Rakhel says, "She's fine. I have to get the water," and walks quickly away from the inquisition of his eyes. She rushes back past him as fast as the boiling pot of water allows her to move without scalding her own hands and feet. With her back to him, she places the pot on the floor, cracks the door open, pushes the pot through, and slides in herself.

Ibrahim waits as the afternoon drags its weight, each minute going so slowly that it seems to forget nightfall. Sometimes, it appears to him that time does not move at all. That time notices the insistence of his own path and, tired of the drudgery, sits down in the shade of the willow tree by the well, so that the shadows remain changeless, the butterflies cease their panic of encroaching death and settle on honeysuckles, unhurriedly extending the curl of their nectar-seeking tongues and dip their heads into the sanctum of the flower to drown in the possibility of infinite being. Time ceases for Ibrahim and his wife's screams orchestrate the motion of all things, the sound of the other women in the room, the birds in the courtyard, the footsteps of strangers passing in the streets.

In the room, Rakhel stands beside the servant girls. She holds the pot of water in her hands, uncertain of what to do with it. Finally, she places the pot on the floor and crouches on her heels beside it. She clears her throat a couple times, but Naneh Adeh does not notice her. In fact, no one notices her return. *As though I am invisible,* Rakhel thinks. *The servants more necessary than I.*

Naneh Adeh tells Khorsheed to rest a moment. The girl's chin settles on her chest, drops of beaded sweat dripping from her nose. "Just let me be," she pleads. "Please, let me be. Just let me be." Her legs give way and the women release her arms so that she can steady herself on her hands and knees. Zolekhah dips a rag into the bowl of rosewater, twists the excess water from the fabric, and places the cool cloth on Khorsheed's back and neck. "Let me be," Khorsheed screams.

"Child," Naneh Adeh says, "it isn't good for the baby to be taken back so many times. This time, give him up into the world. I promise, no harm will come to him."

Khorsheed throws her head back and clenches her teeth. She strains, her breath whistling. She attempts to squat again and all the women rush to lift her. The old midwife turns to Rakhel and says, "Come, child, this is no time to stand idle, bring over that pot of water, my hands must finally welcome our guest." Rakhel lifts the pot of hot water and walks slowly, hesitantly toward Khorsheed.

Then, suddenly

a head, soft hair covered in film, a face, eyes clenched, nose crinkled, shoulders, the fold of the flesh of arms, clenched fists, tiny fingers, the chest, buttocks, the two legs, bent, tiny toes, a long black dripping cord, the whole body wet, shaking in the wrinkled hands of the old midwife, whose expert fingers dip into the toothless mouth, then turn the baby, and

Then, suddenly

a piercing cry. And everything falls into motion. The specks of dust that paused momentarily in the stream of sunlight resume their dance again. The birds in the trees, the women's voices, the animation of the streets, begin again.

"A son," the old midwife says.

"A son?" Zolekhah asks.

"If memory serves me." Naneh Adeh takes a knife from her belt and cuts the cord. She holds the trembling, screaming baby and rubs his body vigorously with a dry cloth. "Ten fingers, ten toes. Fine arms and legs." Zolekhah rushes to the window and pulls the curtains aside. She pushes the window open.

"Ibrahim? It is a boy! A son for my son!" Zolekhah shades her eyes with her hand and searches the courtyard for Ibrahim. He rises from beside the pool and runs to the window.

"Really? Mother, really?"

"Yes, Ibrahim. A son, you have a son. May G-d bless him. May He see my Asher also fit for such joy!"

Ibrahim covers his face with his hands. For several moments, he remains silent, then looks up, wipes his eyes with the back of his hand and says, "May I see him?"

"Not yet. Let us clean the room. Wait a few moments here." Zolekhah closes the window.

Rakhel watches as the rest of the women gather the soaked blanket beneath Khorsheed and wash her arms and legs, between her thighs, her face, beneath her breasts, her back. Naneh Adeh picks up the afterbirth and wraps it in a cloth, all the while muttering to herself. "It is best for the husband to wait," Naneh Adeh says. "Allow time for the power of the birth to dissipate. Men frighten easily." She takes the baby from Zolekhah and places him on Khorsheed's chest. The child, blindly, with the hunger of his lips, finds the nipple and clasps with such force to the young mother that she gasps and moans while the baby suckles. "It will hurt less once your nipples toughen up," Naneh Adeh says as she pinches the swelling pink of Khorsheed's other nipple between her fingers and chuckles. "A little olive oil, though, will help. Rub it in good, after he feeds."

"I'll bring in Ibrahim, now," Zolekhah says. She walks by Rakhel without even seeing her, to the door and opens it wide into the courtyard. Ibrahim walks in hurriedly, almost knocking Rakhel over in his haste. He stops a moment, mumbles an apology without looking at her, then rushes to the side of the bed.

"Is this him, this mewing creature, this miracle?" Khorsheed nods wearily and smiles. The baby struggles to find her breast again. "You have done well, Khorsheed," he says. "You have done well."

Naneh Adeh walks about the room as if looking for misplaced objects. "Forty days, child, you are impure to your husband's touch. And see that someone is with you during those forty days, at all times. Keep a lamp burning throughout the night." She stoops beside Khorsheed's bed, reaches beneath it, and takes out a large pair of iron scissors. Then she hands them to Ibrahim and motions to the alcove above the bed. "These should be placed up there and not removed. Only boiled water, if she must drink at all. And sheep fat, as much as she can stomach. And on the fourth day, a broth of rooster and hen, cooked together. I'll be back on the sixth day." The old woman walks out without looking back. "Your son has a birthmark like a snake. He'll turn whatever he touches to gold. Put a little soot on his face," she says. "To keep him safe."

Rakhel picks up the pot wordlessly and walks after her. "Not yet, child," Naneh Adeh calls out. "I have business with that water." Naneh Adeh turns toward Rakhel and walks slowly in her direction. She stops, looks Rakhel in the eyes, then blows three times over the surface of the water. "To protect the mother and child," she says to Rakhel. "Against the evil eye." She winks, then nudges Rakhel toward the garden. "Wait for it to cool, then pour it out at the base of a fruiting tree, daughter, and pray with a pure heart, so that you too may yield."

The ceremony requires that the mother of the infant boy hand the child to another woman, one who is childless, and this woman carries the infant to the father, who in turn will place the baby in the arms of the man honored, usually the father of the father, who will hold the baby in his lap as the rabbi proceeds with the covenant. Ibrahim decided that the honor of holding his son during the ceremony belonged to Asher, who was like a father to him, and so it could only be that Khorsheed herself placed Yousseff in Rakhel's arms on the morning of his Brit Milah, who walked the boy over to the chair and gave him to Asher.

Mahboubeh tugs at a vine that grows at the base of one of her rosebushes. The leaves are hardy, green, with fine hairs that irritate the skin of her hands. "I don't remember planting you." She follows the vine to its root, digs with the tips of her fingers into the soil, and pulls the vine out. She throws it on the small pile of similar weeds she has spent the morning uprooting. She rises heavily from the ground. The rosebushes are bare. She picks the dead leaves of a stem. "Spring will come," she says. "And with it, the blooms." She stops and looks up at the empty skies, then turns back to her roses.

Ibrahim must have instructed Khorsheed to give Yousseff to Rakhel on that morning. Perhaps the first time Rakhel held him. Mahboubeh looks up at the cloudless blue skies again, as though waiting for a sign. A distant airplane. Crows flying toward the brown mountains. She imagines Rakhel waiting impatiently, watching Khorsheed and her child with a heart brim full of longing.

Khorsheed bends her face down to smell the perfume of her son's head as he sleeps in the cradle of her arm. Rakhel steps forward to take the child from her into the crowded room, toward Asher, who waits in the ceremonial chair. Khorsheed hesitates a moment. In between Khorsheed and Rakhel, in the ray of light that separates them, the baby sleeps.

Khorsheed ignores the waiting guests, the impatience of her mother-in-law, the haste of the rabbi. She looks at the infant's clenched fist, the delicate curve of his nostril, the stir of his breath. She marvels at his perfection. He is just that, perfect. For seven days, when she is not asleep beside him, she studies him, the shimmer of his fingernails, the pattern of the hair on his head, the glow of his skin. *Not human,* she thinks, *angelic. Or human as meant to be before the dust of this world settles and dulls the shine.* This morning she asked Ibrahim, again, even though she knew it must be, if they must circumcise him. "But he is so beautiful as he is," she said. "All of him." He did not respond to her but continued to dress himself in preparation for the event.

"But, Ibrahim, what about the pain?"

"Not another word," he said. "What nonsense to even think of."

So she carries her baby gently and whispers into his sleeping ear, "Yousseff, you must be brave. I will be here to hold you, after. Rakhel will carry you to the chair and back to me when all is done, because she is childless and this act may bless her with a son of her own." She steps to the door of the great guest hall and Zolekhah tells her to hand the baby to Rakhel. Rakhel will carry her son and give him to Asher, who will sit, holding her baby upon his lap, and wait for the prayers, who must hold the infant still until the blood and then. . . .

"Then he will be pure," Ibrahim told her.

"But he is pure," she said.

Khorsheed continues to stand in the doorway holding the baby and a hush falls upon the room. Rakhel waits, her arms extended to receive him.

"Khorsheed," she whispers. "Give him to me."

Khorsheed looks up from the sleeping baby in her arms at Rakhel, at the frantic look in her eyes, and she leans in, almost touching Rakhel's chest with her own, and gently places the sleeping infant against Rakhel's breast. Outside, a fine rain begins to fall.

"He is my heart, my whole being," Khorsheed whispers. She looks into Rakhel's eyes and smiles. She steps back to watch Rakhel walk away with her son.

Mahboubeh stands in the kitchen, staring at her mud-caked shoes. She's scraped her knees. Her dress is ruined. She sobs and hiccups, sucking her thumb.

"A girl of nine and your finger still in your mouth?" Rakhel says. "What man will want a bride like you, huh?" Rakhel pulls on Mahboubeh's arm.

Mahboubeh whimpers in protest. She hears a distant ringing.

"So a group of goyim boys chased you home from school and taunted you, eh? Pushed you in the mud, eh? I told you to stay home. Stay home, learn to keep a house. A girl who sucks her finger and reads. Fine bride you'll make. Covered in dirt. Don't know a thing about cooking. Couldn't darn a sock."

The ringing in her ears continues. Mahboubeh stops crying. "Your father got beat, too. When Yousseff was just born. A whole group of them beat Ibrahim like a mule in the streets, a group of goyim men, a whole mob of them," Rakhel says. "We found him outside the door bleeding, half-dead."

There is an urgency to the ringing. Mahboubeh continues to look at her shoes, ashamed for sucking her thumb, ashamed for her father being beaten.

"They hit him too hard in the head," Rakhel says, knocking on her own head with her fist. "He stopped doing much after that. Let my husband do all the work, and just sat around and read all day. What man sits all day long and reads? Can you answer that?"

Mahboubeh's cheeks burn hot. The ringing becomes louder and louder.

"And all you got today was a little taunting, huh? No bloody nose? No broken ribs? Go on. Go bury yourself beneath your books. Don't bother me with your sniffling."

The telephone.

The kitchen is dark. Mahboubeh starts for the phone. "Hello?" she says. "Hello?" She waits for a moment. No response. She puts the receiver back down. She turns on the lights. The propensity of familiar objects. The bulk of the refrigerator, kitchen table, stove. The reassurance of cabinets, drawers. The sink. The kettle. *You are here, not there.* She touches the kettle to solidify this fact. It is cold. She turns on the faucet to listen to the sound of running water. She cups it in her hand and splashes her face. It feels cool. She has been crying. "Foolish old woman," she says. "Talking out loud to no one and nothing, even crying about it." She looks at her shoes. They are caked with dry mud, her legs splattered with it. Her dress is torn at the hem. Her knees hurt.

Ibrahim told her that story once, and only once, the day she asked him if it was true, if a mob of men attacked him and beat him in the streets. "Like a mule, Father. Dada said like a mule."

He looked at her for a moment. There should have been anger in response to even repeating such a sentence, but Ibrahim just looked at her, then began talking about what had happened.

"It happened during the rains," he told her. "A rain that started during Yousseff's Brit Milah and lasted days and days," he said. "I was walking home from the synagogue one morning, when I bumped into a Muslim man. Maybe he was a common merchant . . . perhaps an artisan of something."

Mahboubeh imagines Ibrahim walking. He gazes at the ground, at the puddles reflecting the clouds and sky. Rain dampens his face and hands. He listens to the sound of his own feet against the cobblestones. He does not see the other man turn the corner sharply, and since Ibrahim's attention is on the reflection of the sky in puddles, he collides with the man. Ibrahim looks up and the two men's eyes meet. Ibrahim mumbles an apology, and in the dream state of his thoughts, fails to see the quick flash in the other man's eyes. Ibrahim continues walking slowly in the direction of home, his hands clasped behind his back, nodding his head in response to the dialogue in his head about G-d's ability to work divine wonders. But the man turns and follows him, reaches out and grabs his shirtsleeve.

Mahboubeh decides, as her father tells her this story and each time after when she imagines the event, that the man who grabs Ibrahim's shirtsleeve is a tailor. While this tailor can recite some suras of the Quran, mostly by rote memory without understanding the meaning of the Arabic words, he is probably illiterate. He does simple business calculations using an abacas, but this particular skill, as of late, causes him much anxiety. The numbers he notes in the margins of the book he keeps from the years of a business he inherited from his father add up to one truth . . . he isn't making money. The price of wheat increases weekly. Another winter approaches. He sees men in the streets wearing *farangi* shirts, poor quality, that tear in a season or two, while his own stock gathers dust. The night before this accidental collision, while his family slept, he concluded that he must begin to look for another line of work. And since all he knows is the art of tailoring, his only option is to become a common laborer. This morning, as he walks around the bend of the tight winding street, clutching the heavy key that opens the door to his shop, shaking his head at the prospect that his own son will not have a business to inherit, he walks right into Ibrahim.

Judging from the Jewish man's shirt, his qaba, the quality of the cloth of his pants, the tailor deduces that the Jew before him must be wealthy. He has heard, at Jomeh Masjid, sermon after sermon claiming that the wealthy Jew is in joint venture with the farangis to impoverish Iran. Perhaps a nagging part of the tailor questions the sermons, and he wonders if these speeches full of wrath against the Jew are aligned with the Rahman and Raheem, the gracious and compassionate nature of Allah, but then he remembers his son, and imagines his child a common laborer, and he wonders about the wealth of the man before him.

"The Najis Laws that dictated everything from how Jews must dress, to what they must do when it rains so that the filth of their bodies does not contaminate Believers, hadn't been in effect for decades, but culture is a beast slow to learn. There was that rain, and I was wet, and my body touched his body in passing," Ibrahim said to Mahboubeh. "He beat me without compassion, beat me an inch from death and then he incited a crowd of other men, who also participated in the beating. The mob finally dragged me to a mullah. I remember hearing the men say over and over, *Jude najis.*"

"That is what the boys called me," Mahboubeh told her father. "That is what the boys said as they chased me home from school, Jude najis."

"Jude najis," the tailor repeats. And the mob responds like one body, its faces contorted with anger, its fists and feet dancing with rage.

The mullah interrupts the men. "Silence, please," he says. "One cannot hear the subtle words of the Lord above the angry voices of men."

The mob slowly settles.

"Now leave, please, so that I can pray and contemplate the situation. And let the Jew stay here. I will see to him."

Reluctantly, one by one, the men leave the mullah's sitting room. The tailor is last to go. He looks at Ibrahim trembling on the floor, his knees drawn to his chest, his face covered in blood. Then he looks at his own hands, hands that crafted such fine shirts, hands that learned from the hands of his father. The tailor studies his palms, upturned as if in prayer or supplication. He looks at the lines, the scars from the accidents of his early years, the padding of his fingers thickened so that a prick of a needle hardly draws attention anymore. He looks at his hands with wonder in his eyes, as though he is recognizing them for the first time. Then he turns to see the man on the floor, who weeps and moans quietly, and his hands begin to shake. The tailor opens his mouth to say something, but the words fly away from him like startled mourning doves. He looks to the mullah, who watches him steadily, kindly. The tailor turns and runs out of the door.

The mullah waits until the muezzins sing the afternoon azan. He waits until the town settles for their rest.

Then, he lifts Ibrahim tenderly and places him atop his mule. He covers Ibrahim with a blanket and leads the mule past the mosque, through the streets, to the Jewish quarters of Kermanshah. He asks until he finds Ibrahim's home. Once outside the door of the estate, he carefully lifts Ibrahim off the mule and gently leans him against the wall. He knocks once, then turns and walks slowly in the direction of home.

The light filters through the dust of the windows. Ibrahim watches the curtains billow out with the breeze, then settle back again and he thinks *glass, dust, lace. Before that, the limbs and leaves of trees, and clouds. And the great expanse of the heavens. From its source before this light reaches me, how many other distortions?*

In the yard, the women come and go. If they did not speak a word, he would still be able to identify which of them passes his window by the sound of their feet on the brick of the andaruni. The shuffle of one, the staccato of another. He hears them, and their faces rise to the surface of his mind. All day, the women walk back and forth in the same enclosed space, now with this task, then with that, and sometimes, aimless, sometimes, it seems, in perpetual circles.

In his lap is the Old Testament, his finger rests on a sentence. "Here I am," he whispers. "Here I am." He closes his eyes. Again, he sees the men's feet. Some wrapped in rags and bits of leather in place of shoes. Some barefoot.

First, there was pain. Then, the men's voices sounded like distant music. He didn't feel anything much, after that. And each motion, each kick seemed so graceful. The street wet with rain, droplets of water rising into the air, the foot, the fall, the thud. No hands, no fists, just the feet. And stones. They dragged him, finally relented and held his arms and legs. He saw their hands. Their faces. They kept their eyes from him. Glances, short, curious. Shy, perhaps. He rested as they carried him. Until they came to a door and a courtyard and threw him to a floor. They stood about him, listening to a man with a gentle voice speak. He watched them leave. Some quickly, others with reluctance. A last one and then only the man with the gentle voice remained, who crouched beside him and looked him in the eyes and said, *with gold we test our servants and with fire, we test our gold.* Ibrahim allowed himself to fall into darkness, then.

As soon as he could sit again, Ibrahim asked for his books. Attar, Sana'i, Hafiz. He looked through the pages of the Mathnawi' Masnavi. He searched and searched the pages of the Talmud, the Torah, the Bible, the Quran. The rabbi visited him, too, and Ibrahim asked, "Why?"

"G-d saw it fit."

"I am a good man, a G-d fearing man. Why?" Ibrahim said.

"There is something in this for you to learn."

"Compassion?" Ibrahim sneered.

"Yes, son, compassion."

"For the men who beat me?"

"They, too, suffered. More than you. Through their brutality, they distanced themselves from Hashem. That is a sad, terrifying place. A lonely, desolate wilderness."

"And so I must consider their pain? I, with my broken ribs, my broken pride?"

"Ribs mend. Pride another subject for another time. But how does one regain their humanity, once lost? How does man heal a darkness in his heart?"

Ibrahim continued searching for an answer. He read book after book. He'd look up from the book in his lap, repeating what he had read, over and over and over, until the words he spoke became nothing separate from the ray of light that seeped into the room through the dust-covered glass, through the veil of the curtains, until the words were the breeze, the beat in his own chest, the breath of his nostrils, the page in his hand, his hand, the dust of his skin. He read until he became word and word became him and he didn't know if he spoke or if he was spoken.

Asher returned in the evenings form the caravansary with his own answers. He'd knock on Ibrahim's door and enter. *Brother, I found one of the men who beat you. He will receive a visit from some guests soon.* And again, each night, *Brother, I think I found another of the men.* Ibrahim always listened to Asher with his head down, his eyes on his hands clasped in his lap. He felt ashamed to look Asher in the eyes. Ibrahim had never witnessed anyone raise their voice against his brother, let alone their hand. He felt that the beating was somehow his own fault, a weakness in him that allowed for such shame. As Asher spoke about the need for retribution, Ibrahim nodded his head silently, a book open in his lap, a pile beside his hand, upon the table, upon the bed.

Ibrahim looked up one evening and asked Asher, "Is this what G-d intended? For men to behave like dogs to prove themselves men? One more savage than the other?"

"This is not a question of G-d's intentions, brother," Asher said. "It is a question of honor."

After that, Ibrahim just listened and after his brother had spoken for some time, always with a rising anger, always with a sideways glance at him to see if Ibrahim, too, shared his rage, but Ibrahim could only say, *Forgive me, brother, I am tired tonight.* And Asher would shake his head, sigh, and rise to leave.

Ibrahim puts his book aside, rests his head on the pillow and thinks *the Lord, Himself, is not shy to acts of violence. With such ease, He turns men to salt, women and children, too. Teases the thirst with blood. With such ease, He strangles the firstborn. With such ease, He raises the waters to swallow entire armies of men. With such grace. In the Torah, when He asks of Ibrahim to sacrifice his own son, is that not an invitation to the man to try his hand at being G-d through unthinkable violence? And since G-d's time is not man's time, but eternal time, having no beginning nor end, is He not sacrificing His own son, as the Christians say, breaking his ribs, nailing his hands to a crucifix in the same moment that he invites Ibrahim to try this same act . . . but why? Why this savage love of His?*

Outside he hears Khorsheed's footsteps in the andaruni. He lifts the edge of the curtain to peer out. Khorsheed sits at the ledge of the fountain, and brings Yousseff to her breast. She begins singing, "What will your meals be? Bread, rice, and halvah, and manna sprinkled all over." Her voice, sweet, clear, rings through the yard, carries to the street. Ibrahim feels an overwhelming desire for her, for the soft of her body, the warmth of it. This urge silences the other voice in his mind, the one that asks insistently, and seeks, and seeks. He shuts the window quickly and reaches for a book. The poetry of Rumi. Ibrahim closes his eyes and opens the book to a random page. He looks down and reads, "Like Yakov, I am crying, for the beautiful face of Yousseff is my desire. Without you, the city is my prison. Wandering, the mountain and desert are my desire."

Six

⚜

The birds are a commotion of song in the naked branches of the trees. Mahboubeh stands by the kitchen window, a plate of bread crumbs in her hand. She looks at the seamless gray skies outside her window, then opens the kitchen door and walks into the bare garden. She puts the plate of bread crumbs in the grass for the hungry birds and walks along the perimeter of her yard. She spots a bit of green. It is that vine that creeps along the soil, and climbs the stalks of her rosebushes. She kneels down to uproot it. She holds it up in the morning light and shakes her head. "Unwanted," she says. "And you persist."

"If he didn't know the value of his own son, his firstborn, what makes you think he'd want a daughter? And you still persist?"

Mahboubeh rises from the ground, shakes the dirt from her skirt, and keeps her eyes on her shoes. If she looks at the ground long enough, Dada will stop speaking, and walk away.

"You are already eleven, old enough to be married and sent away, and you stay here, another mouth to feed, a burden on everybody?"

If Mahboubeh shuts her eyes tightly, the tears stay in. If she holds her breath, and stills her heart, it doesn't burn so much.

"I tell him and tell him to find you a husband, and you, with your own ideas, come each morning to tell me you are off to school? A few chores you do and you think it earns you a place in this home? Go to your school, then. Useless, stupid girl."

"Do you hate me because I am a girl?" Mahboubeh asks out loud. Dada does not reply.

Mahboubeh looks up. Seamless gray skies. She stands in the middle of her yard, the small space of it, a bit of soil and grass, a few trees, and four brick walls, above which stretches the endless, endless sky. Someone knocks on the street door. From the corner of her eyes, Mahboubeh watches Dada turn and walk away to answer it.

The old rabbi waits in the street, leaning heavily on his walking stick. "A bit of haste, daughter, I'm closer to the

grave than you," he says. The rabbi taps Dada's leg with his
wooden walking stick and she moves aside to allow him in.
He stops to look at her face, squinting his eyes in the late
morning sun until they almost disappear beneath the folds of
wrinkles on his face. He nods his head at her once and walks
slowly past her toward the courtyard. Before noon every
Friday since the day they found Ibrahim broken and bleeding, Rakhel hears the rapping of the rabbi's stick against the
street door and each time she answers, he tells her about the
need for her haste and his own proximity to the grave.

She follows the old man through the outer gardens and
into the courtyard. The trees in the outer gardens are naked,
but at the tips of their branches tiny buds wait to reveal their
flowers and new green leaves. As the old man walks beneath
these trees, Rakhel watches his bent back, the curve of his
legs, each step a delicate approximation of the next. She does
not walk ahead of him for fear of offending him, but his pace
inspires in her the desire to jump and run like a spring colt.

The rabbi speaks to her without turning. "I imagine
you've been anticipating the arrival of your guest?" he asks.
"Remember, daughter, that G-d smiles upon the obedient
and dutiful wife."

Rakhel smiles politely, but she is not certain who he
means. Zolekhah did not mention that they'd have guests
this Sabbath, nor did Rakhel notice any preparations for
guests by the servants.

When they finally reach the courtyard, Rakhel walks
quickly past the old rabbi, who nods at her again, and enters

Ibrahim's room to announce his arrival. Zolekhah sits beside her son, holding his hands. She breathes in heavily and shakes her head. Ibrahim pats her hand with his.

"Rabbi is here," Rakhel says.

"I'm going to take my rest," Zolekhah says. She pushes on her knees to stand. Then, she picks up a few pillows from the floor and places them against the wall at the head of the bed, and helps Ibrahim sit up and lean against the pillows. By the time she turns to walk out, the old rabbi shuffles into the room. He mutters Shabbat shalom as he walks past Zolekhah toward the bed. Rakhel hurries to place a chair beside the bed for the old man. Zolekhah stands waiting by the open door, the morning light behind her radiant.

"Asher knows what he is doing, Mother. Please, just trust him. He calculates the costs and risks of everything before making a decision," Ibrahim says. Zolekhah listens without turning. She waits a moment, then says Shabbat shalom to the rabbi and leaves. Rakhel follows her quietly into the courtyard.

"Naneh Zolekhah?"

"The girls already left for the day. Can you see to the chai, Rakhel?"

"Fatimeh made it. I will serve it. Naneh Zolekhah?"

"Yes, daughter?"

"The rabbi said something about guests. Are we expecting company for Sabbath?"

Zolekhah shakes her head, then turns to face Rakhel. "Yes, a guest. A guest is coming, though not for Sabbath."

"Who is coming?"

Zolekhah places her hand on Rakhel's shoulder, then looks up at the trees behind Rakhel. "Asher took Kokab as a wife on Wednesday. She will arrive here the day after to-morrow." The old woman does not look at Rakhel when she speaks but keeps her gaze at the tops of the trees as though she were announcing the news to them. She finally looks at Rakhel for a moment, then turns and walks away. She continues talking as she makes her way across the courtyard.

"I know it will be hard for you, child. But nothing can be done. Asher needs a son, or else all he has built will be lost to the wind. You must be strong, dear. And welcome his new wife, for the sake of whatever peace remains in this household."

Rakhel waits for Zolekhah to leave. She stands alone in the empty courtyard. Clouds rush overhead. Outside, a man whistles. She listens to his song until she can no longer hear him, then she turns and walks to the kitchen. She stops in the doorway for a moment and watches the orange fire through the grille in the belly of the black stove. Rakhel walks closer to the stove. She takes one more step forward and then places her open palm on the hot surface of the grille. She grits her teeth and holds her hand on the burning metal. Rakhel removes her hand and bits of her skin peel off, sticking to the surface of the stove. She turns and walks back to the courtyard to sit beside the pool. Zolekhah peers out from the open window of her bedroom.

"Rakhel, have you served the tea?"

"I was about to, but I burned my hand."

"Why G-d has chosen you for such black misfortune?" Zolekhah looks up to the sky and shakes her head. She comes out of her room and walks toward the kitchen. "Is it very bad?"

Rakhel looks at her palm. She studies it for several moments. Her flesh is red, the white of it revealed in some places. "It will scar," she says.

Zolekhah walks past her without looking at her. "I'll peel some cucumbers for the guest and leave the skins on a plate for you in the kitchen. Put it on the burn," Zolekhah says. "Go get some rest with Khorsheed. She is asleep with the baby in the sitting room. I'm sure this news has you worn. I'll tend to the rabbi and Ibrahim myself."

Rakhel walks toward the sitting room. The air stings her raw flesh. She shakes her burned hand and opens the door quietly with the other. The curtains of the room are drawn and the room is dark, save for a sliver of light that falls across Khorsheed's face. Khorsheed lies on the rug, her black hair loose over a pillow, her body curled around the baby asleep at her breast. Youssef clutches with his small hand the collar of his mother's shirt so that Rakhel sees the rise and fall of the girl's chest as she sleeps. A streak of light wavers across Khorsheed's full lips, and she sighs deeply in her sleep, shifts her shoulders and wraps an arm around the sleeping baby. The baby nestles his head farther into the flesh of his mother's breast.

Rakhel enters the sitting room quietly and sits beside

Khorsheed. The baby stirs and wakes, then looks up at her face, blinking. Khorsheed opens her eyes, yawns, and smiles at Rakhel. Rakhel gives her finger to Yousseff, who clutches it in his small hand. She wiggles her finger and says, "It was my place to bear the first son of this family."

"Don't talk like that, Rakhel."

"He should have been mine."

"Spit three times, Dada, so some awful thing doesn't happen," Khorsheed says. She sits and takes the baby in her lap. She holds Yousseff up in the air and gazes at him, before pulling him toward her face, then kissing his eyes, his nose. "You know as good as I what happens if you look at some-one wanting what they have, regardless of who you are or how much you love the other person."

Rakhel jumps to her feet and glares at Khorsheed and her baby. "Worried I have the evil eye for your baby?" She watches Khorsheed's innocent surprise, the way she presses Yousseff to her chest protectively, and a strange pleasure takes hold of Rakhel. She closes her eyes for a moment and breathes in deeply, then looks at Khorsheed again, cowering before her, and says, "You're right, Khorsheed. I am full of envy, overflowing with it. So much, it's going to flood the whole damned world. See what comes of it."

Mahboubeh watches the warblers dart in and out of the bare rosebushes, eyeing her with suspicion, eyeing the plate of bread crumbs she's left for them, then looking at her again.

She remembers how Rakhel used to walk to that well to talk to her djinns and curse her enemies. She and the other children hid and listened, holding their breaths for fear that she'd name one of them. And whomever she did name came to some misfortune, one way or another. So no one ever crossed her. Everyone always did what she asked. Mahboubeh walks back into the kitchen and closes the door. She presses her forehead against the cool of the glass. She watches the little birds outside gather around the plate. A small war ensues among them.

Mahboubeh remembers the night Rakhel suggested the neighbor's son as a potential suitor for her. Mahboubeh was home on holiday from the college she attended in Tehran. She announced to the whole family, at the Sabbath dinner, the news that she had just been selected for a scholarship to further her studies in mathematics in France. Rakhel looked at her. Then she turned to Ibrahim and mentioned Elchonon's eldest son. He owned a shoe store with his brothers. He had even studied up to the eighth grade, knew how to read and keep numbers. His mother had come calling.

"No," Mahboubeh said.

Six months later, Rakhel led Mahboubeh, weeping, to the altar.

Mahboubeh sits down at her kitchen table and looks at a portrait of her husband on the wall. A tall man. Sad eyes. Smooth skin. A faint smile. He wears a fine tailored suit. The photograph is in sepia and soft white, but his cheeks have a slight rosy tint and his eyes a hint of green, the stroke of the photographer's paintbrush. She closes her eyes and sees him as he was the first few mornings after their wedding. He sits before her, at the table she set for him, the steam of the chai rising in swirls between them, the bread still warm. He clears his throat, but she does not look up. It is she that speaks, first.

"I want to work as a teacher," Mahboubeh says. "I will make my own money. So that my will is my own."

"Yes," he says.

She has not asked him for permission. She simply stated a condition for the life they will lead together. He looks up to meet her eyes and nods his head. She looks back at him with fierce resolve. He chuckles. He brings the glass of chai to his mouth to hold back the laughter, but it escapes him. He laughs for a while, then looks at the bewilderment in her eyes and laughs again.

"Yes, Mahboubeh. Clearly, your will is your own," he says. She smiles. He stops laughing and looks down, his cheeks red. Then he stands abruptly and says, "Thank you for breakfast."

"You will be home for lunch?"

Her kitchen is silent. The click of the refrigerator. Mahboubeh looks about her, lost for a moment. She sees the portrait. "So much respect you had for me," Mahboubeh says. "You came to me for advice, when men in your time thought of their wives as something they owned." He died young, her husband. In her arms, of a stroke. She closes her eyes, releases her breath sharply between her teeth.

He appears before her, tall, awkward, silent. She sees him thus, in that captive moment before the rest of life washes over her. Mahboubeh opens her eyes and shakes her head. The birds outside bicker among themselves. She walks over and stands before his portrait. Then, she closes her eyes and places her hand on the glass of the frame, over his chest. She can feel it, almost, the warmth of his hand over hers, the course of his life beneath her palm. She holds her hand there.

"Mahboubeh," he says, and nothing more.

An urgent knock sounds against the heavy wooden door, the resonance of a man's knocking. From behind the drawn curtains, through the crack that allows in a sliver of daylight, Rakhel watches Fatimeh rush across the courtyard, one hand pushing the wisps of white hair that fall out from beneath her chador back into place, the other gathering the black fabric over her head and throat. Rakhel clenches her fist, then winces at the pain from her burned hand. She watches Fatimeh all morning. Asher told the servant to keep her tasks close to the door, so that when Kokab's brothers bring her, the old servant could let her in immediately.

When the knock finally sounds through the silent estate, Fatimeh jumps in alarm, overturning the pot of rice she's been sifting for pebbles and pests. Sadiqeh and Zahra peek their heads out of the kitchen and laugh into their hands. Fatimeh hears them and shoos them back out of sight. They wave at her and gesture lewdly, pushing out their chests, shaking their hips. The old woman waves them away with both her hands until they retreat into the kitchen. Fatimeh then leaves the andaruni for the outer gardens leading to the street. When Fatimeh returns to the empty andaruni, a cloaked woman walks beside her. Fatimeh holds the knotted bundle of the woman's possessions firmly with both hands and motions for Kokab to follow her.

From behind the drawn curtains of her room, Rakhel watches the movement of Kokab's black chador, the fabric folds shifting as she enters the courtyard. Fatimeh places the bundle down and Kokab sits on the edge of the fountain. The servant walks away in a hurry to find Zolekhah and announce Kokab's arrival. Rakhel watches Kokab withdraw a slender white hand from beneath her chador and touch the surface of the water with her fingertips. When Zolekhah arrives, Kokab rises. The two women exchange a few sentences and Zolekhah leads her in the direction of Asher's house.

Zolekhah and Kokab ascend the stairs, walk past the purple blossoms of the wisteria, glide down the breezeway toward the farthest room. Hidden behind the curtains, Rakhel watches them walk by her window. Rakhel tries to catch a glimpse of Kokab's face behind the ruband, to see a lock of her hair. She looks at the drape of the fabric and tries to discern the shape of the body veiled beneath it. Zolekhah opens the door to the room at the farthest end of the building and waits for Kokab to enter, before she walks in herself and closes the door.

By late afternoon, the courtyard is still empty. Fatimeh finishes preparing dinner and retires to her own room to say her evening prayers. Sadiqeh and Zahra take their leave for the day. Rakhel watches them go from the slit in the drawn curtains. They walk with their arms about each other's waist as they whisper. They laugh out loud and turn to look over their shoulders in the direction of Asher's home. Rakhel darts away from the window. She touches the flesh of her burned palm with a forefinger. Her lips are cracked, her throat is dry and her stomach empty.

Rakhel did not intend such a vigilant fast to mark the arrival of Asher's second wife, but after Asher left that morning, she stayed in the tangled sheets of the bed, her knees pulled into her chest. Her husband had risen from bed, finished his ablutions, and dressed as he always did. But when he took his leave, he paused for a moment, his back to where she sat, his hand on the door latch. She waited for him to turn, to take her in his arms, but he only stood there. He sighed, shook his head and left without looking back.

She wept then. Wept most of the morning. She buried her face in his pillow and inhaled the scent of his sleep. She crawled out of bed to where his nightshirt lay crumpled on the floor and held it against her cheek, repeating his name until her voice cracked and she felt a sharp pain in her throat. Then she took up her station at the window and waited and watched the comings and the goings of the household. Everyone had forgotten her, even Khorsheed. No one knocked to ask if she was thirsty, if they could bring her some water, if she needed witness to her suffering. The day proceeded like any other day, except for her absence and the anticipation of Kokab's arrival.

By dusk, Rakhel sits motionless on the floor, spent of crying. She thinks about Kokab sitting in her room, dressed in fine clothes, adorned with jewels, waiting for Asher. Rakhel tries to imagine Kokab's body, the feel of her skin. She pictures Kokab's arms embracing Asher, and the thought shakes her so violently that she falls into another fit of hysterical curses, damning Kokab, her own barren womb, and the G-d that created her for this life of suffering. Exhausted from her fury, she lies back down and takes up her weeping once more.

Rakhel hears muezzins all across the city begin the evening azan. She sits up to pray, mimicking Fatimeh's gestures, prostrating over and over, chanting Arabic words she doesn't understand, but hopes that G-d will hear and either take mercy upon her or strike her down in His wrath. In the silence that follows the muezzins' song, Rakhel finally hears the sound of Asher's voice in the courtyard. She reaches under her shirt to where she keeps the iron key tied about her waist. She clasps it and shuts her eyes. "Please, please, please," she whispers.

She runs to the window to see Asher through the crack

in the curtains. He lights a lantern and walks across the courtyard in the direction of her room. She hurries to the mirror, wipes her nose with the end of her skirt, then pulls her fingers through her hair. By the time he reaches the door, Rakhel is standing behind it, straining to hear his footsteps. He knocks once and she catches her breath. "Rakhel?" She can hear his breathing behind the closed door. "Rakhel?"

"Yes?"

"I came to say that I am home. Did you help Kokab when she arrived?"

Rakhel clutches the key at her waist with her burned hand and winces.

"Rakhel?"

She breathes in gulps, tries to pull enough air into her lungs so that she can say something. She touches the smooth ungiving surface of the wood. She imagines Asher's hand on the other side of the door. She presses her lips against the wood, strains to feel, through the surface, the stroke of his fingertips.

"Rakhel," Asher begins, a tremor in his voice, but the sentence ends there. "Listen to me," he says, this time with a firmer tone, "I won't be seeing you tonight. Go to sleep."

Rakhel bends forward and wraps her arms around her body. Tears drip from her nose and chin, her sobs audible now. She hears the cold steel of the latch lift and she holds her breath. She waits, but he does not push the door open. She listens to him whisper to himself. Then, the cold steel of the latch settles softly back, and Rakhel hears the rustle of Asher's qaba and the sound of his feet recede down the breezeway in the direction of the farthest room.

Mahboubeh holds the tip of the pomegranate branch close to her face. She touches the small, hard red buds gently with her forefinger. "So much longing," she says, "all here, enclosed in this sheath, waiting to blossom." She smiles and releases the branch. Her garden is on the brink of blooming. A few more weeks. A bit more sunshine. And then, one morning, she will wake to tender green leaves. And blossoms. She sees the green vine that has been climbing her rosebushes all winter, insistent in its path. She holds it, the fine hairs irritating the skin of her hand. "You, too, will blossom soon," she says. She does not tug on the vine to uproot it but lays it back gently in its path. "We'll wait, then, to see."

Mahboubeh sits in a chair and looks at her garden. Kokab's arrival must have been something like this. On the end of winter, with so much life held fast within her. They said something awoke in Asher Malacouti when she arrived. Something opened in him and he changed. Mahboubeh imagines her uncle waiting hesitantly before the door of that farthest room, the moment before Asher opens it that first night when Kokab enters his home. He holds the lantern and breathes in once. He straightens his shoulders. Then, he cracks the door ajar and peers into the dim room.

Kokab sits before a lit candle, her hair veiled. The candle provides the only light in the room and its dimness comforts Asher. He places his own lantern outside and enters quietly. Kokab remains seated, staring at the flame. He stands before her, hesitating. Perhaps he should sleep this first night in his bedroom with Rakhel, give the woman some time to settle, ease Rakhel's anxieties. He needs to be more diplomatic, he thinks. Then he notices that Kokab sways slightly back and forth. The folds of her skirt gather beneath her, allowing for a faint outline of her legs. The skin of her throat is bare, gold in the warm light. *Though not the skin of fresh youth,* Asher reminds himself. *This act is a mitzvah,* he thinks. *Certainly no other man would have her, if not for the scandal, then for her age.* He continues to study her sitting before him, quiet, motionless, as though willing herself invisible. Her lips are still moist, though, and the thick of hair beneath that veil. . . . When he realizes his trance, he clears his throat and calculates that she has perhaps fifteen years of childbearing left. Enough time, no doubt, to bear a son.

The silence becomes too ponderous. He steps forward and speaks. "Would you rather be alone tonight?" he asks, though he isn't certain if he has spoken at all. "Are you comfortable?" He tries his voice again, still uncertain if the words he forms in his mind leave his lips. "Have you had dinner?"

He realizes that the woman sitting before him refuses to acknowledge his presence, or hear his questions, and so his sentences fall to the floor, unheard. The blood rushes to his face. "Would it have suited you better if I had left you in your brothers' home? Always ashamed, always the source of shame?" These words feel sharper in his mouth, he waits for a response to their edge, but they, too, meet with her silence. "You are now my wife, it does not matter anymore that you have been divorced, because you are now Asher Malacouti's wife."

Kokab turns her face away from him. The veil slips off of her head and onto her shoulders, then off of her shoulders and onto the floor. She does not move to replace it. The candlelight illuminates the black of her hair. Asher can discern a multitude of colors gleaming in that blackness. "My wife," he repeats. He turns to face the wall, to steady himself. He breathes in a few times, closes his eyes. *Why this light-headedness?* he wonders. He shakes his head, straightens his shoulders, and turns to look at her, again, sitting before him as though she is made of stone.

"You are now my wife. You will have my children, you will befriend Rakhel, she will help you raise them, you will live without any want, you will eat well, you will dress well, you will grow old well." At these words, she shudders. He softens his tone. "They will forget that you were ever married before me, you will be known only as my wife, the mother of my children. What more do you want?"

Kokab does not answer. Asher paces the room. His shadow looms treacherously on the walls. When he sees the monstrous form of himself cast on the walls, he puts his hand to his temples and turns away from her again. He keeps his back to her for a few moments, watching the shadow of her profile, her shoulders bent forward. She raises her hand, brings it to touch her cheek. The hand falls limply onto her lap. *I have frightened her,* he thinks. *I am, after all, a stranger to her.*

"Forgive me," Asher says. He waits a moment, look-ing down at the top of her head, the white of the scalp a thin river, the lobe of one ear visible. He sits down across from her. He wonders if her skin is warm to the touch, soft, like fine gold you've held in your hand for some time. He watches her for several moments and tries to find words to comfort her, to assure her that he means no harm, that in-deed, he intends on helping her. Finally, he reasons it best to allow her the silence until she feels ready to address him.

Several more minutes pass as Kokab looks at the flicker of the candle. Asher listens to the slight crackle of that hum-ble flame, to the crickets outside, to the occasional voice of strangers passing in the street, to the subtle breath of this woman sitting before him. Then, Kokab speaks, "There is the story of the three moths dancing around the can-dle flame." She says her words slowly, her eyes still on the candle. Asher feels the darkness expand and believes, for a moment, that all that exists rests in the orb of light between them. He lowers his eyes to look at his own hands, clasped in his lap. "The first moth spins madly in his ecstasy, draw-ing nearer and nearer to the fire, but he stops when he feels the warmth and pulls back, and remains content to look with longing at the light from a distance," she says. "The second moth, in his fervor, singes the tips of his wings and in fear, flies away. And there is the third moth. This one, so enthralled by the light, throws himself fully into the flame and burns." Silence, again, between them. Asher listens to the rustle of leaves outside. After several minutes, she raises her face and looks at him for the first time, her eyes steady. He feels as though he is looking into the expanse of a deep, deep well, at the bottom of which he sees himself, diminutive, drowned.

"You are that flame," he says. "And am I the moth that will burn?"

"The flame doesn't know the moths, Asher. Neither the moth gazing from a distance, nor the one burning." She does not turn away from his gaze. He looks at the resolution of her lips, the strength of her chin. He swallows. Then frowns. He looks down at his useless hands, then up at her eyes, again, her deep, unforgiving eyes.

"My father died when I was just a boy. He left me some land. It wasn't much. But something to build upon. Some earth to create upon. The land brought me fortune and I made with that fortune a greater fortune. And through this, you see, through this . . . Something of him continues. But I have no child, no son, to give the work of my days any meaning." He brings his face closer to her face, leans in because he feels that these words should not be spoken with distance between the person who utters them and the one who hears. "I . . . I want you . . . " He pauses, weighs the consequence of those words. He starts again, in almost a whisper. "I want you to give me children, to give me hope."

"Children you may be able to wrest from my womb, but hope is not something I can give."

Asher flinches. Kokab looks at him another moment, then looks down at the candle between them.

"This is not what I meant to say," he says. "There is more than this. More reasons than this for why you are here, why I have taken you as my wife." Sitting there before him, she is lost again in her solitude. *Perhaps she is not here at all,* Asher thinks. *Perhaps she is a phantom of my mind born from these many years of longing.* He considers reaching across the vast space between them to take hold of her slender hand and pull her into himself, pull her into being, for him. A moment passes, then another, and with each passing second, that space between them becomes greater and greater. Asher panics that he may never reach her. He leans forward again and says, "Every day, I wake and I walk to the caravansary. Every day, the sound of the same merchants, the haggling, the clicking of the abacas, coins and coins and coins. In my hands, they feel so weightless. Inconsequential. And I buy things. Beautiful things, valuable things from around the world. This house is filled with beautiful, valuable things." He looks around himself desperately, as if searching for the shape of his cumbersome possessions in the dark. "And each night I come home, I walk to my study and stand in the darkness, among the shadows of my gilded horde, and all I can think of is the dust that it is gathering. Dust." His voice cracks on the last word. He can feel his eyes burn with tears. He waits until it passes, then says, "I want to know that there will be something left other than dust, something living after this tedium of night and day. Something to show that I was. Alive. Once."

She looks at him as he speaks. He is there, again, small in the black pupil of her eyes. He turns his face from her. Then turns back to look into her eyes once more. "And there is more, still. More that you must know. Kokab, for years, you have been standing in the cool water of that pool for me, beneath a hot sun, bent over and washing apples. I can still hear you singing. For years, your song has haunted me. I've dreamed of being the water against your calves. I've imagined being the drop of water that traveled down your spine when you put your wet hair back. I have been living in the wake of that August morning, an eternity in that moment when you first looked at me." He looks down, his hands clenched in his lap. He shakes his head at his own weakness, at the words he has just spoken. It is too late, now, to stop. Enthralled, he thinks, by the light caught in the gleam of her black hair. He leans into her and says, "You burn with life, Kokab. I want to feel the world through you."

Kokab brings her face close to his, so that her lips are a breath apart from his. "You want to feel through me?" she asks.

"Yes."

She raises her hand and he looks down at her forefinger as it draws close to the candle. She holds her finger in the flame a moment, then extinguishes the light. Asher flinches and quickly takes her hand, putting her fingers to his lips. In the darkness of the room, he holds her fingers to his mouth and kisses them once, then inhales the musk of her wrist. Gently, Kokab pulls her hand back. The taste of her skin, a trace of the salt of her remains in Asher's mouth.

"What can I give you?" he asks. "Ask for anything, anything in the world, and you shall have it."

"I want my solitude."

Asher pulls back as though she has slapped him. He hesitates. She is so close. He should take his arms, the leaden weight of them, and grab her shoulders. He should draw her with force toward his body and kiss her open mouth, run his tongue on the flesh of her neck. He raises his hands to clutch her shoulders, then hesitates and stands up abruptly, instead.

"As you wish, Kokab. Tell Zolekhah if there is anything you need," he says. "I will return tomorrow night." And with that, he walks briskly out of the room and into the cool night. He waits a moment, with the door into her room ajar behind him, then he closes it gently.

Asher stands in the breezeway, beneath the painting of Mount Zion and the feverish dance of the tribe. He sees the darkness first, then the still courtyard. Slowly, he recognizes the scent of night jasmine, the crispness of the air. He hears the low moaning of a cat in the street. His soul opens its eyes and he sees the splendor of the night. He feels the need of his own body. He walks back toward the room he shares with Rakhel, reveling in the power of his legs. *Rakhel will be happy to see me,* he thinks.

Khorsheed hears someone singing in the courtyard. She rises from her bed and looks out of the window. In the yard below, Rakhel hoists a bucket of sour plums into the fountain. Khorsheed opens the window and leans out, resting her forearms on the sill. "That's how I like to see you, Dada, working and singing like a peasant."

"Not all of us are born to eat and sleep the day through," Rakhel says.

"Certainly no. Only those of us of certain refinement," Khorsheed says. "So you are done with the mourning?" Rakhel walks to the window, wiping her wet hands on her skirt. "Good thing, too, Dada. I've been meaning to tell you. Your nose gets all swollen when you cry too much."

"I was only a bit anxious," Rakhel says. She stands beneath Khorsheed's window, rises to the tips of her toes, and reaches for Khorsheed. "Though it seems there was no need. Asher didn't even spend a minute in her room last night, came straightaway back to me. Come closer so I can pull you down by the rope of your hair."

"And when I break my neck, who will mother my boy?"

"Myself, of course. And a better job I'd do of it."

"You'll be too busy wiping the bottoms of Kokab's brood to care for my little prince."

"Yousseff would be the apple of my eye. That woman can tend to her own litter."

"Have you spoken with her yet?"

"To say what?"

"I don't know, to befriend her somehow."

"I'd befriend her soon as I befriend the mare Asher buys to mate with his steed."

"Please, Dada, she may hear you. I'm not interested in living with an enemy."

"I hope you are not planning on becoming her friend?"

"I just don't want trouble with her."

"You know, Khorsheed, it's best to keep away from her. You heard about why Eliyahoo divorced her."

"Rumors, Dada."

"I don't know, Khorsheed. She seems to have it in her."

"You haven't even met her yet."

"For a reason. It's best to keep from looking into her eyes, directly. I didn't want to tell you, to scare you, but they say she's possessed, you know, by the djinn Al." Khorsheed stands up and looks down on Rakhel. Rakhel looks back at her.

"What are you talking about, Dada?"

"Well, you know Al doesn't just snatch babies from their mothers. Sometimes she takes the form of a beautiful woman, who lures men away from their wives. And from the stories I've heard about her . . ."

"Enough, Dada. She's a mother, herself."

"I've heard stories about her daughter, too."

"Stop creating trouble, Rakhel."

"That's the real reason Eliyahoo divorced her. To keep the girl from learning the mother's lewd nature."

"Enough, Rakhel."

"I'm just warning you, Khorsheed. I don't think she'll seduce Ibrahim, she seems to have her eyes on my husband alone, but I'd be careful with your baby. It makes sense, no? All that sorrow for losing her own child might make her eyes full of envy for yours, right?"

Khorsheed takes a step away from the window. She turns to look at Yousseff sleeping on the bed. She turns back to Rakhel.

"Don't worry, though. Just be cautious," Rakhel says. "Put a little soot on his face each time she's about. Better yet, keep him away from her sight. Just to be safe."

Khorsheed frowns. "I have to go nurse him," she says, then begins closing the window.

"I'm just telling you to keep him safe, Khorsheed. I love him as much as you do."

Khorsheed looks at Rakhel from behind the closed window. Rakhel smiles and shrugs her shoulders, then turns back to the fountain and the buckets of sour plums. Khorsheed walks over to her sleeping baby. She kneels beside him and watches the gentle rise and fall of his chest. She clenches her eyes shut. "Please, G-d," she says. "Let no harm come to my baby."

Seven

⚜

Kokab *steps into the dim light of the* study. She stands for a moment be- side the threshold, looking into the courtyard. Then, she closes the door gently behind her. She turns to look at the room. All four walls are lined with towering bookcases. Some shelves hold books, others statues and strange masks. On the topmost shelves are tremendous, heavy vases made of silver with intricate etchings, images of men on horseback hunting gazelles and bare-breasted women holding flasks of wine in the wilderness. Kokab walks from bookcase to bookcase, running her finger down the fabric spines of books, stopping to study strange objects made of precious metal, carved of wood, chiseled in rock. She picks up a stone sculpture of a nude woman, the size of her hand. The head and half the legs are missing, the breasts prodigious over an orb of a belly. She turns it in her hand. It feels cold and heavy. She places it back and turns to the desk facing the window overlooking the courtyard. Fierce dragons are carved into the woodwork of the desk, the whole of it painted a deep emerald green. On the desk is a leather-bound book, which she opens. Inside, beneath meticulous writing, she sees rows and rows of numbers, page after page after page. She closes the book and walks around the desk to a table that holds a gramophone. She puts her palms on the large trumpet and peers into the hollow.

"Do you want to hear it?" Asher asks. He enters the study and closes the door behind him. She does not greet him but turns to the window, instead, and places her hand on the glass. He walks to her. She feels him, close enough to reach out his hand and touch the fabric of her skirt. "After a day of haggling and buying, sometimes on my walk home through the streets of the mahalleh, I feel as though my limbs are slowly turning to lead." She faces him and looks into his eyes. Without taking his eyes off her, Asher turns the crank, places the needle of the gramophone down and there comes a *kheshkhesh* as the record turns, before sound pours out into the silence of the room. "I panic in those moments that if I don't move fast enough, that cold will touch my heart and I will never arrive at my home." He steps beside her and looks out of the window at the courtyard. "It is a race to beat this slow suffocation. I come to my study first, always, and put a record on this contraption. And when that first note sounds, I open this window into the courtyard so the rest of them, too, can hear the music. It fills the gardens. And death is not so solid, then." He places his hand on the glass beside hers. "This that you are hearing now is by a man named Beethoven. *Moonlight Sonata*. I received it the week I married Rakhel, from a dealer I correspond with in Austria. The music reminds me of you. The sweet longing in it." Kokab moves away from Asher and leans against the desk with her back to him. Asher follows her.

"Did boredom lead you here?" he asks.

"The desire to know who you are."

"Do you know, now?"

She turns to face him and says, "You want desperately to believe that life can be measured in what it yields."

Asher laughs. He steps closer to her and fingers the collar of her blouse. Kokab pulls back abruptly. Asher's hand falls to his side. She watches a red creep up his neck and into his face. He steadies his breath and asks, "Have you met Rakhel yet?"

"No. I saw her working in the courtyard from the window of my room."

"And you didn't go to say hello?"

"How do you imagine that conversation?"

"Well, the two of you will have to meet eventually."

"In due time, when she is ready."

"Are you ready?"

"To meet her? Yes. But I am the enemy."

"I won't allow that. You needn't worry about her."

"She is hurt."

"That is not your concern."

"I have to live with the guilt of her suffering."

"It is her own fault. She will have to learn to adapt."

"And me? Will I learn to adapt?" Kokab asks. Asher takes hold of Kokab's shoulders with both hands.

"I pray that you will find this to be your home," he says.

Kokab becomes rigid at his touch. "But you know that despite your efforts to beat death, there is something that escapes you," she says. "Something that cannot be measured, something beyond your grasp."

"Pardon?"

Asher turns and lifts the needle off the record, silencing the music. Kokab strums her fingers on the leather-bound book. "I imagine that you are waiting for the yield of your investment," she says.

"I won't demand anything of you that you will not give willingly."

"What is the weight of one's will in a prison?"

"I should hope that is not how you deem this home."

Kokab laughs. She places her palm on Asher's cheek. Asher closes his eyes and tilts his head down slightly toward her. "Asher, tell the old servant to bring my dinner to my room. I am not ready to join the family yet. And I am tired. I hope to go to bed promptly after eating." Asher's jaw tightens.

"How long do you plan on pulling me in such a fashion?"

"Forever."

"I am a patient man."

Asher begins walking out of the room. "In the future, this is my private study. The women do not come in here unless I invite them and that is a rare occasion." He stops and, without turning, says, "You remember the direction of your room?" Kokab walks past him silently. She continues to walk down the breezeway. She knows that he watches her bare heel against the marble, her hips sway beneath the folds of her skirt. Without looking back at him, she disappears into the darkness of her room.

A package arrives for Mahboubeh in the mail. Too big to fit in the mailbox, the mailman leaves it behind her door, rings the doorbell, and leaves before she has time to answer. She opens the door to find a box, wrapped in white paper, lying on her doormat. It is from a man in London, a certain rabbi, the husband of a distant relative. She closes the door to the empty streets, walks to her dining table, and opens the package to find photographs, handfuls of pages, the writing in diligent blue ink, carefully formed words, questions, dates, and a mass of pages taped together, when unfolded, revealing a family tree. There is an envelope, too, with a letter inside, addressed to her from the rabbi. She reads it once, then again. He asks several questions about the family history in his letter. Mahboubeh puts the letter down and looks at the family tree spread out upon her table. Beside Asher's name, joined to him by the branch that indicates marriage, there are two boxes. In one, the rabbi writes *Rakhel,* in the other, a question mark. Beneath both boxes is the word *childless.* In the careful blue script of his letter, the rabbi asks if Mahboubeh might know the name of Asher Malacouti's second wife.

"Kokab," Mahboubeh says. "But who remembers her anymore?"

Beside her father Ibrahim's name there are three branches, one for each of the wives he wedded, then buried. Those women lived in that home beneath Rakhel's reign, neither their will nor their children belonging to them alone. Mahboubeh places her finger on Khorsheed's name and closes her eyes. The other women's faces she can recall, but of Khorsheed all she has is a name, and the question of how she died. Mahboubeh looks beneath her father's name at a multitude of branches, children, grandchildren, great-grandchildren. She looks past that, up to see Zolekhah's name, and finds beside it a small image. Quickly, she shuffles through the bundle of photographs the rabbi has sent, and there it is, a photograph of her grandmother. *Zolekhah,* the rabbi writes beneath the image, *lived to be one hundred years old.*

Mahboubeh remembers Zolekhah as a bent old woman. Quiet. Unobtrusive. Perhaps even apologetic for the space she inhabited, the corner of the room where she sat all day, watching the family come and go in her silence. But this portrait is of a younger Zolekhah, in her late forties, perhaps. In the image, her face is like the bark of an oak tree, the frown sealed by the creases of the forehead, the chin pulling down on the corners of lips, which appear to have been supple in her earlier youth, now pursed, in controlled sternness. Her eyes are soft, though, or softened. There is a subtle kindness in the depth of those eyes, an understanding. Zolekhah wears a white head scarf, and through it, where it parts at the chest, a sequined blouse catches the light. She wears a coat of velvet, or mink. The costume and the face are incongruous. It is the face of a great chief, a sexless face, time worn into the skin. And the blouse, the coat? Certainly her grandmother would have dressed in such finery, her sons the richest merchants of the caravansary. And yet, Mahboubeh cannot imagine Zolekhah in any other dress than the one she wore in her old age, made of simple cotton, modest blue flowers, darker hues, her sparse white hair wrapped in a head scarf. On the day of this portrait, Zolekhah must have dressed herself in wealth to indicate her power within the household, to insist on it through the ages. Mahboubeh imagines Zolekhah as she sits for the photographer in the courtyard of the old family estate, and holds still for the time it takes for him to steal his head beneath the black cloth, and set her image to gelatinous silver. Zolekhah prepares for this occasion Asher has arranged for her with her thoughts elsewhere, and in the two-minute meditation as the camera captures the sepia leather of her skin, the firm pride of her cheekbones, she thinks of her son's ache for a child. She thinks about Kokab, alone in the farthest room, and for a moment, she allows herself to hope that the solution might be in that woman. When the photographer indicates that he is done, she rises from the chair and wanders to the kitchen to ask one of the girls to bring the photographer some tea.

From the kitchen, Zolekhah hears hurried footsteps in the courtyard and looks out to see Asher leaving Rakhel's room. She goes back into the kitchen to save him the shame of having to explain to her why, a week after Kokab's arrival, he has not yet consummated the marriage. When she hears the *clickclock* of the horse's hooves pass the kitchen and the dull thud of the heavy wooden street door close, she steps out. The courtyard is empty. The photographer must have left with her son. Zolekhah walks to Ibrahim's quarters, and quietly opens the door to find Khorsheed sitting on the floor beside the bed where Ibrahim sleeps, the child at her breast. "Did you sleep last night?" Zolekhah whispers.

"He kept me up."

"Let me take him from you when he is done nursing. You go to Rakhel and tell her I need to see her, to come to the kitchen as soon as she is dressed, it is a matter of urgency." Khorsheed rises heavily from the floor and lifts the baby. She hands Youssef to Zolekhah and leaves for Rakhel's room.

Zolekhah, with the baby in the nook of her arm, climbs the marble steps to Asher's home, and walks down the breezeway to the farthest room. She raps gently on the door, then opens it slightly. "Kokab?"

"Zolekhah Khanum?"

"May I come in?" Zolekhah enters without waiting for a response. Kokab sits beside the window, looking out to the gardens.

"Did you see Asher leave?"

"This morning?"

"Yes, from the window. Did you see him leave?"

"Yes."

"He did not stop to bid you a good morning?"

"No."

"He has not, yet, slept in your bed?"

Kokab turns her face back to look out onto the garden. Zolekhah walks to her. "Take this child from me." Kokab takes the baby and Zolekhah lowers herself to sit on a cushion on the floor. "Age is getting the best of me," she says. They sit for a while in silence, Zolekhah looking out the window at the skies and Kokab rocking the baby in her arms until he falls asleep.

"He smells of milk," Kokab says. She kisses the top of the baby's head. She studies him in the soft blue of the light that filters through the window, then kisses the baby's head again. "He smells of milk."

"There is only so much time we can afford our sorrow, daughter," Zolekhah says. She watches Kokab place her finger in the baby's open palm. Yousseff clenches her finger in his sleep. Kokab brings the baby's hand softly to her own lips and holds them there, her eyes closed.

"I lost my husband several years ago," Zolekhah says. "I

don't remember my parents, very well. I was a child when I married. He was a child, too, in the way men are children even when their beards suggest otherwise. In the beginning, he thought it his duty to beat me. By the time I handed him Asher, he had learned. He became a good man, and tender toward me. He died before my sons reached manhood. I was alone, with two boys. There was no time for weeping. The boys had to become men and I was both mother and father for them. Now, they are who you see before you. Good men. Hardworking, honest men." Zolekhah stops talking and watches Kokab cradling the baby. Kokab keeps her head bent toward the child, clicking her tongue softly.

"Asher suffers terribly for want of a child. The longing for one has changed him. He withdraws from the family more and more. He increases his wealth, his lands, and the success makes him even unhappier," Zolekhah says. Kokab does not look up from the baby.

"I know you've suffered much and your heart aches for the child you have lost," Zolekhah says. "But Eliyahoo will not let you have her back. You must accept this loss. G-d does not take without giving. You are fortunate to be married again. You will have more children. The pain of your loss will never abate, but soon you will bear and love other children. It is a blessing, this chance to start new."

Kokab shakes her head no, biting her lips. The child startles in his sleep and Kokab pulls him closer to her breasts and begins humming again. Zolekhah watches her. The child settles back into sleep. They sit for a while in silence, looking at Yousseff. Then Zolekhah rises and Kokab hands her the sleeping baby.

"Go to the hammam. Tonight, join us for dinner. Allow him to be a husband to you. It is the time for living."

Rakhel sits beside Khorsheed in the courtyard and waits for Zolekhah. She watches Zolekhah emerge from Kokab's room with Yousseff in her arms. She nudges Khorsheed. Zolekhah walks toward them, slowly as to not wake the sleeping baby. Khorsheed, her eyes round, her face drained of color, stands up and takes Yousseff hurriedly from Zolekhah.

"Where did you take him, Naneh Zolekhah?" Khorsheed asks.

"Nowhere, child. Go, I must have a word with Rakhel."

"Did you take him to Kokab, Naneh Zolekhah?"

"For a moment, daughter. Go, now."

"Why?" Khorsheed asks.

"What nonsense, child. I took him with me for a moment."

"Did she touch him?"

"Khorsheed?"

"Did she touch him?" Khorsheed inspects the sleeping baby in the light of the morning. He opens his eyes and reaches for her face. She kisses his hand and looks at Zolekhah. "I will burn some wild rue seeds for him. Just to be safe." She turns and hurries to her room, holding Yousseff to her chest protectively.

"The whole household is unsettled," Zolekhah says. "As though some terrible omen, G-d forbid, has come upon us." She shakes her head and mutters a quick prayer, then turns to Rakhel and says, "follow me to the kitchen, I must have a word with you."

Fatimeh stands in the kitchen peeling and chopping onions. "Where are the girls?" Zolekhah asks.

"I sent them to clean up the chicken coop and gather some eggs."

"Go see if they are doing it correctly, Fatimeh, you know those girls." Fatimeh wipes her hands on her skirt and leaves the kitchen. Zolekhah turns to Rakhel. Rakhel fingers the hem of her shirt nervously.

"Did I do something wrong, Naneh Zolekhah?"

"No, daughter, not something I have seen, though G-d sees all."

"Why did you wish to speak with me?"

"To talk to you about your responsibilities as the first wife. You understand, don't you, that though Kokab is older than you, you have the authority of the first wife? And with that authority comes a responsibility?"

"I don't know."

"You do. You are to make sure that things run smoothly, not just between you and Asher, but that the whole of the household continues to live in peace."

"I'll try my best, Naneh Zolekhah."

"Rakhel, you are like my own daughter. I am growing old and tired. I cannot continue doing all that I do daily. Cooking and managing the servants, ordering supplies from the markets, keeping an eye on the stock of food, calculating what's left and what's needed." Rakhel watches as Zolekhah takes from the cord tied about her waist the ring of keys. "These are the keys to the cellar and the storerooms of food." She hands the keys to Rakhel. Rakhel stands motionless, the keys a substantial heaviness in the palm of her hand. She looks up at Zolekhah.

"See to things," Zolekhah says. She pats Rakhel's shoulder, then holds the small of her back as she walks out of the kitchen. Without looking back, she says, "Kokab will join us for dinner this evening. You are the khanum of the household now. This is the first dinner you oversee. Make sure you welcome her."

Rakhel stands alone in the kitchen. A copper pot of water boils on the hearth. Eggplants soak in a tub of brine on the stone floor. She looks at the keys. They feel warm, already, from the heat of her hand. She lifts her shirt and unfastens the red yarn that holds her mother's key about her waist. That key wasn't meant for any lock, but held all her mother's hopes for her. If her mother could see, now, this ring of heavy iron keys she holds in her hands. Rakhel slips the bunch of keys onto the yarn, but they are too heavy and the whole of them fall to the floor with a clatter. She stoops to collect them, one by one, holding each to the light. Then she unfastens a length of rope from a bag of rice and strings each key, saving her mother's for last. She fastens it about her waist, the rope rough against her skin. This will do for now, she thinks, until she can find a more decorative cord, one made of braided silk, perhaps. She walks into the kitchen garden, the weight of the keys against her hips. The morning air feels cool, delicate.

In the gold of the light, she kneels among the bitter herbs and fills her skirt with the young leaves of the opal basil, plucks the tender green of the tarragon, clutches handfuls of parsley. She returns to the kitchen humming and places the herbs in a bowl of water, then kneels on the floor to remove their stems. Rakhel looks up from her task to see Sadiqeh enter the kitchen with her shaliteh full of brown-shelled and blue-shelled eggs. Sadiqeh stops at the threshold a moment and looks over her shoulder, then walks into the kitchen quietly. Rakhel stands up and straightens her skirt, then moves to the hearth. "Finish cleaning those herbs for me," Rakhel says.

"Yes, Rakhel Khanum. Soon as I set down these eggs." Sadiqeh takes the eggs one by one from her skirt and puts them into a bowl. "Wouldn't believe how many eggs we found here and there," Sadiqeh says. "Those poor hens, hiding them from us."

Rakhel pretends to mind the pot on the stove. She lifts her shirt to shift the keys and when she is certain that the girl has seen the set of keys at her waist, she says, "Put the eggs in that bowl faster and tend to the herbs. You did not find the eggs earlier because the henhouse is such a mess."

Rakhel worries that the tone of her voice is not flat, the way Zolekhah speaks when she addresses the servants. She will have to practice, later. Sadiqeh pauses, an egg in her hand. She places it carefully on top of the pile in the bowl, then brushes her hands off on her skirt.

"Yes, Rakhel Khanum."

"The henhouse must be cleaned once a week, from now on. The smell is evil and I'm certain it carries disease."

"Did Zolekhah Khanum say so?"

"Zolekhah has asked me to see to things around the household from now on." Rakhel turns abruptly back to the hearth so that the keys dangling from her waist clink against one another. She hears Zahra and Fatimeh approach the kitchen from the garden, talking to one another.

"Fatimeh, they say if she pounds mandrake into a fine powder and sprinkles it in her husband's food, he will become more fond of her."

"Everyone else eats that food, too, child."

"Well, maybe it will help us all. Lord knows I don't like her much myself. Oh, and if she can put the same powder in her rival's food, but add vinegar, Kokab will go crazy." They stand outside the kitchen. Sadiqeh swipes her hand across the table with a rag as though to clean it, pushing a wooden ladle onto the floor.

"And I've heard that if you make halva and mark the surface with a silver ring inscribed with a love talisman . . ."

"Rakhel Khanum, should I wash the herbs first?" Sadiqeh asks, louder than necessary.

Zahra and Fatimeh enter the kitchen to see Rakhel standing by the hearth, wooden ladle in hand, her lips a thin, straight line. Zahra turns red from ear to ear. Rakhel addresses herself to Fatimeh. "I'm seeing to dinner tonight," Rakhel says. "You can finish the coop today with the girls, then send them home when it is clean." Fatimeh looks Rakhel in the eyes. Rakhel tilts her chin up slightly.

"Yes, Rakhel Khanum. You won't be needing old Fatimeh's help with the cooking?"

"Not today. But for tomorrow morning, make sure that the men's breakfast is ready earlier. Asher has been heading out early, lately, and thirsty for tea."

"I'll do it right after my morning prayers, Rakhel Khanum. You'll call me if you need me?" Rakhel nods once and motions with her hand for the servants to leave. She turns her back to them to stir the contents of the pot on the flame. She can feel the women hesitate. When they walk out of the kitchen, she turns to pick up the eggs, one after another, and cracks them into a bowl. She stirs the yolks briskly. She hears an unfamiliar footstep approaching the kitchen. Rakhel knows that Kokab stands in the doorway, but she does not turn.

"Do you need help?" Kokab asks. Rakhel turns, wiping her hands on her skirt. Kokab has the ruband covering her face and eyes. She reaches up and unfastens the cloth, so that Rakhel sees her face. "I hope I didn't startle you. Would you like me to help?" Rakhel looks at the slant of Kokab's eyes, the defined lips, the pale skin.

"No, that won't be necessary. No need for you to sweat in here, I'll see to things." Kokab nods. She smiles at Rakhel. Rakhel strains to return the smile, but her mouth defies her in what she knows must be a menacing grimace. Rakhel turns her back to the woman with the pretense that the pot on the flame needs her tending and says, "You will join us, finally, for dinner?"

"If I am welcome."

"It is certainly more convenient to have you at the table than to serve you in your room." Kokab remains silent. Rakhel waits until she hears her leave. Then she walks into the empty courtyard. The pool and fountain gurgle in the center of the andaruni. The windows of Ibrahim's house are open into the courtyard, their lace curtains catching the breeze. Rakhel looks at the potted plants in front of Zolekhah's quarters, then up to the great hall of the *panj-daree*. She looks at the marble steps leading to Asher's home, the long breezeway to her bedroom, to his study, and farther, until that last room. Kokab may have power in that one room, Rakhel thinks, but I have rule of all this, the cellar, the gardens, the storerooms, the servants, the grand room with all its antiques. She pats the keys and returns to the warmth of the hearth to finish her cooking.

Mahboubeh remembers how Rakhel carried those keys with her until the day of her death. Even after Yousseff's widow sold the family estate and the locks those keys opened didn't exist anymore. Mahboubeh opens another kitchen drawer and rummages through it. She slams that drawer shut. Frantically, she opens another. She takes out the contents, folded dish towels, clothespins, envelopes with yellowed letters, batteries. She stops and looks at the items crowding the countertop, littering the ground. So many objects. A panic takes hold of her. She can't remember what she searches for, or how long she has been searching. She closes her eyes and waits for her mind to clear. She opens her eyes, takes a deep breath, and begins putting things back in the drawers and cabinets.

Mahboubeh's dinner sits cold and untouched on the table. Rice, a bit of stewed lamb. She sits down before it, in the silence of her empty kitchen. A spoon. She needed a spoon. She does not rise to fetch one. She has no appetite these days. She cooks rarely, a big pot of something that lasts days. Meals are no longer the events they once were, when her husband was alive, or when she herself was a child, at the family sofre. In those days, Rakhel controlled and allocated the food. The men, of course, Uncle Asher and her father, simply sat down and ate their fill. But the women and the children looked to Rakhel for permission before they ever ate anything.

Mahboubeh imagines Rakhel, preceded by the sound of her keys as she walks slowly through the courtyard after returning from the cellar, eating a handful of something. A group of children surround Rakhel and their voices crowd Mahboubeh's mind, shrill with anticipation, *please, Dada, please, do you have dried mulberries? Please, some for me? Did you bring figs, Dada, can I have a fig?* Rakhel reaches into her pocket and takes out a handful of sunflower seeds, puts one between her front teeth, cracks it, flicks the shell, and eats the meat. And another, and another. The children become more frantic. *Some for me, Dada, some for me?* Mahboubeh stands among them. She is hungry. She bounces from foot to foot. In her haste, she forgets and grabs at the hem of Rakhel's shirt. Rakhel turns and slaps her hand away. Mahboubeh's eyes sting with tears. She looks at the untouched plate of food before her and pushes it away.

A car passes in the street outside. Dusk settles. The kitchen grows darker. The crickets take up their song. Mahboubeh rises from the table, turns on the kitchen light, and scrapes the food on her plate into the trash, then places the plate in the sink. She turns on the water. The sink fills with warm water and Mahboubeh dips her hands in, closes her eyes a moment as the steam rises.

Rakhel sits quietly at the sofre and watches the steam rise from the mound of saffron rice, from the bowl of eggplant and okra stew. She looks at the basil and green onions she arranged in the fine silver tray used only for the most special occasions. Asher sits at the head, in his usual place, and Ibrahim beside him. Zolekhah, at the other end. And Khorsheed beside her. Then, Kokab. Rakhel tries to keep her eyes on the food, and find a way to busy herself with eating.

She reaches for bread, but then she notices Asher glance at Kokab, a quick spark in his eyes. Rakhel's hand remains outstretched until Asher clears his throat and startles her. She grabs a piece of bread and puts it in her mouth, almost choking. Asher looks away from her and resumes his dialogue with his brother.

"So when do you think you will be well enough to return to the caravansary?"

"I am sorry, Asher. My ribs are still mending, I can sit and stand with little assistance. Though I ache to lift or walk."

"It is the wheat harvest, soon. I will need to leave for the villages to oversee the farmers. Do you think you might be able to manage in my absence?"

"In a week's time, I should be on my feet again."

"Not much is needed from you but to make sure we are not robbed."

"Yes, yes . . ."

"It will not be physically taxing."

"No."

"Why don't you come with me to the caravansary, tomorrow. You can rest there, too, and see how things are faring."

"I'm not sure . . . If I can walk the distance."

"Take one of the mules."

"Asher, the jostling of that beast will kill him," Zolekhah says. "What is your hurry, the farmers have been harvesting the wheat for centuries without you overseeing them. Allow Ibrahim a bit more time to convalesce. Besides, you have your own business at home that needs tending to. This is certainly not a time for you to leave, with Kokab just arriving."

Asher turns to his mother. He inhales deeply and closes his eyes, then looks at her and says, "Thank you, Mother, but perhaps it'd be wiser for you to see to other matters and allow me to care for the business and the lands."

"Yes, son, certainly. As a matter of fact, Rakhel, you can help me clear the plates, and Khorsheed, why don't you help your husband to bed?"

Khorsheed rises dutifully from the table and reaches to assist Ibrahim. Ibrahim looks apologetically at Asher, but Asher glares at Zolekhah, instead, his jaw tight.

"Perhaps I may come with you tomorrow, brother," Ibrahim says as he stands. He leans on his wife and walks slowly toward the door. "Perhaps a good night's sleep will have me feeling more capable in the morning."

"Well, Rakhel?" Zolekhah says. She kneels and brushes crumbs with her hand. She stacks one plate on top of another. "Get up, daughter, and help me."

"I can be of help, too, Naneh Zolekhah," Kokab says.

"Not you, dear. You stay here and keep Asher company. His sour mood needs some sweetening."

Rakhel does not move. She looks at the plate before her. She can feel Zolekhah waiting for her to do as she has been told, but her legs are treasonous and she worries about what her hands might do. Should she reach for a plate, she might drop it, just to hear it shatter.

"Rakhel?"

She looks up slowly and sees the look of warning in her mother-in-law's eyes.

"Have you gone deaf, Rakhel?" Asher asks. "Does Mother need to repeat her request more than once?"

Rakhel shakes her head no and rises. She picks up the pile of plates Zolekhah has stacked and walks out of the room.

Outside, the night is silent, black, with the scent of impending rain. Rakhel walks to the pool, places the plates on the ledge and sits on the edge of the fountain. She turns her back to Zolekhah and puts her fingers in the water.

"Rakhel?" Zolekhah says.

"I'm here," Rakhel says.

"Asher will spend this night in Kokab's room," Zolekhah says. "You understand why it is necessary for him to do so?"

Rakhel looks at her feet. She holds her breath.

"Rakhel?"

"Yes, Naneh Zolekhah?"

"Do you understand why he needs to do so? Because you cannot give him a child and he is not a man to sacrifice all he has built for want of a child."

"Yes, Naneh Zolekhah."

"It will get easier with time, Rakhel. This first night without your husband may seem long, but it will get easier with time. You have seen to breakfast for him in the morning?"

"Yes, Naneh Zolekhah."

"You did well with dinner, I am very pleased. I know

you have the capacity to be the khanum of this estate, to take the role of the first wife with grace."

Rakhel remains silent. She can stop breathing at will, whenever she chooses. She continues to look at her feet. Zolekhah reaches out and lifts her chin. She bends close and kisses Rakhel's cheek. Rakhel sobs once, then holds her breath again, but she cannot stop her tears.

"Time, daughter, time is a salve upon an aching heart. I will tell Khorsheed to come out here and keep you company. Better to busy yourself with a task, than sit alone and think. And better to be with a friend." Zolekhah rises to fetch Khorsheed.

In the stillness of the courtyard, Rakhel looks at the lit guest hall. Asher stands by the window. Kokab stands beside him.

"Rakhel?"

"Did you see that?" Rakhel asks without turning to look at Khorsheed.

"See what?"

"Are you deaf or blind?"

"Why?"

Rakhel wipes her face with her shirt, then turns to Khorsheed. "Didn't you see what she has done to Asher? Haven't you noticed the changes in your own baby? She is taking what she wants from us, my husband and your baby. Right before our eyes."

Khorsheed takes a step back. She pauses, then picks up a plate. She scrapes the contents into a bucket. "What are you talking about, Dada. She has done nothing to my baby. Yousseff is fussy lately because he is teething."

"Some mother you are. This very afternoon the poor lamb screamed like someone was tearing his liver out of his body."

"Well, it hurts to cut teeth," Khorsheed says. She picks up another plate. It slips from her fingers, but she catches it. She breathes in heavily and dumps the remains.

"Khorsheed, you've seen babies cut teeth before. Have any of them ever suffered like Yousseff?"

Khorsheed doesn't respond for some time. She continues to scrape the food off dishes and stacks them by the fountain with her back turned to Rakhel.

"Well, have they?" Rakhel asks. "Isn't Yousseff's pain different?"

"I don't know."

"Think for a moment."

Khorsheed takes another plate from the pile. She holds it for a moment. Then she tilts her head to the side. "That's him. He's crying again," she says. She places the plate down and walks with haste back to her room.

"Lord knows what she plans for him," Rakhel calls after her.

Khorsheed rushes into her room. A warm light comes from inside. Rakhel waits in the still darkness. She wipes plate after plate, deliberately. After several minutes, Khorsheed comes back out to join Rakhel.

"Did she stop tormenting him?"

"He just needed a little milk to soothe him, that's all. The little sparrow misses me when I leave him."

"Probably because he senses something menacing. You noticed Asher, too, no? The spell she's put on him? Like a man walking in his sleep."

"He is a bit distracted." Khorsheed grabs a handful of spoons and dips them into the pool. She hands them to Rakhel, who shakes them dry.

"I'm doing what I can to bring him out of it," Rakhel says. "You can't be naive, Khorsheed. You have to do your part. You are a mother, and that helpless little sparrow depends on you."

"Rakhel, I'm not stupid. You are saying this to make me dislike her."

"Like her all you want, Khorsheed. But don't come running to me when black calamity comes your way."

"It won't. And I won't come running to you if it does, either."

"You don't have to be mean."

"Who's mean, Dada? All you do all the time is try to frighten me. From the very beginning, when I was pregnant with Yousseff, without regard for me or my baby, you'd do things to scare me. To hurt me. And now all this talk about Kokab being a djinn. You know, I'm nursing, and fear turns my milk sour. It can even dry me."

"Nonsense."

"Happened to my aunt."

"No, I know that. Nonsense that I'm trying to scare

you. You are my only friend, Khorsheed. More than that.
My sister. I'm saying what I say to protect you, and Yousseff,
whom I love as much as you do. Don't worry, though. I
know you won't believe me. Who'd believe a woman's ac-
cusations against her havoo?"

"Oh, Dada, just stop worrying. Asher hasn't even been
with her, yet. If he wanted her so much, he'd have taken her
by now. He just brought her for one thing only, and he'll do
what he needs to when the time comes, and he'll be done
with her after that."

"So you don't see what I see?"

"Maybe you see what you see because you are jealous."

Rakhel turns swiftly toward Khorsheed, a plate clutched
in her hand.

"I am not jealous of that harlot, Khorsheed. And I'm
certainly not jealous of you."

"You know what I mean."

Rakhel raises the plate and hurls it to the ground. It
shatters, the sound crystalline in the night. Shards of porce-
lain scatter about.

"What do you mean, Khorsheed?"

"What was that?" Zolekhah asks from the window of
her room.

"Just dropped a plate accidently," Rakhel says.

"Be careful," Zolekhah says and closes the window.

Rakhel grabs Khorsheed's wrist. Khorsheed tries to
twist her arm out of Rakhel's hold, but Rakhel doesn't let go.

"Listen to me, Khorsheed."

"Let go of me, Dada."

"I am not jealous of anybody. I have everything, Khorsheed. You know what Zolekhah gave me, right? All the keys. You know what that means, right? I'm in charge. Not Zolekhah. Not that harlot. And not you. What do I have to be jealous of?"

"Let go of my hand or I'll scream."

Rakhel releases her hold. Khorsheed pulls back and nurses her wrist.

"You hurt me, Dada. You know, your envy is really getting the better of you these days. Sometimes, I don't even want to be around you."

Rakhel turns and slaps Khorsheed. Khorsheed cries out. Rakhel grabs her neck and places her hand over Khorsheed's mouth. Zolekhah peers out of her window.

"Tell her it was a rat," Rakhel whispers. Khorsheed struggles. "You tell her it was a rat or you'll pay dearly." She removes her hand from Khorsheed's mouth.

"Just a rat," Khorsheed says. "A dirty, little rat." Khorsheed looks at Rakhel quietly. Then, she turns and walks away.

"Where are you going, Khorsheed?" Rakhel asks. "Did I tell you that you could leave?"

Khorsheed walks into her room and closes the door. Rakhel stands alone in the empty courtyard. She looks up at the night sky. Not a single star. Rain in the morning.

"Go ahead," she says. "Abandon me like the rest of them. I don't need You."

Eight

✦

Asher remembers a zoo he visited as a
child with his father, at the foothills of Doshan Tepe in Tehran. In
his memory, the colors are muted and warm. It
was before Ibrahim's birth, one of Asher's earli-
est memories. He recalls seeing a fox, curled on
the packed earth beside an amputated tree trunk,
behind the thick iron bars of a cage. And the fluid
movement of a leopard, the contrast of those bars
against the black spots of the animal's skin. And a
fly's impunity against a wolf. And that pacing lion.
Its cage not much longer than his own body. One
step, two step, turn, one step, two step, turn.

What is this pulsing urge to live, to breathe? Asher thinks. *In the confine of four paces, the lion still gnaws the bare meat of the donkey's head thrown it, tears at the meager flesh of the cheeks and ears to sustain his own life, even when wanting is a wide, wide savanna. When wanting is louder than the thunder of a thousand hooves. Why not just lay the head down on the cool of the earth, gaze at the clouds rushing overhead, the insistence of the sun, the perpetual games of the moon, watch quietly until you reach the edge of days?*

Asher walks across the four paces of the room. *The flesh, in essence, is a prison,* he thinks. Asher kneels before Kokab and takes her hand in his hand. Something breaks open inside him. He brings her fingers to his lips.

"The days pass so slowly here," Kokab says.

Asher inhales the musk of her wrist.

"Today I watched a flock of gray pigeons against the gray skies," she says.

He leans in to her hair. He breathes in and exhales against the lobe of her ear. He notices the rise of the fine hairs on the contour of her neck in response to his breath. He buries his hand in the thick of her hair, holds it out at arm's length, and watches the gleam of light captured in its blackness.

"You would not think their flight so majestic, to see them," she says. Then, she pulls back and looks at him. "You will take what you want from me, but it is not something I choose to give."

"Then push me away."

She looks at him silently. He catches the quickness in her eyes. It is a melting darkness. Had he not been kneeling beside her, he thinks, he might have fallen to his knees. "Then burn for me," he says. He places his finger against her mouth before she can speak. He touches the moist softness of her lips. He traces his fingers on her skin to the smooth of her throat and notices that his hands shake, subtly. She tilts her head back slightly and he feels an explosion of heat inside his own body, a ripple that passes from the skin of this woman into his own hand, and from there, fast toward his heart. Suddenly, he feels the proximity of his own death, but the terror of this thought abates to his hunger to taste, again, the salt of her skin.

One night passes, then another. At first, each evening before dinner, Asher visits Rakhel in her room and asks about her day. She prepares chai for him and he sits before her, impatient to leave, sipping his hot chai quickly, his eyes distant. Often, she catches him as he glances at the door. He clears his throat before he begins the formalities of good-bye. Then, he leaves hastily to see Kokab in her room.

So that each night Rakhel might recount for Asher reasons why she is indispensable to him, she spends her days from dawn to dusk engaged in household industry. And when Asher asks her about her day, she begins a detailed account of her preserving, stewing, pickling, brewing, sewing, cooking, and carrying on without a pause until Asher pats her hand and says, "Well done. Well done, indeed." She closes her eyes when he touches her hand, briefly. The way you might pet a child upon the head. His hand feels cold on her flesh.

One night, in desperation to keep him a moment longer from leaving, Rakhel says, "Asher, the valley you say you pass before reaching the village of Gahvareh, don't only goats and sheep graze there? If the shepherds move them up into the mountains, you can buy that land and have the farmers plant wheat in that valley, too, no? I remember my father used to say that the man who holds the grain is the man that has power. No matter what happens, everybody still needs to eat bread."

Asher stops a moment in his incremental escape of her company and looks directly at Rakhel for the first time in weeks. "You think I should expand the lands where we grow wheat?" he asks, amused.

"Yes. Purchase that valley near Gahvareh and plant more wheat."

"Purchase that valley and plant more wheat?"

"Then, you can grow and sell more wheat."

"Well, why not," Asher says. He says good-bye to her and takes his leave. The following day, when he returns from the caravansary, he remembers her suggestion and smiles. That night he tells her, "It is a sound idea. To buy that valley and plant more wheat fields."

Rakhel's suggestion proves profitable, and when Asher tells her this, she begins a determined search for ways to counsel her husband on investing. At first she steals into Asher's study and looks through all his books, but unable to read or understand his calculations, she abandons the venture. Instead she decides to listen closely to the men as they speak. She eavesdrops on visitors in the yard or in Asher's study. She talks to peddlers about what they see in their routes from village to village. She even listens to the gossip of the visiting women about who has met hard times. Thus, she gathers information and sits alone in her room at night thinking and rethinking, shaping her argument for Asher. She arranges her requests in a fashion palpable to her husband's ego, cautious of what she suggests and when. A Tabriz rug the Cohenzadehs need to sell, a ruby medallion worth tenfold of what they are asking. Then, after acquiring those jewels and antiques, she spends several nights listening to him talk to her of the market before she says, "What if we buy the lands east of Tofangchi, too?"

"I built his empire," Rakhel told Mahboubeh as a child. "I made Asher Malacouti richer than rich." Rakhel repeatedly recounted for Mahboubeh the story of how she first suggested the valley near Gahvareh. Mahboubeh remembers the jewels, the coins, the rugs, the vases Rakhel kept in her rooms, behind locked doors. Sometimes, she'd take Mahboubeh into one of those storerooms and show her an antique pendant, tell her its value, and the price she paid for it. In truth, the wealth belonged to Asher, but after his death, that wealth, the lands, and all those priceless antiques became their son's inheritance, and since Yousseff was not yet married, Rakhel managed to gain even more control of what was bought and what was sold.

Then, Yousseff died. His children were still young when his heart gave out. The Kurds from the villages came for his funeral the way they had for Asher's death, and for Rebbe Yousseff's, before him. They chanted and pounded their fists against their chests. Some even hit their backs with chains. And there was Rakhel, louder than any of them, weeping, and screaming and clawing her face. She'd pull out handfuls and handfuls of her hair. All day long, she'd *shivan,* until night came and she fell asleep from exhaustion. Then Mahboubeh took a broom and swept up her hair. Tufts of it, like small animals, on the floor. At sunrise, Rakhel started again. For months, she mourned him. Then she stopped crying when Yousseff's young widow started to sell the antiques, one by one. And parcels of the lands, too. Rakhel took to yelling, then. Yelling and screaming up and down the street that Yousseff's widow was a thief, selling *her* antiques, selling *her melk.* But all that wealth belonged to Yousseff's boys by inheritance, and since they were still too young, his widow could do as she saw fit.

But before the loss of her melk, the act of advising her husband and helping him invest begins as Rakhel's attempt to keep Asher in her room a bit longer, to win back his approval, to earn a place for herself in his home. She praises his profits, his acquisitions, lists for him how his wealth grows and grows. Sometimes, Asher pauses a moment and looks at

Rakhel intently, as though looking at a new acquaintance, intrigued.

Regardless of Rakhel's endeavors, however, Asher never returns to her room to spend an evening. After dinner, she sits beside her window, looking toward the light that escapes the curtained windows of the farthest room until it is snuffed out. In the mornings she rises early and looks out again to watch for Asher to leave. And it happens, often, for the morning to advance, sometimes approaching noon, before Asher steps out. By then, Rakhel has been working in the courtyard for hours, orchestrating more and more household projects that engage the maids to the brink of exhaustion. She labors, herself, alongside them. Asher walks past her, toward the stables, and nods a greeting in her direction. He leads his horse out without looking at her once.

Rakhel keeps her gaze down and busies herself with the task at hand so that the girls don't see her hot shame. After he leaves, she turns to Zahra and Sadiqeh with a controlled fury, and explains how their work is inadequate, careless, unsatisfactory. It must be redone, with greater diligence and more speed. And the girls exchange a quick glance, a smirk, before continuing their work with exaggerated zeal until Rakhel leaves their company. Only then does she hear their hushed talking, their laughter. She imagines them aping her, and her face burns with rage. She walks faster, toward the well, thinking of other laborious projects for them to begin. She reaches the well, her hands trembling, and sits beside it, her back against the cool of its stones. She closes her eyes and sees Kokab's face, perhaps just rising from sleep. She imagines Kokab's thick hair disheveled, and the movement of her limbs across the bedclothes where the impression of Asher's body still rests. Rakhel imagines how Kokab leans in to smell his scent on the pillow. How she rises from the tangle of the sheets and walks to open the window to allow for a breeze.

In the mornings, after Asher leaves Kokab for the whole of the long day within the household, she stares out of the window for hours. At the gray days, the steady rain, the shift of clouds, the sudden gold and the world illumined before dark clouds again, the white flash of lightning, the roll of thunder. She watches the birds come to settle on the naked branches that scratch at her window. She saves crumbs of bread from dinner in the pocket of her skirt, and leaves this small offering on the sill. She watches the birds look at the mound of crumbs skeptically, first with one eye, then another. And she watches the naked branches, scratching at her window, until she opens it one day to look closely at the small buds on the branches. She closes her eyes and pictures her daughter. The glow of her eager face in the mornings.

"Look at the branches, my love," Kokab whispers. "They are not bare. The blossoms are simply waiting." She thinks about her daughter's dimpled hands. If she could hold those hands now . . . She throws her head back and a cry escapes her lips. She shuts her eyes tightly. If she could hold those hands now, she'd guide them along the branch, to the tips where the buds are still enclosed in their tight sheaths, the tree aching with the desire to push forth the petals.

"And afterward, those petals will come down on us like snow," Kokab whispers. "And soon after, green leaves. So new, they'll shimmer in the sunlight."

Kokab catches a glimpse of herself reflected back in the glass, alone in the room, talking. She laughs. She raises her fingers to her cheeks. Tears, again. Endless. *There is dust, too, she thinks. Dust that settles on the leaves. That dims their shine. And time dries them, breaks their bones. Burns them red, orange, gold. And winds that push them until they can't hold any longer to the limb, relent. Let go their grasp. Float. Settle in puddles to be trampled by man and beast.* She shakes her head. "Even in this, my love," she whispers, "even in this a spectacular grace."

Kokab waits through each passing day for the evenings. When the sun begins to set, she feels, despite herself, a flutter in the pit of her stomach. Soon she will hear the gentle rap of his fingers against the door. Each evening, Asher walks in and dispels the quiet birds of her sorrow. He fills the cold room with the warmth of his body. He asks her to stand in the candlelight, to stand naked and trembling, so that he can look upon her. And she stands for him. She stands for him in the golden flicker of that light, and she watches the shadows pass over his face. She watches him watch her with so much longing, the way she watches the sky, the moon, the rain. And in these moments of his rapture, she feels herself become tree, sky, moon, rain, the shift of clouds, the sudden gold, the illuminated earth.

Rakhel stands pressed against the garden wall. The night is moonless, and the stars litter the black sky. She shifts her bare feet in the wet grass. Across from Rakhel the willow tree hangs low to the ground, swaying each time there is a slight breeze. Beneath the tree rests the well. The shadows that lurk in the peripheries of Rakhel's vision whisper to her, masking their voices as the sound of leaves. She hears a rustle come from the old walnut tree and she stands erect, the potential of motion pulsating in every muscle of her body. One more unknown sound in this darkness and she will lose her resolve, run back to her empty room and pray for forgiveness.

She takes a step forward, then two and approaches the well, her whole body shaking. She braces herself, tilts her head to the side to listen for footsteps, then she takes another step and listens again. Nothing but the sound of the wind in the trees. She places her hand on the low stone wall of the well and looks into the black emptiness of its opening.

"Can you hear me?" she asks. Her question rings down the well and multiplies itself indefinitely. She waits for a sign. The wind falls still. The leaves silence their whispering.

"Can you hear me?"

She brings her face closer to the opening, her question a response to her own question.

"You must eat the child that grows in her belly," Rakhel says. She listens to her own voice travel, echo in the circular tunnel. "If she has a baby, I will lose everything," Rakhel says.

Some bird of the night laughs from a nearby tree. Rakhel jumps back from the well and looks around frantically. She holds her breath, her heart lurching against her chest. She waits until the night resumes its silence, and turns back to the well.

"Kill the baby that grows in her belly, and give me a son," Rakhel says. "No matter the cost. Give me a son."

She breathes heavily, shuts her eyes, and reaches under her blouse to unfasten the rope about her waist. She shifts through the keys and finds the one that belonged to her mother. She slides it out and holds it between her fingers. She brings it to her lips and kisses it, then leans over the edge of the well. A thousand stars float around the dark shadow of her reflection in the still water. Rakhel opens her fingers and drops the key into the well. It breaks the surface of the water, shattering the night sky. The stars elongate and separate in the waves of Rakhel's offering. When the water in the depth of the well is still again, she turns and walks back to her room. Once inside, her fingers are clumsy in lighting the lantern. She sits on the rug and takes a gold hand mirror, brings it to her face, and looks fiercely at the reflection of her own eyes.

Rakhel rises from the floor and opens the door leading into the breezeway. She walks beneath the picture of Moses striking his staff before the pharaoh and his court. The staff turns into a hundred snakes. She comes to the room at the end of the breezeway. A light escapes from the window between the slit of the drawn curtains. Rakhel presses her face to the glass and in the gold light of the room, she sees the naked back of her husband, sitting, and around his neck, Kokab's long, white arms, spilling on his shoulders, the lush of her black hair. Rakhel watches the face of the woman in her husband's arms. Kokab's eyes remain closed, her lips apart. Rakhel watches Asher throw his head back, a look of pained agony on his face. She watches them become still. She waits for them to separate.

Rakhel wakes with a start. She sits up in her bed. It is not yet dawn. She hears a door open and shut. She listens to the footsteps in the courtyard. The splashing of water from the shallow pool. She rises from the bed and walks across the room to the window facing the courtyard. She pulls the curtains back slightly to see Khorsheed standing beside Ibrahim. Ibrahim motions for her to return to her room. Khorsheed leaves, reluctantly. The knot in Rakhel's throat turns into a slow burning. These days, whenever Rakhel tries to speak to her, Khorsheed replies with cold, polite formalities.

"Damn you," Rakhel says out loud. She raps her knuckles against the glass. "Damn you and your lack of loyalty."

Another door opens and shuts. Rakhel hears the familiar footsteps on the marble stones of the breezeway. Asher walks across the courtyard to the stables. He does not look in the direction of her window. *It is as if I have vanished,*

Rakhel thinks, *that nothing of me remains, not even the room I inhabit.* A few minutes later, he returns leading the horses. The two men each take the reins of a horse and walk out of the courtyard, through the narrow passage leading to the door that opens into the street.

The previous night, to disguise the strained silence of their dinner, Ibrahim told stories about the harvest in the villages. Rakhel tried to listen, but each time she started to see the fields of wheat and the men swinging sickles with sweat on their brows, she'd remember that Kokab sat directly across from her, and she knew that if she looked at Asher, she'd see him entranced by Kokab masticating.

The first few nights after Asher left her bed, Rakhel had sat down to the family meals resolved to stop eating and waste away. But when she noticed that nobody paid her slow death any heed, she developed a ravenous appetite. While Ibrahim spoke about the villages, Rakhel ate voraciously, smacking her lips, licking her fingers, leaning over to help herself to a second, a third helping.

"Even the women with new babies work," Ibrahim said. "They leave the infants in the shade of a tree, work behind the men gathering wheat, and when it is time to nurse, they return to the shade."

"What if wolves eat their baby?" Khorsheed asked.

"Wolves wouldn't approach such a large group of people," Ibrahim said. "Besides, Asher and I have seen these men wrestle. Each night, they hold contests. Should a wolf come, thirty men would fall upon the poor beast."

Khorsheed giggled. Rakhel felt a wave of nausea and decided to conclude her meal noisily with a tall glass of water.

"The village heads host our stay. They spread the best of their bedding for us to sleep, and each night, their wives prepare stews with lamb meat. They do not eat so lavishly themselves. They slaughter a lamb when we arrive and treat the three days of our stay as a feast. It is a pity to miss it, this year. I feel terrible regret." Ibrahim looked to his brother, but Asher did not notice, or perhaps even hear his brother.

"I wish I could go, just once," Khorsheed said. "I'd leave the baby in the shade and try my hand at gathering."

Rakhel snorted in response. Khorsheed paused and looked in her direction. Rakhel reached out to tear a piece of bread and soaked it in the pot of stew on the sofre, then stuffed it into her mouth. Then, she rose abruptly and gathered Khorsheed's plate on top of her own.

"Rakhel, you seem to be in a bit of a hurry," Zolekhah said. "We are still eating."

"I'll just take these," Rakhel said and she left the room.

The sun crests over the mountains and the sky outside is pink and gold. It will be a warm day. Rakhel turns from the window and walks to the mirror. She stands before it and weaves her hair into two thick braids. She remembers the previous night at the well, her offering, her prayer. Something must change, now. She straightens her skirt and turns her thoughts to the day's tasks.

The farmers brought in the grape harvest a week ago.

If Rakhel waits any longer, mold will ruin the year's wine. Rakhel saw to it throughout the week that the girls string up hundreds of clusters from the ceiling of the cellar. She stood in the dim light of the cellar to oversee their work. Zahra and Sadiqeh worked silently. When she addressed them, they responded with as few words as possible. *Clean those bushels to make bottles of syrup. Yes, Rakhel Khanum. Extract the juice of the unripe ones and bottle that for stews and sherbets. Yes, Rakhel Khanum.* Khorsheed avoids Rakhel, and Rakhel's conversations with Zolekhah are sparse, so that some days the only sentence uttered by another in response to what she has said is *yes, Rakhel Khanum.* She spends days in this silence, under the hot sun, standing over the servant girls as they quietly burn the grapevines and boil down the ashes, then boil the yellowish water to dip clusters in for raisins. *There are still the bushels of* rang-e kishmish-e siyah *and* methqali *for wine making. We cannot do that, Rakhel Khanum.* And Rakhel knows this, that it is blasphemous to their faith to make wine, but she says it regardless, asks them why not, drags reluctant words from them, pulls and tugs at the conversation to make it stretch until she knows it cannot go any further. Then she assigns them another task, and retreats to her room.

Rakhel must make the wine soon and she decides to do the arduous work alone. She brings up the buckets of grapes from the cellar one by one as the sun climbs to its zenith. She licks the salt of her own sweat from her upper lip. Her shirt sticks to the dampness of her body, the hair at the nape of her neck is wet. In the few moments of her rest, she feels the thud of the heart in her chest and the pulse of blood in her veins. *Like the almost imperceptible motion of a fly's wings,* she thinks. So she works harder to keep from thinking.

If she had a child, Rakhel reasons, even a daughter, she might carry along with the rest of the world around her. That child, her child, will have another child, and another child will be born of that, so that through them, she might forgo such insignificance. But she has no child. She is the ending point of generations that stretch back to the beginning of time. She stops in the middle of the courtyard and places the buckets she carries on the ground. She looks up to the sun, dazzling white in the blue skies. Her eyes tear, but she keeps looking at the flaming disk.

"I will make things grow, the wealth of the estate, its abundance," she says. "I will build a kingdom. At least this will remain of me, not the objects themselves, but the knowledge that I made them proffer. And the wine for the Sabbaths this year will be my own secret reminder, the product of my will and strength. It will be my hands that wash the grapes, my feet that press them, my diligence to nurse the fermenting liquid. I will funnel this wine of my labor into glass bottles to keep."

She looks at the skies a moment longer, then turns and walks to the stables to drag a tremendous basin back to the center of the courtyard. She rolls up the cuffs of her tumban and the sleeves of her shirt. She goes to the pool and washes her arms and legs, her hands and feet, and sits for a moment on the ledge for the sun to dry her skin. Yes, it will be the wine she has pressed that Asher will bless and drink. Rakhel jumps to her feet and hoists bucket after bucket of grapes into the basin. She feels the strain of the work in the muscles of her arms and back, in the tension of her thighs. Her clothes are wet with perspiration, she can feel the sun on the ridge of her nose. A fly hovers near her face. She swats at it and it returns. Rakhel looks at the basin full of red grapes, holds her breath and steps in. An explosion of grapes beneath the soles of her feet. Cold against her calves.

"Whoever drinks this wine will also drink the resolve of my heart," she says beneath her breath.

She begins stepping up and down, one and two, a rhythmic dance. She keeps her hands on her hips. She thinks about Kokab, she sees the vision of her in Asher's arms. She pounds her feet harder, brings her legs up and down faster, breathes heavily.

"You will see," she says out loud, kicking and thrashing the pulp. "You will see what I am worth!"

She slips to her knees, throws her hands forward instinctively. The liquid pulp is beneath her chin. If she could just overcome the impulse to breathe . . . She clutches grapes in her hands and squeezes them, the juice dripping from between her clenched fingers, the pulp falling from her closed fists. She grunts and stands, her clothes stained deep purple and dripping with juice. She begins pounding the grapes beneath her feet, again. She thrashes wildly about the basin, the liquid sloshing back and forth violently. She slips again and yells, jumps to her feet and resumes, kicking her legs, dripping with juice.

"Rakhel, G-d be merciful, have you gone mad?" Zolekhah says.

Rakhel turns to see Zolekhah's bewildered face. Khorsheed, Kokab, and the servants stand behind her, their mouths agape.

"Fine, fine, Naneh Zolekhah. Just seeing to the wine, that's all."

"Now? In the heat of the noon?"

"Allah forgive us, Rakhel Khanum, you will die of heatstroke," Fatimeh says.

"Don't worry, I'm capable enough to do this task alone."

"Rakhel, three grown men couldn't do this task. Get out of that basin before you bring black calamity upon us."

Rakhel continues to step up and down, now with a measured pace. She steadies her voice and says, "If we let the grapes go any longer, they will spoil, and if I leave the task now, the grapes will cook. Someone must see to this year's stock of Sabbath wine?"

"I can help her," Kokab says.

Rakhel stands in the basin. The liquid settles around her calves. She looks down to where her legs disappear in the juice and pulp. The skin above the line is stained purple. Her clothes are sticky. She looks up and sees the women staring at her expectantly.

"Yes, Kokab jan, and Khorsheed, too," Zolekhah says.

"Zolekhah Khanum, Khorsheed, the poor child, is a nursing mother. You put her in this sun to do this work and, G-d mute my tongue for uttering these words, she will perish," Fatimeh says.

"Well, then, Kokab and Rakhel can share the work."

Kokab bends to roll the cuffs of her tumban. She steps into the pool and washes her legs and her arms. Khorsheed looks at Rakhel and lifts her eyebrows. Rakhel shrugs her shoulders and looks away.

"Rakhel, step out a moment and rest. Kokab will take over," Zolekhah says.

"Naneh Zolekhah, really, I'm already stained and doing the work, no need—"

"Out, Rakhel."

Rakhel takes one leg out, then another and stands in front of the basin, barring Kokab's way.

"Thank you for allowing me to help," Kokab says.

Rakhel ignores her and walks to the pool. She hears Kokab step into the basin. Rakhel bends and splashes water on her legs and arms.

"Rakhel, your clothes are ruined," Zolekhah says.

Rakhel does not respond. She sits on the ledge of the pool and turns to look at Khorsheed. The two girls stare at each other for a long time, then the baby begins whining and clutching at his mother's hair. Khorsheed turns her attention to Youssef, and Rakhel finally looks in the direction of the basin, to watch Kokab stepping on the grapes.

Kokab moves with slow, deliberate steps. She closes her

eyes and tilts her chin up slightly. She places her braceleted hands on her hips. She lifts one leg, presses down, lifts another. Rakhel imagines Asher's hand on Kokab's legs. He will think the beauty of her white calves heightened by the stained skin.

"Strange sensation," Kokab says and smiles with her eyes closed.

Kokab's upper lip glistens in the sun. Sweat beads on her forehead. She shakes out her hands, and the jangle of her bracelets startle Rakhel from her trance. *There is something in Kokab's face, something in her expression,* Rakhel thinks. Then she imagines that same look on Kokab's features, in Asher's embrace. *Here, before all these witnesses,* Rakhel thinks, *she is polluting the Sabbath wine, sweating into it her wicked thoughts, the scent of her sinful body.*

Rakhel imagines Asher reciting the kiddush. She imagines him pouring a glass of the wine for the prayer. She sees Kokab in the glow of the Sabbath candles. Asher puts the translucent garnet of the liquid to his lips, closes his eyes, and drinks. And Kokab spreads warm inside him, flows deep into his veins. He opens his eyes, only to see Kokab. He passes her the glass, one hand to another, red black wine wetting their tongues, in their mouths. And Rakhel, too, would have to raise that glass to her own lips and believe in the sanctity of wine, Sabbath, prayer, marriage, even though she bore witness to the profanity of this moment, now, where the grapes are being pressed beneath Kokab's feet. She sees herself in the dark of the cellar, each morning and evening, a slave to the fermenting liquid. Her fingers stained purple as she draws off the fluid from the settled refuse. She sees herself kneeling, funnel in hand, doggedly filling bottle after bottle with the wine of the woman who has intoxicated her husband.

Rakhel jumps to her feet and runs to the basin. "That's enough, you will tire yourself," she says. Kokab stops to look at her.

"Rakhel, Kokab just started . . ." Zolekhah says.

"No, no, it's fine. Get out. Get out, now."

Rakhel leaps forth and grabs a handful of Kokab's hair. She pulls hard and the woman loses her footing and falls forward. Zolekhah grabs Rakhel's shoulders and tries to pull her back, but Rakhel doesn't release her hold.

"You've done enough," Rakhel screams.

Kokab struggles to stand in the liquid. Rakhel pushes down on her head until Kokab's face submerges in the juice and pulp.

"Khasveh shalom, you are killing her!"

"Allah protect us, Allah forgive us this sin!" Fatimeh says. She pulls Rakhel's arms and pleads, "Rakhel Khanum, let go, let go!"

Rakhel finally releases her hold and steps back. Kokab raises her face, coughing and gasping. There is a clear, still moment. The women around Rakhel wait to see what she will do next. Rakhel looks to the sky, then opens her mouth as if to scream.

At first the women hear a sound like the rumble of low

thunder, then it becomes a shrill pitch that fills the whole sky. The women look at Rakhel in bewilderment, then look up to where she gazes. A thick moving cloud covers the sun. It looks like a torrential flapping of birds' wings, until the cloud splits apart and they see the luminous gray-green armor of the insects, the thick of them settling in the trees, plummeting like hail at their feet. The women scream and run in the direction of the sitting room. Rakhel ignores them, and watches, in stillness, the downpour of the locusts, undisturbed by the large insects that settle on her hair, on her arms, on the grass, splash into the pool and bring the hungry fish up to the surface to feed. She stands and watches as though she had been waiting all along for this answer to come falling from the mute blue skies.

Zolekhah and the women watch Rakhel with horror from behind the windows of the guest hall. The locusts land on Rakhel, crawl on her arms and legs. Khorsheed begins rapping on the glass frantically and screaming, "Dada, Dada!" Yousseff wails and Zolekhah bounces the child absently, clucking her tongue.

"Ya Imam Hossien, the girl is out of her right mind. Those insects will eat her face," Sadiqeh says.

Khorsheed pounds harder on the glass with her fists. Zolekhah puts a hand on her shoulder. "You are upsetting your baby. I'll get her," she says.

Zolekhah knocks on the window to get Rakhel's attention, but the girl does not respond. Zolekhah looks around the room and spots a broom.

"Fatimeh, hand me that broom, I'm going out to get that girl."

"Zolekhah Khanum, those insects will eat the broom. I've seen them before, they'll eat right through that straw, maybe down to the stick," Sadiqeh says.

Zolekhah pulls her chador over her head so that only her eyes are visible. She braces the broom in one hand and steps to the door. Khorsheed stops crying and the women turn to watch Zolekhah.

"Zolekhah Khanum, it is thick as fog out there with those insects," Zahra says. "Leave it be for a while, until they clear."

"The poor, poor child," Fatimeh says. She looks at Rakhel, frozen by the pool, and clicks her tongue. "It happens this ways, sometimes, when a woman suffers too much."

The women look at the storm of green bodies, the *thud thud* of them against the window. A few crawl on the glass, revealing the white of their bellies, the clasping forceps of their mouths, the nervous twitch of antennas, their red eyes.

Zolekhah hits the window with her knuckles. "Come this way, Rakhel, come inside!"

Rakhel looks at them. She raises her hand to wave. Then she looks at the back of her hand. A locust crawls over it, to the palm and out to the tips of her open fingers, then flies off. Rakhel drops her hand limply to her side.

"She's going inside," Zahra says.

An hour later, armed with the broom, Zolekhah braves the journey to Rakhel's room to see what has become of the girl. She sweeps her path clear of the bodies of insects, carefully treads her way across the marble. She enters the room to find Rakhel sitting beside the window, still wearing the torn, stained clothes, staring vacantly at the courtyard.

"Rakhel?"

Rakhel turns slowly to look at her.

"Say something, child, you're aging me."

"They came because of her."

"Who came, child?"

"They came to cleanse her sins from the earth."

"What nonsense are you speaking, girl?"

Rakhel looks out of the window again, places the tips of her fingers on the glass where locusts crawl. "She is evil."

"Who?"

"Kokab."

"Rakhel, you're not yourself."

"No. I have seen her wickedness. In the clear light of day."

"What wickedness, poor wretch? She is a sad woman, trying to find a place in this world, pining for the child she's lost."

"She is destroying Asher."

"Enough, Rakhel, enough."

"She is, but I won't allow her."

"What has the poor woman done to you? She is here to help you and Asher."

"She's bewitched him."

"Nonsense."

"He walks in a dream state, he has forgotten everything else."

"You are speaking from jealousy."

"He cares for nothing but her."

"She is a new wife, it is natural for a man."

"He is trapped by her spell. They say Eliyahoo divorced her for this wickedness. She brought him near the brink of insanity. And he wasn't enough. She lured other men, common men."

"Rumors started by Eliyahoo's sisters to save face."

"The truth is before our eyes. He spends all his time in her room, leaves late, sometimes never leaves for near the day, the whole of the day."

"It is normal, Rakhel. She is new to him. He will tire of her soon."

"She will be his death."

"Asher needs children, Rakhel."

Rakhel turns to look out of the window again. The locusts hit the glass, crawl over its surface, cover the sill, cluster on the pots of flowers on the ledge. Outside, the trees are covered with breathing, glittering leaves. The grass of the courtyard crawls and clicks, the vegetable and herb garden of the kitchen is already bare down to the black soil.

"It's a hunger that leaves the earth barren," Rakhel says.

"What?"

"This longing."

Nine

❦

It will stop, do you hear me?

She looks out of the window at the garden.

Do you hear me?

She wants to rise from the chair, to walk into the morning air.

What would you prefer me to do? Spend every night with you? Send her away?

Her legs feel leaden. Her body aches. She is tired. Early morning and she is tired.

I need children. Do you understand this? And what will my future be if I don't have a son? All I work for?

If Mahboubeh does not work in the garden,

now, if she misses these early mornings, the day will come when the garden becomes unmanageable.

Where will all my melk, all that I have built go after me? I, alone, must be the man for this household, and my position undermined by a girl of fifteen, sixteen?

The weeds will be too many, too strong. The rosebushes untamed. The fruit trees less productive.

I am not made of stone! Every day I leave this home, I know full well that any street beggar, any ruffian could beat me the way they beat my brother! My brother, abused in the street like a dumb beast! And no one stopped them!

Mahboubeh thinks about rising from her chair, but her legs hold fast to the ground.

Do you know how hard it is to work with men for years and years, men who take your money, but still deem the touch of your hand to be najis? I see these men each day at the caravansary, and whenever it rains, they stay away from me for fear that the water will spread my contamination. Jew. Jew. They whisper behind my back like the word itself is filth in their mouths. Do you know what this does to a man? Shamed by men less than me? And now, by my own wife?

"Stop," Mahboubeh says quietly. "Stop telling me." She knows that no one is with her, that she is alone, all alone, in a home in a place too far away for this story to unravel itself at her feet, and bind her to her chair to keep her a prisoner to its telling.

My home is the only place I have peace. Where I can be respected, and you . . . You disrespect me with your childishness!

She is my wife, too. A woman ten years older than you! What if this story gets out? That I can't control my wives? Did you ever think of the effect that would have on my name? Stop crying. Stop! Look at me. I will do whatever it takes to maintain the peace of my household. Do you understand what I mean? Do you understand what I mean?

"Let me be," Mahboubeh yells into the silence of her home. "Let me be."

Rakhel sits alone in the corner of her room.

"She has gone mad," the girl servants whisper from behind the door.

"She is possessed," they whisper, then turn to run.

Rakhel wakes up screaming. It is night outside. The bed is wet, her body on fire. The door opens to her room. Asher runs in, behind him Zolekhah. Darkness. Rakhel opens her eyes. Daylight. Zolekhah's face before her. The old woman asks her something. Darkness.

Rakhel stands in the courtyard. Beneath her feet, a chasm opens. She looks into it. No bottom. Khorsheed beside the window. She waves. She smiles. The men hold Khorsheed, their big hands on the length of her arms. They pull in the opposite direction of each other. Khorsheed splits, her body tears. Black bleeding. Khorsheed turns to stone. Time passes. Stone becomes soil. Time passes. From this black soil grows a pomegranate tree. It blossoms, fruits. One falls to the grass, splits open, pours forth her ruby-coated seeds.

Rakhel wakes up lying on her stomach, her back is

bare. She struggles. Somebody holds her arms, there is a weight on her legs. She sees Naneh Adeh looking into her face. The old woman holds a horn-shaped glass over an open flame. Then she places the glass between Rakhel's shoulder blades. Rakhel hears herself scream. It feels as if her skin has been torn off and her flesh is melting. She turns her head to see a red rose blooming on her back. Darkness.

Kel na refa na la. The voices of women respond, *Amen.* Someone lifts Rakhel until she sits. Someone lightly slaps her face. Rakhel opens her eyes to see the room full of women. The old rabbi folds a small scrap of paper full of writing in black ink. He drops it into a glass of water, stirs until the water is blue. He moves toward her. Someone tilts her head back, holds her face with one hand, presses hard into her cheeks with a thumb and forefinger. When Rakhel opens her mouth to moan, they bring the glass quickly to her lips and flood her throat with the ink water. She drowns. The torn paper lodges in her throat. She swallows and swallows words. She sees Khorsheed standing in the far end of the room, holding Yousseff. *A son. A son for me.* Darkness.

Rakhel, wake up, please. Dada, open your eyes. Dada, please, please, open your eyes. Look, Yousseff is holding your finger. If you open your eyes, I'll show you how he can stand when I hold his hands. It's lonely here, without you. Remember when we ran out in the rain? It's been raining. Raining and raining.

Thunder. Rakhel stares into the chasm that opens between her feet. No bottom.

When she opens her eyes, the light is a dusty blue. She

tries to swallow, but her throat feels full of sand. She sees a glass of water beside her bed. She tries to lift her hand. She whimpers with the effort.

"Rakhel Khanum?" Fatimeh stands beside her.

Rakhel tries to say water, her tongue like stone in her mouth. She looks frantically to the glass beside her bed. Fatimeh places an arm behind her back and raises her, then brings the glass to her lips. The water is cool. She gulps and gulps. She pulls her head away from the glass when she finishes.

"Rakhel. Rakhel, open your eyes, you must eat. A week has passed. Rakhel. You must eat."

Zolekhah lifts her head. Fatimeh places pillows behind her back until she sits upright. Khorsheed appears. She carries a bowl full of steam. She sits beside Rakhel.

"Soup," Khorsheed says. "Made from the most beautiful rooster you have ever seen. Green feathers and a proud red comb. He jumped into the pot willingly, when he heard you screaming all that nonsense. I'll blow on it. Open your mouth. Good. Open your mouth. Good . . ."

The broth is warm. Rakhel feels it go down her throat. It spreads all across her body. She sees Yousseff, crawling across the floor.

"In The Book, G-d gives Yousseff to Rakhel," Rakhel says.

"What do you mean, Dada?" Khorsheed asks.

"Let her rest. She'll drink the rest of the soup later," Zolekhah says.

Rakhel looks at the women in the room. She opens her eyes again and they are gone.

In the moonlight, the courtyard appears blue. Asher stands beside the window, looking at the frozen trees, the snow-covered ground. He looks up at the sky. Black clouds move to cover the moon, veiling parts of her, then passing to reveal the white orb of her body, before concealing her again. He stands for a long time in silence, aware of Kokab sitting behind him, but lost in the currents of his own thoughts.

Without turning, he says, "This moon, comes into fullness and waxes and wanes, I've watched so many of them from this window, and still . . ."

"Sometimes it takes time," Kokab says.

"Enough time has passed, now."

Kokab says nothing in response. Asher waits, expectantly, for a word, a promise, something to ease the growing fear that lurks in the corner of his mind. He presses his forehead against the cool of the glass. "Kokab?"

"Yes?"

"What if . . ."

"It is no use, Asher, to think about it. It is out of your hands."

"But what if I can't . . ."

"Then that is the destiny G-d has written for you, your qesmat."

Asher reels around to face her. His brows furrowed

deep with anxiety, he clenches his fist and pounds it against his chest. "Then my life amounts to nothing. The value of what I have built is nothing. It would all have been in vain." He searches her face to see if she shares his suffering. Her face is empty. "Don't you want a child, too?"

Kokab turns her face away from him.

"All these nights, in my arms, isn't that the yearning? The fire between us, isn't it the longing to create?" Asher asks.

Kokab stares at him for several moments, then looks down and shakes her head.

"What is it for you?"

"Perhaps to burn the past, to forget."

Asher covers his face with his hands, then looks up furiously at Kokab. "You don't want to give me a child?"

She watches him, her eyes full of pity.

"Don't look at me as though . . ."

"Asher."

He buries his face in his hands, again, his body shaking. She rises off the floor and approaches him and places her hand on his shoulder. He moves out of her reach and turns his back to her. He holds his face a moment longer, then wipes his eyes with his sleeves.

"Don't you want to be a mother? Isn't it a natural inclination for women, to want to bear a child, to nurture a child? Desire is a means to that end. Unless, like an animal, you act on that desire for the sake of the act itself?" Asher asks. Even after the words are spoken, he hears the waves of them crashing over the woman who stands before him, and she is suddenly carried beyond his reach. Her eyes look past him, past the courtyard, beyond the moon.

He places his hand on her arm. "Kokab?" Her eyes remain distant. "Kokab?" He shakes her arm with his hand. "I did not mean what I said, forgive me. You must understand. Kokab?"

She looks at him, a look so empty, that in her looking, he feels himself erased, the touch of his hand ethereal, the nights of his embrace gone. "Please, I have enough to consider, don't make more of my words than they were meant to be." He squeezes her arm. The suppleness of her flesh, its response to his touch, feels cold. For a brief moment, Asher imagines her as an apparition of the moonlight, and wonders if the nights that passed between them only existed in the dreamscape of his mind. He shakes her again, this time more forcibly. "Woman, stop this selfishness, I am not in the right mind at this moment."

Kokab sits heavily on the floor, her hands folded in her lap. "I cannot tonight, Asher."

Asher looks down at the top of her head. "You don't consider me," he says.

"Please let me be, Asher."

"For you, I am nothing but a distraction."

"Asher."

"So you don't have to think about how you have failed . . ."

"Asher, please . . ."

"As a woman."

Kokab throws her head back, her eyes clenched shut. In the silence of the room, Asher hears her breathing, short inhalations, short exhalations, like rapid, dry weeping. Asher kneels beside her. He touches Kokab's arm. She does not respond, again, to his touch. He flinches. "All day, when I am away from you, I am mad with longing," he says. "I cannot think to count. I lose words amidst sentences exchanged with clients. I make errors, simple errors at the scales, because my eyes do not see the thing before me, but are lost in the contemplation of you. All I can think of . . . you." Asher looks to Kokab to see if his words touch her. He yearns to pull her into his arms and bury his face in her hair. "Something must be born of this desire, no?"

"Layli," Kokab says.

"What?"

"My child. Her name is Layli. You have never asked. The child I have lost, my daughter . . . Her name is Layli." Kokab keeps her eyes closed. "I know what being a mother means, Asher, I know it well." Kokab wraps her arms about her own shoulders and buries her face in their fold.

Asher looks back out of the window. Black clouds cover the moon completely. The poplars by the garden walls sway in the wind.

"I miss smelling the musk of her when she rises from the damp of sleep," Kokab says. She bites her bottom lip to keep it from trembling. She sways gently back and forth. "I wake from sleep, sometimes, thinking that I have heard her voice, calling me." Kokab looks up at Asher. A long moment of silence stretches between them.

"If the only value of my whole life is in those moments that she slept in my arms," she says, "against my chest. If all that I have done was to soothe her, to hold her . . ." Kokab's voice breaks, she presses her closed fist against her lips, then bites her knuckles.

"And I don't know . . ." she says. "I don't know, now, when she startles from her sleep and calls for me . . . only the endlessness of the dark night greets her . . . I don't know . . . if she even calls for me any longer . . . if she is afraid and thinks that I have left her of my own will . . . that I have left her to the despair of night and that terrible man . . ." Kokab's voice trails off. She looks to the window, the light of the moon illuminates the rivers upon the earth of her face.

So old, Asher thinks, *she looks so old.* "Have I not made you happy?" he asks. He pulls her into his chest and holds her tightly.

"What joy can I feel, Asher?"

"Don't tell me you have not felt joy, Kokab, don't tell me that. I have seen you. I have held you."

Kokab struggles to pull out of his arms. "I am your prisoner, Asher, your slave. Should I feel joy in this life? Should I feel joy for these crumbs of bread you throw at me and believe to be enough to satisfy the hunger of my soul?"

Stunned, Asher releases her and looks at his arms in the blue light of the room, then looks at the woman sitting

before him as if seeing her for the first time. Suddenly, he
feels a revulsion, a bitterness in his mouth. All that he has
given her, all he has done for her. He rises to his feet. He
bends over and clutches her arm, then pulls her to her feet.
She stands before him and looks into his eyes.

"Enough. Enough self-pity," he says. He pushes her
against the window so that her face is pressed against the
glass. He stands behind her. "Enough ingratitude," he says
in her ear. He feels her shudder, but she does not move. He
pulls her closer to himself and bites the lobe of her ear. She
pulls away.

"Asher, you can't."

"Don't tell me I can't. Of course I can, it is my right."

"I am in the state of my impurity."

Asher stops. He steps back. He holds his forehead in his
hand, shaking his head. He looks at Kokab. Then he turns
and walks abruptly to the door.

"I will spend the next two weeks with Rakhel. When
you can, attend the miqveh. When you are clean, we will
try again."

He hears the sound of the trees, branches snapping in
the wind. He steps into the cold, cold dark without looking
back.

Rakhel does not need to turn to know who enters her room.
She knows the sound of the metal latch followed by the
firm step. She listens to his heavy breath, the rustle of the

qaba falling off his shoulders, the guttural sound of his throat as he raises his arms to lift the shirt over his head, the crumpling of cloth against the floor. She knows he stands behind her, naked in the moonlight, watching the mound she makes beneath the bedclothes. An eternity of waiting and he does not even announce his arrival with words. He simply pulls the blankets back and settles behind her.

She tries to even out her breath, to feign sleep, but she fears that he hears the thudding of her heart. He raises her dress shirt above her thighs and she feels his hands explore her flesh, the heat of his breath on her neck, the urgency of his want against her legs. He doesn't wait for her to speak, doesn't speak her name, gives her no time to cry against his chest, to demand an explanation for why he forgot her for so many nights. She weeps, silently, as he finishes, turns and lays on his back.

"I will sleep here for a while," he says.

Then, more silence until the soft snore begins in his throat. Only then does Rakhel allow herself to turn and look at him. She studies the outline of his face in the blue twilight. She leans over and smells the scent of the other woman on his skin. She brings her face closer to him, to find a trace of herself. She wants to reach with her fingertips and touch the flesh of the arm he folds beneath his head, but she hesitates, her hand midair, and brings it to her own face instead. She watches the rise and fall of his chest until her eyes close and she slips into a dream.

Mahboubeh stares at the ceiling of her bedroom, then turns to the clock on the bedside table. Rakhel won Asher back, once Asher realized that he would never beget children. But he needed a reason to divorce Kokab. And she gave him just that, the day she went to the wheat mill. Mahboubeh remembers that this was one of the stories that Rakhel liked to bring up, from time to time, even after so much time had passed, the day Kokab went to the wheat mill, a place no respectable woman would be seen, and Asher divorced her in order to save the family name from shame.

The minutes pass so slowly that time seems to unwind itself before her, at once present and the past. In this tangled darkness, Mahboubeh finally allows the ghosts to come and go as they please, loud with the urgency of their stories, begging her to give them voice, to explain, to her, to the audience of eternal silence, what happened once upon a time.

Kokab has not emerged from her room for many days. She no longer comes to the sofre for dinner. Rakhel watches from the courtyard as Fatimeh takes food to her. The old servant walks into the farthest room with a tray in her hands, then comes out quickly, muttering *Allah Akbar* to herself and rushing back toward the kitchen.

"Fatimeh, is everything all right?"

"Too much suffering, Rakhel Khanum. That poor

woman suffers too much. She is somewhere else, her body empty of spirit," Fatimeh says. She shakes her head and looks back in the direction of the room. "The look in her eyes makes the hair on my arms stand. It's no good. I know this by the white hair on my head. She's allowed too much sorrow to settle in her heart."

"Does she eat?" Rakhel asks.

"Eat? Like Imam Hussein in the desert of Karbala, poor woman. I go to take another tray and pick up the last with the food untouched. Not even a sip of water from the glass." And the old woman turns and walks away, shaking her head and wringing her hands.

Rakhel returns to her room and sits for a long while. The morning creeps toward afternoon, and Rakhel just sits quietly, looking at the motion of the shadows on the wall. But as the hour approaches for Asher's arrival from the caravansary, Rakhel begins to become more and more agitated. Finally, she jumps to her feet, throws open the door of her room, and runs toward the farthest room. After several minutes of waiting behind the door, Rakhel finally opens it and stands there, holding her breath. Kokab, who sits in a corner and rocks gently, stops, looks up at her and says, "You have finally come to visit me?" She invites Rakhel into the room with a motion of her hand. Rakhel takes a hesitant step, and closes the door quietly behind her. She waits with her back pressed against the door.

"What news do the blackbirds bring from the neighbor's garden?" Kokab asks.

"That you are no longer welcome here."

"Asher has sent you to tell me this?"

Rakhel remains silent.

"He does not need to, does he? It is clear that he is done with me."

Rakhel clenches her teeth and walks up to where Kokab sits on the floor. "You cannot stay here," she says. "You no longer have a place here. You are just a burden now. A sad reminder to Asher. Another mouth to feed. It is best if you go."

Kokab looks away, shakes her head sadly, and says, "Where can I go?"

Rakhel straightens her back and tilts her chin up. Her breathing is heavy. She must remain stern, authoritative, she reminds herself. She will not run, she tells herself, this is the time to act. "Perhaps you can kill yourself," she says.

Kokab watches her for a while, then says, "I want to live for my daughter, if there is a chance I may see her again . . ."

"Then return to your brothers' home," Rakhel says.

"They would wish me dead, rather than returned once more," Kokab says. She looks out of the window. "You are not cruel, Rakhel," she says. "You are a child, and desperate. You could have been my own daughter, trapped where you are, afraid of losing the little bit of earth G-d has allotted you."

Rakhel can no longer keep calm. She moves from foot to foot, at once trying to move closer to Kokab, then pulling back. Asher will be home soon. He will ask what business Rakhel had with Kokab. Perhaps Kokab will tell him what they said. And if he goes back to her, despite the fact that there will be no children . . . If he decides to return to her, even still . . .

"Will you go? Please?"

"I am not free to go as I please, Rakhel."

"You must give Asher reason to divorce you," Rakhel says. "Give him reason to send you back to your brothers' home. It doesn't have to be something big, just an act to give him an excuse, and save him face. Asher will be happier once you are gone. And my life will be better, too. And the family will not have this turmoil. And your brothers are blood to you, you have more a place in their home than here. And your daughter, maybe the day will come when you can see her. If you leave, maybe then everything will be fine. If you go, maybe everything will be fine, again." Rakhel does not look at Kokab as she speaks, but at her own hands, then the walls, then out the window, any other place, but Kokab. When she stops talking, she finally notices Kokab's eyes, soft with tears. Kokab shakes her head and sighs.

"So this is how we finally make one another's acquaintance?" Kokab says. "All this time, I wondered what we might say to one another, once alone."

Rakhel looks away. She does not respond, but she cannot keep her body still. Her hands fiddle with the hem of her skirt, her feet step back and forth. Her body refuses stillness, and so she starts to speak again, to quiet the rest of her self. "If you go to a public place. You don't need to do much else. You don't need to create a reason for going, or explain what you did. Just be seen there, alone, with no business. A place where only men go."

Kokab looks at Rakhel, bewildered. And then she laughs. "Is this how my life plays out?" she asks. "My qesmat written by the hand of a girl child?"

"The wheat mill. Will you go there?"

"Such a serious gamble, Rakhel. The consequences so irrevocable. And why the wheat mill, Rakhel, why the wheat mill to crush your rival?"

"Because no one will be able to think of any reason for why you have gone there, other than the worst reason."

"Of course. And if he kills me?"

"He won't."

"How do you know?"

"You have known him, too. He won't."

Kokab nods her head. She draws her knees into her chest and wraps her arms about them. She rocks gently, then places her cheek against the wall and closes her eyes. After a while she turns to look at Rakhel. She studies her for some time and finally says, "Don't look so worried, Rakhel. I'll go. There is no life for me here, but for you, there may be a chance."

Rakhel looks down at her own hands, which hang limply now, tired after their frantic dance. She feels so tired. Her body aches for sleep. She wants to fall to the floor, right before Kokab, draw her knees into her chest, and cry. Kokab reaches out and takes hold of Rakhel's hands in her own. With effort, she draws Rakhel into the fold of her arms.

Rakhel fights for a moment, then collapses into the embrace, burying her face against Kokab's chest, where she weeps and weeps. They sit thus for some time, Kokab cradling Rakhel until she is spent of crying, until she hiccups with sobs every so often, and then settles into a calm half-sleep. The afternoon advances. The shadows grow longer. The air cools. The muezzins begin to sing the evening azan.

"Go now," Kokab says. "Go before someone sees you here. I will leave for the mill in the morning."

Rakhel clutches Kokab's hand with both of her own. She brings them to her lips and holds them there.

"Go to your room, go prepare yourself for your husband," Kokab says. "Go, before he arrives. No one but you and I will ever know."

Rakhel releases Kokab's hands and wipes her face with her sleeve. She rises with haste, then turns to Kokab. They look into each other's eyes, speaking wordlessly, because there are no words, any longer, between them. Kokab nods her head. Rakhel looks down, then leaves.

Mahboubeh remembers another story about Asher, as a young man, before he married Rakhel. It happened that one day Asher decided to visit the farms in the outskirts of Kermanshah. Perhaps on a morning in late spring, a day much like this. Mahboubeh reaches down to pull from the earth the green vine that spreads, unruly, from the stalk of her trees to the walls, from there to the stems of her roses, then creeps through the dirt, and grows among the vines of her grapes.

On that day, mist rose from the mountains, the dew evaporated from the tips of the tall grass and wildflowers, the whole landscape appeared dreamlike. Asher rode his mule on the narrow path that went up the mountain. The path was full of small rocks the size of a man's fist.

The mule lost his footing, began to slide down the slope of that cliff and Asher jumped off the panicked animal, wound one hand tightly in the reins, grasped the harness with the other, dug his heels into the earth, threw the weight of his body back, and pulled with all his might.

Mahboubeh rises heavily from the ground. She looks at her hands. Dirt beneath her fingernails, in the creases of her skin. Blood, too. She has cut herself, in numerous places. She tries to remember when. She shakes her head and brushes her hands against her blouse. Her blouse is filthy with mud stains. She tries to remember when she changed it last. Surely it was clean this morning? She looks up at the sun. It must be noon, at least. Has she eaten? She can't remember. She is not hungry. Just thirsty. Very thirsty.

Asher pulled until he saved that mule, but he tore something in his groin with the strain of his effort. Mahboubeh turns on the garden hose, holds it with one hand, and cups her hand with the other. She splashes water onto her face, then drinks from her cupped hand. She drops the hose, and walks away, forgetting to turn the water off.

This is the story the women told when anyone asked why Asher was unable to beget children. Somehow, perhaps shortly after Kokab left, this story found its way into the mouths of all the merchants, the clerks, the maids. It was repeated in gardens and kitchens, whispered between prayers at the Sabbath services, told by women in the public baths, by men in the *zoor khane,* perhaps even reached the Kurds in the provinces. Generations later, this is the story they repeated, that Asher tried to save a poor, wretched beast, and his act of kindness cost him his progeny.

Mahboubeh walks toward her house slowly. "It was Asher Malacouti's kindness," she mutters to herself. "His mercy toward a dumb beast that cost him so dearly. And that is why, they said."

Ten

✦

Kokab *went where?" Zahra asks. The* chickens cluck and peck at the grain at her feet. She holds a handful and turns to look at Sadiqeh in the early morning light.

"To the mill," Sadiqeh repeats.

"To the mill? What on earth was she doing there?"

The chickens look at her hand expectantly. Zahra remembers to throw the grain and reaches into the bucket again without taking her eyes off of Sadiqeh.

"I heard it from Fatimeh myself. Zolekhah

sent her secretly to follow Kokab when she saw Kokab leave without asking permission to go. Fatimeh followed her clear to the edge of town, until she reached the mill."

"And Kokab went inside? What on earth for?"

"She stayed inside for more than an hour."

The chickens cluck and pace about the girls, waiting.

"Did anyone see her inside the mill?"

"Everybody saw her."

"How can they be sure?"

"She removed her ruband. And showed her face."

Zahra places the bucket down and brings her hands to her mouth. "She removed her hijab in front of all those men?"

The chickens scurry to the bucket, stretching their necks over the rim to reach the grain. They hop onto one another to find a place to stand. Sadiqeh shoos them away with her broom and picks up the bucket. She hands Zahra the broom and begins to throw the grain to the dirt ground.

"Does Asher know?"

"If he doesn't know, he will find out soon."

"Well, Rakhel may become the sogoli of her husband yet, once he finds out what her havoo has been doing behind his back."

Zahra sweeps absently. The chickens keep away from her broom. She stops and looks at Sadiqeh. "What will become of Kokab?" she asks.

The chickens cluck hungrily. "What will become of her?" Zahra asks, again.

The chickens tilt their heads up at Sadiqeh, who stands still, holding the bucket for a long, long time before she reaches in again and throws more grain to the earth for them to eat.

Zolekhah stands in the breezeway before Asher's study, holding the lantern. For a few years now, she feels the approach of the seasons in her bones. Winter stiffens her knees. She knows the approach of rain by the ache of her joints. *This is the body preparing to become one with the earth,* she thinks. She looks up to the fresco. Moses holds the stone tablets in his arms. Zolekhah shudders. *The correct course of action is clear,* she thinks to herself. She looks back to the painting of Moses. Here, the artist must have thought the greatest moment of illumination, Moses's hair wild from his days in the mountains of Zion, his eyes burning with truth. Yes, she tells herself again, truth is the correct course of action. She raps on the door to Asher's study. "Asher?" He does not respond. She knocks again, louder. She sees him from the window, sitting at his desk, facing the window looking out to the outer gardens. She waits a moment, then opens the door. "Son, why don't you answer?"

Asher turns to face her. "Sorry, Mother, I didn't hear you knock."

"I came to discuss a certain matter with you."

Zolekhah walks into the room. She looks at her son

sitting behind his desk, fingers absently moving the beads of the abacas in his lap back and forth, back and forth. "Asher, are you all right?"

Asher looks down. He shakes his head. A moment passes in silence.

"It does no good, son, to keep the pain in your heart. Tell me, tell your old mother what has you so heavy these past weeks."

"Mother . . ." Asher stops and presses the knuckles of one hand against his mouth. Then he removes his hand and looks to the ceiling. He draws in his breath sharply. "Mother, I am incapable of fathering a child."

"Is that all? Son, Kokab is not as young as she was, that is why. When a woman's age advances, it becomes more difficult for her to conceive."

"No, Mother. The problem is with me."

"Nonsense, of course."

Asher stands abruptly and walks to the window facing the courtyard. He presses his forehead against the window. Zolekhah walks to him. She places her hand on his shoulder. She looks out of the window, too. Her son's breath fogs the glass, so that the fountain is at once visible, then gone. "Mother, I am not man enough to . . ."

"Hush, son, hush."

"Please, Mother, let me speak the truth, at least between you and me."

"Don't say it, lest, G-d forbid, it comes to pass."

Asher turns to face his mother. "It has passed, Mother, it has already passed."

She takes his face in her hands. He lowers his face and she pulls him into her chest.

"Mother, I will never have a son."

"No, my dear, no, you mustn't say such things. You are simply anxious, that is all. It is not you, but her womb. Her womb is old. It is your bad luck, that's all. She is no good. We will find another woman."

Asher pulls away from his mother and wipes his eyes with the back of his hands. "What other woman, Mother? A third wife? And when she doesn't get pregnant? The whole town will speak of my failure. Though they will speak of it soon enough, regardless, as time passes and Kokab remains barren. The most common man will feel that he is more man than I am. And he is. He is more man." Asher holds his forehead in his hands. He clenches his jaw. "These farmers in our villages, blessed with so many children. Small, ragged little boys, scabs on their knees, sticks in their hands, running behind their goats and sheep in the fields. And these fathers . . . their eyes shine when their sons speak to me. They grow taller, these peasant men. They grow before my eyes. Their shoulders straighten, the tiredness of their muscles melts away, the burden of their loads lightens. They become so, so . . . proud."

"Soon, my dear, soon you will be proud, too."

"It won't be long before every peasant at the caravansary knows, every bastard walking in the street. All of them whispering behind my back at the synagogue, the women with pity in their eyes. And Kokab, here, in that room, to remind me . . . that I am no man at all."

Zolekhah turns from Asher and draws in her breath. "Son, I came here to talk with you about Kokab."

"It is no use, Mother, I know the fault is with me."

"No, Asher, something else." She straightens her back and turns to face him. "She went to the wheat mill. She left without telling anyone. After she left, Rakhel came to my room and said she feared for Kokab, that the woman might do something to harm herself. I told Fatimeh to hurry and follow Kokab. She walked all the way to the mill. Fatimeh saw her enter. She waited over an hour in the street before Kokab came back out."

"Why . . . what business . . ." Asher stops, the color drains from his face. He turns wildly and with one move of his hand, wipes all the objects of his desk onto the floor. The abacas breaks, the beads bounce and roll across the rug. "She has done what? Gone where?"

"Son, please—"

"Already taking my shame to the street? Already cuck-olding me before the public?"

"Asher, I have not asked her, yet, why she went. I wanted you to ask her, to give her an opportunity to—"

"To deceive me? To make a further mockery of me?"

"Asher, we don't know why she went."

Asher grabs a vase from the shelf and smashes it against

the ground. "Perhaps to have her grains ground to flour, Mother?" He picks up another vase and hurls it against the wall. "To have it sacked and stored for the cold winter months?" He takes the book of his accounts, pulls off the cover, tears and crumples handfuls of pages with fury. "I should have known. I saw it, I've seen it in her eyes." He throws the book at the window and groans, holding his head.

Ibrahim rushes into the room. "What's happened?" he asks, a wide-eyed Khorsheed peering from behind him.

"Go from here," Asher says. "Let me be. Let me be before I drag that whore here by her hair and kill her with my bare hands."

Zolekhah tries to embrace Asher again, to calm him, but he pushes her away.

"What's happening? What's happened here?" Rakhel asks. She pushes Khorsheed aside to look into the room. Kokab walks in after her and stands behind Rakhel.

"You," Asher says and points his finger. "You shameless harlot!"

Asher lunges toward her and Rakhel covers her face. He pushes past her and grabs Kokab's arm, pulling her into the room.

"Wait, Asher," Kokab says.

"Shut up, you whore, you wretched whore." Asher shakes her violently. "Look at me, look me in the eye."

Kokab looks at him, her chin firm, her eyes steady.

"No shame? Not a bit of shame? You deceive me and then look me in the eye without a hint of shame?" Asher pushes her away from him, then slaps her hard across the face. Kokab's head jerks and her lip splits. Blood trickles down her face and neck. She touches her lip, looks at the blood on her fingertips, then looks back at Asher.

"Enough, Asher," she says.

"Enough? I'll say when it is enough, woman."

Asher grabs her throat with one hand. Kokab clutches at his hand. He takes hold of her wrists with his other hand and whispers close to her face, "Tell me, I leave you for a few nights and the hunger gets you, like a filthy cat in heat, huh? You go searching, huh? Or did you find your way out before, too?"

Kokab struggles to free herself. Ibrahim grabs Asher's shoulders. Asher releases Kokab and turns with rage to face his brother. "Let me do what I must do!" he says.

"Brother, please, wait a moment, allow her to speak."

"Move out of my way so I can break her neck."

"Mother, get the women out of here," Ibrahim says. "Brother, please, do not act in anger."

Zolekhah starts pushing Khorsheed and Rakhel out of the room. She turns to grab Kokab's hand and pull her along, but Kokab remains still.

"Come, child, come before he does something terrible. Come, there will be time for explanations, later."

Kokab looks at Rakhel, who still stands by the door, trembling. Rakhel looks up and their eyes meet. Rakhel turns to walk out but then stops and walks back toward Kokab.

"After all my husband has done for you," she says to Kokab. Rakhel looks to Asher, then turns and spits in Kokab's face. She leaves, without looking back.

Asher glares at Kokab. "You," he says, "you are an animal. At least an animal follows its appetites so it can procreate. You are lower than an animal."

"Son, allow her a moment to tell us what happened," Zolekhah says.

"It is between me and this whore I have taken as a wife," Asher says. Then he spits in Kokab's face, too. Kokab closes her eyes and moves her head back, as if he has struck her again. She opens her eyes and looks at him.

"Asher, you have known me."

"Yes. Yes, I have known you. A fool I am to think that an animal might go against its own nature. You are inclined to such baseness."

"Asher, you have known me."

"Deception and lies. A fool you have made of me. Was I not man enough for you, either? Or is one man not enough for you?"

Asher pushes Kokab to the floor. He stands over her and clutches a handful of her hair. He pulls back his fist to hit her. Kokab looks up at him.

"The truth is before you, Asher, you choose to be deceived," Kokab says.

Asher stops for a second, frozen by her words. He looks at her open mouth, blood still flowing from her lip. "I choose to be deceived?" he asks. Then he hits her with his closed fist. "I choose to be deceived?" he asks again, and hits her once more.

"Please, Asher, she is a woman, after all," Ibrahim says. He places his hand on Asher's shoulder and Asher turns wildly to face him.

"Honor is a thing to be protected," Asher hisses. "At all costs, honor is a thing to be protected."

Zolekhah runs to help lift Kokab off of the floor. Kokab pushes her hands away and raises herself to her arms. She gets up slowly off the floor and stands before Asher. Zolekhah tries to pull her away from her son's fury. "Come, woman, come before he kills you," she says.

"I have been murdered, already. A thousand times," Kokab says. Kokab turns and walks away slowly, holding onto the wall for support. She stands for a moment and turns to look at Asher, then walks in the direction of her room.

Asher pushes past Ibrahim to chase after her. He stops when he reaches the door. He paces back and forth wildly for a moment, then sits heavily on the floor and buries his face in the palms of his hands.

Fatimeh rises for the morning azan. She unrolls her prayer rug and unwraps the black prayer stone from its embroidered kerchief. She rubs the cold stone between her fingers. The writing on the stone is worn smooth. She places it on the mat and stands so that her heart faces Ka' bah. She raises her arms and brings her hands beside her face, palms turned out to the world. She moves through the motions of her prayer, but her thoughts drift back to the night before. She had stood by the courtyard pool long after she finished rinsing the plates and watched Asher, Ibrahim, and Zolekhah through the window of the sitting room from the dark. She listened to pieces of sentences that rose above their tense whispers. Asher was to leave early this morning, accompanied by Ibrahim, and stay in the village of Tofangchi for several days.

Fatimeh kneels and prostrates. She keeps seeing Kokab's swollen eyes. Blue at first, after a few days, bruised well into black. She tries to forget the look in those eyes, to focus on her prayer instead, but her mind keeps roaming back to Kokab, sitting in the dark of her room, silent, motionless. Fatimeh sits back on her heels and beseeches the Lord for mercy. She sits for several moments in thought, and then rises heavily from her rug. Perhaps Allah will forgive an old woman her indolence, and accept her prayers, imperfect as they are. She peers cautiously out of the window of her small room beside the kitchen. The men must have already left.

Fatimeh sees Zolekhah come out of Kokab's room and close the door behind her with one hand while she pulls her black chador over her hair with the other. Fatimeh walks quickly out of her room to the pool under the guise of having to do her ablutions, just in time to walk across Zolekhah's path.

"Zolekhah Khanum," she says, "what are you doing up at Allah's hour, even before the roosters have had a chance to blink open their eyes? Everything is fine? You are not sick? The girls are not sick? Kokab, something become of her?"

"Fatimeh, can you fetch the mule?"

"Certainly, Zolekhah Khanum, but you don't mean to go outdoors at this hour?"

"Better this hour when the town and their wagging tongues are still silent."

"What is the urgency, Zolekhah Khanum? You know I've been a servant to this family since my girlhood. I have given my life to this family. For what reason beneath heaven do you need to leave the house at this hour for?"

"I'm returning Kokab to her brothers' home."

Fatimeh looks at Zolekhah, her back already bent with the years, the whites of her roots a stark contrast to the midnight of her dyed hair. "Zolekhah Khanum, this is the task of her husband," she says.

"Asher has left for an urgent business matter in one of the villages. I will take her back." Zolekhah looks at Fatimeh, a firm determination in her eyes, but the corners of her lips betray her. Fatimeh sighs deeply and wipes her hands with her chador.

"But Kokab's brothers, they will seek revenge to save face."

"I will take her back."

"But what if they harm you?"

"They will not harm an old mother."

"What plans does Allah have for us wretched women?" Fatimeh says. She turns to walk to the stables. Her legs feel heavier this morning, and when she reaches the stables, the mule refuses to budge. She takes the broom resting by the stable door and slaps his hind quarters from a good distance, but the beast senses her own fears, and Fatimeh does not begrudge the creature his hesitation.

"Pshh, psshh," she says, "Ya Allah, you have a delivery to make."

The mule snorts and tosses its head. Then he steps forward and Fatimeh takes hold of the rope about his neck and drags him toward the courtyard. She leaves him standing by the pool and rushes to her own room to put on her street chador and ruband. She comes out to find Zolekhah waiting beside the mule.

"Zolekhah Khanum, I'm coming with you."

"It's not necessary, Fatimeh, their house is not so far and my task won't take so long."

"No, Zolekhah Khanum, it is better for three women to travel at this hour than two, and better that you have a Muslim with you. No knowing what her brothers will do."

The two women wait in silence by the pool. They hear a door open, and both turn expectantly in the direction of Kokab's room. She emerges already covered in black, her face veiled, clutching the bundle she arrived with. She walks a few steps and stops, then crumples to the floor, a cascade of black fabric flowing about her. Both Fatimeh and Zolekhah run in her direction, but by the time they reach her, she rises again, supporting herself with the wall, and picks up her bundle once more.

"Child, you are weak. Let me carry your burden," Fatimeh says.

Kokab drops the bundle and keeps walking slowly toward the pool. Zolekhah and Fatimeh stand close beside her, one at each side, ready to catch her again if she falls, but neither of them dare to touch her. The mule looks nervously over his shoulder at the approach of the three black figures, sniffing the air for danger. Kokab stops at the pool.

"Do you need help, child?" Fatimeh asks.

Kokab shakes her head no and mounts the mule. Fatimeh hands her the bundle of her possessions.

"Daughter, you have not eaten for days. Let me fetch you a piece of bread for your journey," Fatimeh says.

Zolekhah holds on to Fatimeh's arm and shakes her head. Kokab does not respond. The women leave the courtyard wordlessly and head toward the heavy wooden doors that open into the street.

When Fatimeh pushes the door open into the street, the morning sun already casts shadows from behind the buildings. She peers her head out and looks in both directions. Not a single soul walks the tight street of the Jewish mahalleh. She turns to Zolekhah and motions with her hand. Zolekhah steps forward, holding the rope about the mule's neck. She pulls the beast and its sad burden out. Fatimeh runs behind them and shuts the door. She looks once to heaven and says, "Bism' Allah."

They walk but two steps when they hear the creek of another door and a man, prayer tallith about his neck, steps out into the street. Then, it seems as if all the doors in the neighborhood open at once. Men appear, merchants set out their wares, street peddlers shift their bundles from one shoulder to another and amidst all of them, the two women walk with their heads down, pulling along the mule, a woman in black riding atop it. The men stop to watch the women pass. They do not step forward to ask what business the women have on the street at so early an hour, where their menfolk are, if they need help. The two old women carry such a somber air in their passage that the men simply stop in their tracks for a moment and watch them go by, silently. Then, they shake their own heads and resume their business.

Fatimeh and Zolekhah wind their way through the mahalleh. By this time, the street crowds with men and boys, who step aside to watch the women pass. They finally arrive at the home that belongs to Kokab's brothers and Fatimeh reaches out to the brass knocker on the right that announces the arrival of a woman. She knocks once and steps back from the door. They wait a moment. Then Zolekhah steps forward and knocks three times rapidly, but the door opens before she pulls her hand away. A young woman stands before them, wrapped in her indoor chador.

"Good morning," she says. She looks at Fatimeh and Zolekhah, then at the figure atop the mule.

Zolekhah reaches and unfastens the ruband covering her own face and looks the young woman in the eyes. "I am

Zolekhah Malacouti, the mother of Asher Malacouti. I have come to return this woman to her home for she has shamed my son and ruined our family name," she says.

The woman takes a step back, her mouth open. Then she turns and runs, crying, "Agha joon, come quickly!"

Fatimeh realizes that the doors to the homes around them have opened and heads peek out. Women come to stand in their doorways, men stop to watch. She turns to motion for Zolekhah to enter and the two walk across the threshold, pulling along the mule. A man comes running out from the andaruni of the home, another man closely at his heels. Zolekhah stands firmly, staring at the two men, though Fatimeh notices a tremor in her hands. Fatimeh unfastens her own ruband and stands beside Zolekhah. Kokab moans once and slumps forward, but before she falls, one of the men runs and catches her in his arms.

"Stand up," he says. He pulls the ruband off Kokab's face. "Stand up."

He shakes her until she stands on her feet. Kokab buries her face in her hands. He pulls her hands away from her face and looks at her. Kokab's eyes are sunken in and black. Her face seems unnaturally white in the sunlight and her lips tremble, but she keeps her eyes on the man who stares furiously at her. He raises his hand and slaps her hard across the face.

"Go," he says.

Kokab turns to walk in the direction of the andaruni. She stumbles to the ground, too weak to rise. He follows quickly behind her and kicks her once. She remains still for several moments.

"Allah help you, daughter," Fatimeh whispers. "May He forgive you. May He take pity upon you."

Kokab rises from the ground with great effort. She stands, finally, and the morning sun shines brilliantly around her. The birds sing madly from treetops. She looks at Fatimeh and Zolekhah. "Even in this," Kokab says. "Even in this, a spectacular grace." Then, she turns and walks until she disappears in the andaruni of her brothers' home.

"So Asher had his way with our sister and wasn't even man enough to bring her back himself when he was done?" the taller man says. He brings his face close to Zolekhah's face, his mouth tight, the veins in his temple bulging. "Well, then, his old mother will have to be the man and take back our response."

He raises his fist and hits Zolekhah in the jaw. The old woman topples backward and falls to the ground. Fatimeh screams and runs to help her up.

"Don't hit the goyim," the other man says. "Best not to have the police involved."

"No, my business is only with Asher. And since he cannot be here, his representative will have to do."

He approaches Zolekhah and kicks her hard in the stomach. Fatimeh screams again and rises to pull the man away. With one hand, the man pushes her against the wall and kicks Zolekhah again, who lays on the ground, moaning, gasping for breath.

"You'll kill her!" Fatimeh says. "I'll call for help, step back! Help! Ya Abolfazl! He's killed her! Help!"

The man steps forward and with one deft move, grabs Zolekhah's arm and lifts her off the ground. He pulls her toward the mule and like a sack of corn, throws her on top of the beast. Then he takes hold of the rope and walks toward Fatimeh.

"Here," he says, handing her the rope. "Take the old bitch to that *na'mard* and tell him we look forward to his visit, unless he has an aunt he wants to send instead."

Fatimeh takes the rope hurriedly and heads toward the street. When she sees the neighbors peering in, she hurries back over to Zolekhah, who labors to breathe, and pulls the woman's chador over her face so that no one recognizes her. Then she fastens her own ruband in place and pulls the mule out of the yard. The crowd parts slightly to allow her passage, then surrounds them to watch as Fatimeh mutters prayers and pulls the rope to get the mule to move.

The crowd disperses slowly and the old servant pulls the mule away by its rope. Silence. Mahboubeh slaps her hands against the hard wood surface of the kitchen table, palms open. She does this again and again. Then she turns to look out of the window.

Silence. The air is still. Outside, dusk settles.

All the windows remain shut. Mahboubeh cannot remember if she just closed them to turn in for the night, or if she never opened them at all, and just sat in this stagnant air from sunrise through sunset, listening to nothing, nothing at all.

Silence. She cannot remember any other stories of Kokab after this. Her history is limited to the scandal of her divorce, the fact that her husband takes her daughter and never allows her to see her child again, that Kokab becomes Asher's second wife for a brief period, and is divorced for going to the wheat mill. From there, Kokab disappears from the family stories.

Mahboubeh rises with effort from the chair and walks to the kitchen window. She opens it, then opens all the living room windows. Only a small report about Kokab's daughter. When she came of age, the father recognized in her the tendencies of her mother. He immediately sent her to a remote village for nine months, during the time of which no one heard from her or saw her.

Mahboubeh walks to her room and eases herself onto her bed. She remembers when Kokab's daughter returned to Kermanshah. Mahboubeh was a young child then, but she remembers the women talking of her. Her father has subdued her, they all said, no trace of her mother left.

"What have they done to my mother!" Asher roars.

Zolekhah hears him through the open window from her bed. She tries to raise her head a bit, to look out the window, then winces in pain and lays her head back down.

"What have I allowed to happen?" he says.

Zolekhah starts when she hears the sound of shattering glass. The movement cuts her breath short.

"Brother, brother, please . . ." she hears Ibrahim say. She struggles to raise herself in her bed, again. She must reach him, to soothe him. Somehow, she must get out of bed, and walk to his study, to calm him.

"Bring a length of rope and let me end my days. Let me die a coward's death. Bring rope and let me die, to save me, least from facing this shame. My mother beaten, like a mule. My brother beaten, like a woman. And the woman I took as wife, gave my name to, spreading her legs open for any man, any man."

Zolekhah manages to sit in bed, but when she makes the effort to stand, the movement causes a sharp jag of pain throughout her body. She groans, quietly, and holds on to the bedclothes until it passes.

"Brother, please, calm a moment, calm down a moment," Ibrahim says.

"I must go to the brothers' home, I must kill them, or they me, but it cannot stand like this. No. It cannot stand like this."

"Brother, end it here. Enough tragedy has passed for both households."

"Why, Ibrahim? Why must I beget shame, only?"

Through the open window, Zolekhah hears Asher weeping. Choked sobs.

"Please, brother," she hears Ibrahim says. "You are like a father to me, please, I cannot see you thus."

"I am no man, brother. I am no man to be called father."

Zolekhah cries in her bed. She looks to the ceiling. Lord, she prays, please find some way to end my child's suffering, some mercy to end his longing. She hears a soft knock at the door. Zolekhah raises her hand with effort and wipes her face. "Come in," she says.

Khorsheed walks into the room carrying Yousseff. "Naneh Zolekhah, I came to keep you company," she says.

Zolekhah watches the girl's face as Khorsheed sits with effort and places Yousseff onto her lap. Khorsheed's cheeks seem flushed and she keeps the child at a distance from her stomach. She looks up, and the two women's eyes meet.

"How long?" Zolekhah asks.

"Three, maybe four months."

"Why didn't you say?" Zolekhah says.

"There was so much trouble in the household," Khorsheed says. She places the squirming child on the rug and holds her stomach with both hands. Yousseff crawls to the bed.

"Does Ibrahim know?" Zolekhah asks.

"He hasn't noticed yet."

"He will be happy."

"He's too upset about Asher's situation."

Zolekhah considers the girl's words. At this time, for Ibrahim to father another child . . . Neither of her sons will take this news with joy. "You are right," Zolekhah says. "Wait a bit longer for this sorrow to pass."

"When will it pass, Naneh Zolekhah?" Khorsheed asks. "Asher will always want for a child. He will only become more and more unhappy. And my husband, too. Rather than taking joy in his own son, all Ibrahim can do is speak of his brother's suffering. It has come to this, that he does not even take his son in his lap, without some look of guilt coming across his face."

Zolekhah feels Yousseff's little hands holding on to the blankets, trying to use the cloth to pull himself up. Zolekhah looks at Khorsheed and another surge of grief overwhelms her. *Not so long ago,* she thinks, *this one was a child herself and here she sits, anxious over her growing belly, tired already, and so soon?*

"Tired," Zolekhah whispers. She closes her eyes. "Leave, daughter, so I can sleep."

Khorsheed rises to leave. Zolekhah listens to the sound of Khorsheed strain with effort to lift Yousseff, then the slow shuffle of her feet. When Khorsheed leaves the room, Zolekhah allows herself to cry. "Rain down your mercy upon us, Lord," she says. "Show the grace of Your mercy."

Eleven

❧

I brahim hears the sound of the horse in the
courtyard. *Asher is home,* he thinks. The
women will tell him the rabbi is here. He
will not come out of his study until the old man
leaves. Ibrahim turns his attention back to the old
rabbi.

"I don't know," Ibrahim says. "I don't know."

"It is a mitzvah, son. An act the Lord will smile
upon."

"What about the child's mother?" Ibrahim
asks.

"You say she is due with another?"

"Yes."

"Ibrahim, G-d rewards a righteous deed. Tenfold. You will have more children. Many, many more children, G-d willing. Think upon a rich man. What is a loaf of bread to him?"

"A child is not a loaf of bread."

"A child is sustenance for the soul, as bread is nourishment for the body."

"And my brother . . ." Ibrahim looks out of the window at Asher's study. Each evening, his brother walks in through the street door and retreats to his study. He no longer places records on the gramophone and opens the window to the gardens. The dusks pass in silence. If Asher does come to dinner, he eats without a word. If he speaks, it is brief. Business. Formalities.

"Asher is starving," Ibrahim says. He shakes his head and raps his knuckles absently against the wall. He stops and looks at the rabbi a moment. The rabbi meets his gaze, then nods his head.

"What will be the loss for you, son? And what will be his gain?" he asks.

"Yes . . ."

"The Lord still speaks to us, Ibrahim, still as loud as he did when he spoke to our forefathers. It is only the din and racket of this world, our entanglement in greed and selfishness, that distract us from hearing the melody of His voice."

Ibrahim clasps his hands in his lap to keep them still. He draws in his breath and holds it, then exhales heavily.

"And there comes a time when He asks of us to be men. To act with courage, selflessly, to sacrifice for the good of others."

Ibrahim rises from the ground and paces the room. He stops before the window and looks at the empty courtyard, at the shut window of Asher's study, at the empty room that stands farthest down the breezeway. He leans his body against the window and presses his face against the cool of the glass. From somewhere in the courtyard, he thinks he hears his wife singing.

"Ibrahim?"

"Here I am," Ibrahim answers. "Here I am." He holds his face a moment, then looks at the old man.

"I will. It is clear that I must, there is no other way," Ibrahim says.

The rabbi smiles and leans over to pat Ibrahim's knee. Then, he searches for his walking stick and struggles to rise from the chair. Ibrahim takes hold of the rabbi's elbow to help him. The rabbi stares for a moment at the light coming through the curtains. He nods his head.

"G-d will reward you, son, for this sacrifice. You will have many children, and they, too, will have many children. Your lineage will feel the tide of the Lord's blessing for forty generations for such a noble deed."

Ibrahim opens the door and helps the old man out into the sunlight of the late afternoon. The ground is littered with gold, brittle leaves.

"Forty generations, Ibrahim, forty generations will re-

ceive tenfold blessings for this one act of giving," the rabbi
says as they walk slowly toward the street.

It must have been in autumn when Ibrahim made the decision. Mahboubeh sits in the grass, looking at the trees. The
trees naked then, not like this. Not green, like now. She
looks at the leaves shimmering in the sunlight. The garden
must have been empty of roses. Mahboubeh inhales deeply.
She can smell roses. She is here, now. In a garden bloom full
of roses. She hears him talking. Insisting. At first, quietly.
But then, his voice becomes louder and she sees Ibrahim
standing in the room, and Khorsheed listening. Exhausted
from a night of tending to Yousseff, Khorsheed fails to understand Ibrahim's meaning at first. Then, when the words
become solid and heavy, when they become a menacing
presence, moving toward her and her baby like the shadow
of a predatory animal, Khorsheed lifts the baby to her breast
and Yousseff, sensing the danger through the cadence of her
heartbeat, the quickness of her breath, the deft motion of
her movements, startles and begins to wail. Khorsheed runs
toward the door, recognizes that it leads nowhere, stops and
turns, staring wildly about the room for a corner, a place
where the words will not advance any further, where they
will be forgotten and she can tend to the screaming baby.

"Do you feel a falter in your own heart, Father?" Mahboubeh asks out loud, sitting on the earth of her garden,
beneath a cloudless blue sky.

He does not hear her. The room has become very clear for him, filled with the desperate motion of his young wife, clutching his son to her breast, pushing herself against a wall, bending over the child, burying it in the folds of her arm, beneath the black curtain of her hair, hushing, hushing him. Ibrahim stands silent, in awe of what he has done.

Ibrahim begins a series of logical sentences, constructed as though they are bricks in the hands of a blind man trying to piece together his recollection of a house.

"Yousseff will not be far from you," he says.

"You will see him every minute of the day" and "You must take into consideration Asher's sorrow and need. What does he have in this world if he does not have a child?" and "We will have more sons, we will be rich with children, this is an act G-d smiles upon."

He speaks these words to Khorsheed, not daring to step closer to where she kneels in the corner, rocking back and forth, murmuring to her baby. She looks up at him, his hands in a plaintive gesture, in the middle of the room, standing like an uncertain child, waiting to hear the pronouncement of consequences in the aftermath of the shattering. Her look, however, is unfamiliar to him. He has known this woman, his wife, the intimacies of her being, and now, he can't bring himself to use her name, nor place a hand on her shoulder. In the silence of this bafflement, he resolves to move forward with what he does know, that a decision has been made, that there was a promise to his brother and that he must prove himself a man and keep his word.

Khorsheed grasps her child firmer to her body and hisses the accusation, "You want to tear my son from my breast?"

Ibrahim, before becoming stone, trembles a moment, the fine hairs of his skin extending to feel the subtle motions of air that follow her utterance. But this is only a moment, when he listens to her and the depth of the wound he feels proves too much to bear, so, instead, he hardens his body and becomes ethereal, a torrent of words, no longer beseeching. Now, severe, he takes a step forward and she lifts herself off the floor and runs about the room frantically, the baby screaming, and Khorsheed, not finding anywhere to go, sinks to the floor, again, and weeps. She lifts her wild eyes, her face framed by her hair, and she screams for Ibrahim's damnation. She pleads with heaven to turn the day black, to hide her from the mercilessness of her fate.

Zolekhah hears her from her room. She sits up with effort in her bed, her eyes moist, her legs lead, and mutters soft prayers. Fatimeh, too, hears the girl's cries and raises her eyes to the soot-colored ceiling of the kitchen to plead for G-d's mercy. Asher sits pensive in his study, behind his desk, staring at nothing, thinking of nothing.

Khorsheed stands outside of Rakhel's room, her feet bare. Her face unwashed. Her clothes soiled. Dark hollows encircle Khorsheed's eyes. Her long hair knots at the ends. She shifts her weight from one foot to another. She waited that morning until Asher and Ibrahim left for the caravansary before leaving her room. Then, she walked across the court-yard, up the marble stairs, beneath the painting of Moses in his wicker basket, past the sitting room to the door that led to Rakhel's room. The curtains have been drawn tightly for days and the door is always closed. She waits a moment outside and listens. She hears Rakhel talk softly. Khorsheed strains and hears the baby, a low mewing sound. She knocks. Something rustles in the room, but no answer. She knocks a little louder, shifting her weight from one foot to another. She breaks into a cold sweat and pounds on the door. The latch lifts and Rakhel's face appears in the doorway, blink-ing at the sunlight.

"It's time for Yousseff to nurse," Khorsheed says. She pushes past Rakhel into the dim room. Khorsheed looks around the room, her eyes adjusting to the light, until she sees Yousseff beside the bed.

"Why is he on the floor? There is a draft from beneath the door."

"I placed him for a moment so he wouldn't roll off the bed. I don't think he's hungry just yet," Rakhel says. "He hasn't started to cry."

"You shouldn't wait for him to start to cry before bringing him to me. Then he becomes too fussy and can't suckle properly."

Khorsheed picks Yousseff up and begins undressing him frantically. "You've bundled him too warm. He can't breathe like this."

She lifts him to her face and buries her nose in his hair. She closes her eyes and inhales deeply, then presses her lips against his chest, his shoulders, his arms.

"I was afraid he'd catch a cold."

"You don't know what you are doing."

Khorsheed hastily touches the child's clothes. She holds Yousseff up and looks at his legs. "He's wet himself," Khorsheed says.

"I just changed him an hour or so ago."

"The urine has burned his skin."

Khorsheed puts him on the rug and grabs the pitcher of water on the low table by the bed. She pours water from the pitcher onto a corner of her skirt and dabs Yousseff's legs.

"Khorsheed, you don't have to do that, I have clean rags."

"He's been in his own urine long enough for me to wait a while longer for you to find your clean rags."

"They're right here."

Rakhel extends a rag and Khorsheed grabs it from her. Rakhel squats next to Khorsheed. "Let me do it."

"No."

Khorsheed lifts Yousseff to her breast. He turns his head away and Khorsheed turns his face back to her breast, pressing her nipple against his closed lips. Yousseff turns his head again.

"I don't think he's hungry," Rakhel says.

"You only brought him to me once in the middle of the night. He hasn't had milk for hours. He must be starving."

"He hasn't cried."

"Perhaps he is too weak to cry."

"Khorsheed, I won't let him starve. I can sense when he needs milk."

"Not the way I can sense it. My body feels the pull of his hunger."

Khorsheed continues to struggle with the baby, inserting her index finger into his mouth to pry it open a bit, then pushing her nipple against his barely open lips. Yousseff begins to cry. Khorsheed tries to place her breast into his open mouth, but he struggles to turn his face.

"Khorsheed, you're going to suffocate him, he's turning red," Rakhel says.

Khorsheed continues pressing her breast into the wailing child's mouth.

"Khorsheed, stop, he isn't hungry." Rakhel reaches out her arms to take Yousseff from Khorsheed.

Khorsheed looks up with a hot anger in her eyes. "Don't touch my baby, you're upsetting him."

"I'm upsetting him? You are about to kill him. He's crying so hard he can't breathe and you keep smothering him with your breast."

"What do you know about how to care for a baby?"

"I know enough to know when someone is about to kill one. Give him to me, let me calm him."

"What are you two doing, again, making such a racket?" Zolekhah stands in the doorway, then limps into the room and takes Yousseff from Khorsheed. She cradles the baby in the crook of her arm and bounces him gently. "My sons' brides are the talk of the town. Everyone hears this war the two of you make daily."

"I came to feed my son."

"Yousseff doesn't want to feed," Rakhel says.

"What do you know about what he wants and doesn't want? You are not his mother."

"Enough," Zolekhah says. "Enough of the two of you. Khorsheed, we decided that when Yousseff is hungry, Rakhel will come fetch you."

"I don't want to leave my son alone with her."

"Khorsheed," Zolekhah said, "we'll discuss things with Ibrahim and Asher when they get back home. For now, allow Rakhel to care for Yousseff and tend to yourself. Have you forgotten the one growing in your womb?"

"There is a reason G-d didn't see her fit to have a child," Khorsheed says.

Rakhel looks to the ground.

"It will be difficult to adjust to this, Khorsheed," Zolekhah says, "but you must think about the unborn child you carry. This rage is not good for that innocent baby, or this one. When the other one arrives, you will be more than happy to have this one off your hands. The two of you will raise Yousseff together and you will have enough time for the new one. Now leave the room and go tend to yourself. You have neglected your body for too long. G-d forbid, you may harm the baby in your womb."

Zolekhah hands Yousseff to Rakhel. Khorsheed

watches Rakhel holding Yousseff. Rakhel rocks him in the cradle of her arms, clicking her tongue to calm him. Khorsheed narrows her eyes and clenches her teeth. "You are the djinn!" Khorsheed says.

Rakhel looks up from Yousseff and takes a step back. Khorsheed steps closer, pointing her finger an inch away from Rakhel's face.

"Like all those stories you yourself told me! You snatched my baby! You stole my boy!"

"His own father gave him to my husband. I did not snatch him from you at all," Rakhel says.

"That's enough, Khorsheed," Zolekhah says.

"All this time, trying to persuade me of this and that, when you've been watching my child with your envious eyes, plotting and waiting!"

"Khorsheed, that's enough I said," Zolekhah says.

Khorsheed grabs Rakhel's braided hair. "Tell the truth!" she says. "You made this happen! Because of you, they took my baby!"

Rakhel bends her body over Yousseff and tries to free herself from Khorsheed's grasp. The baby starts to cry. Rakhel frees one hand and hits Khorsheed in the stomach. Khorsheed's breath catches and she falls backward. For a moment, there is a frozen silence. Khorsheed remains sitting on the rug, gasping for air.

"See what the two of you have done?" Zolekhah says. "See what the two of you have become? Both of you, like the unnatural mother who stands before King Solomon."

Khorsheed heaves to catch her breath and weeps. "She . . . She is Al. She has taken my Yousseff and she tries to kill the one I carry, too. She will be the death of me!"

Zolekhah struggles to lift Khorsheed off the floor and guides her out. "Come," she says. "Come and pray that the one in your womb still is."

Khorsheed cries in Zolekhah's arms and holds her stomach with both hands. At the door, Zolekhah turns to reprimand Rakhel, but the words catch in her throat. She looks at Rakhel, who cradles Yousseff and coos softly, her face wet with tears.

Mahboubeh does not want to imagine Khorsheed's death, but it is night, and dark, and nothing crowds her mind so that the thought of death creeps in. She rises from her bed and walks to the window of her room, to gaze at the moon. She tries to picture her mother sitting at an open window, gazing at the moon, before they took her Yousseff, before sorrow killed her, when Khorsheed could still dream.

It is a stolen moment in the silence of the night. Khorsheed rests in her bed and turns her attention to the movement of her own body. She feels the shift of her bones and the stretch of her sinews. She looks at the expansion of the flesh of her taut belly and waits for the slight flutter that surprises her each time so that she has to put her hand to her stomach. Only in this darkness does Khorsheed feel that her body, and the fruit of this body, belongs to her alone. She waits each night for her husband to fall asleep, for the lanterns in the household to dim, for the voices in the yard to become whispers, the concerns of the day finally settled by the chirping of crickets. Then, she rises from the bedding beside Ibrahim, removes her undergarments, walks to the window, pushes it open, and sits down to bathe in the cool night air that floods the room and carries in its ebb and flow the scent of orange blossoms in full bloom. Khorsheed sits long enough to watch for the moon to rise, for her to disrobe from behind the cloak of dark clouds, to bare her spectacular fullness in the still black pool of the sky.

It isn't the familiarity of the moon that draws Khorsheed, though. It is the urgency of the orange tree, the desire to fruit so heavy that all living things become drunk with it. She knows this desire, and knows that it is a good thing, and so she breathes deeply and imagines the scent reaching into the small universe of her womb and carrying with it the promise that the loneliness of that existence will end in a paradise where the air itself is of honey.

Mahboubeh wants to reach out the tips of her fingers and touch Khorsheed's cheek. "*Paradise* is a Farsi word, Mother," Mahboubeh whispers. "It means an enclosed space, a garden set aside from the surrounding wilderness."

Mahboubeh sees the seasons pass that orange tree in rapid succession and then, in one simultaneous instant, she sees Rakhel praying, two girls in the rain, Asher lost in the thought of Kokab singing, Khorsheed birthing, Ibrahim bleeding, locusts. A tall mountain. A man waiting beneath the mute heavens, beside a pile of wood, a firestone and the knife in his hand. And then, another birth.

And snow.

"Paradise," Mahboubeh repeats, and tries to picture the courtyard in moonlight, again, the orange tree laden with blossoms. But

Bare feet. Blue. Cracked.

"Paradise," Mahboubeh repeats. She clenches her eyes shut, to shut out the darkness, to keep out the sound of

A door left ajar. Creaking in the wind.

The wailing. Wind.

Khorsheed stands barefoot in the snow. She does not feel the cold, nor does she hear the wailing of the infant in her room. Her eyes are black, swollen. Her eyes. Her eyes are vacant. Hollow.

How did my mother die, Father?

Your mother died from the complications of womanhood.

How did my mother die, Dada?

Khorsheed degh marg shod. From sorrow. Your father killed her, with sorrow.

Milk drips from her breasts. Her thin blouse frozen against her skin. Her nose is running. Her mouth slightly parted. Her breath escapes in small clouds. She stares across the courtyard at the marble steps she is forbidden to ascend, at the door she is forbidden to open.

I just want to smell him. Once more. Just once. Please. Just allow me to hold him to my chest and bury my face in his hair, to

put my lips to the crown of his head. Just his scent. Please. Then just a dirty shirt of his, a shirt he wore? Allow me that? Allow me to hold that to my face?

No.

There is nothing left.

What about your newborn child? Your daughter, Mahboubeh?

There is nothing left.

The trees above her cross their naked limbs. Jagged black lines bar and break a white sky. Her dark hair tangled. Bramble where vines were. Stems and thorns. Broken lips. The howl of the wind. Hers, too. Khorsheed howls, too. She calls him and her voice fills the skies with blackbirds. In the silence that follows, the snow falls.

Youseff, she cries again.

Zolekhah rushes from her room, throws a blanket over Khorsheed's shoulders. Khorsheed's knees give. She falls onto the snow-covered ground. She wails and plunges her hands into the snow, clutches handfuls of it and smashes it against her face. The old woman tries to lift her from the ground. She tries to pull her in the direction of the room where the hungry infant cries for milk, for the heat of her mother's arms. Fatimeh appears beside Zolekhah. They weep and struggle to raise the girl from the frozen earth. The two women finally lift Khorsheed to her feet and drag her back to the room. Across the courtyard, behind the curtains, Rakhel sobs silently, too, and holds Yousseff to her chest.

Twelve

❧

In her garden, the rosebushes have grown thick stemmed, their thorns large, their perfume bewildering. The fig tree leans heavily against the wooden crutch Mahboubeh placed against its trunk for support. The nasturtiums teem in shades of orange. Mint invades any open space. And that vine that grows unruly has bloomed. Blue flowers. It creeps up her trees, crawls along their branches. It strangles rosebushes, tangles itself among the grapes, weaves through the honeysuckle. It allows a uniformity to Mahboubeh's days, the shocking blue of its delicate flowers at dawn. The fuchsia of their wilted deaths by late noon. And time, itself, has become lawless, too, shifting in a moment from afternoon shadows and birdsong to the song of crickets, frogs, the coyotes in the hills yelping, cars on the dark, distant highway without much passing in between.

"There once was a garden, in another home, in Kermanshah," Mahboubeh says out loud. The sun, round and big and red, sets behind the hills. The skies turn orange and pink. Crows become black markings. The house grows unfamiliar. Mahboubeh turns and walks toward it. "That home, in that other place, belonged to two brothers, who would sacrifice anything for one another."

Mahboubeh turns to look, once more, at her garden in the failing light of day. Gladiolus pierce out of the naked earth any which way. The pomegranates, never harvested, hang from the branches, half eaten by crows, empty combs, dry shells. Mahboubeh stops before a rosebush. She brings her face close and inhales deeply, searching in the scent for something she has lost. She closes her eyes and says, "The eldest brother married a woman named Rakhel . . ."

Mahboubeh opens her eyes and notices that the vine, with its beautiful, delicate blooms, holds captive this rosebush, too. She raises her finger to begin untangling the vine from the stalk, but then stops. She looks at her garden, teeming with life. Time passes.

"And when Rakhel failed to conceive, the eldest brother took a second wife, and when she too failed to conceive, the younger brother gave his own son, as a gift, to his brother. And that child's mother . . ." Mahboubeh stops to watch the garden recede into the long shadows of evening. She turns toward the house, its windows dark. "That child's mother . . . she died from too much sorrow. She died from the complications of womanhood."

Mahboubeh stands in the middle of the grass, and wonders if the house before her might be her home. A gentle breeze passes, and the leaves on the trees rustle with their own music, and the flowers shake pollen onto their petals, and the grass ripples beneath her feet. Mahboubeh closes her eyes, and allows that unseen hand to touch her skin, to brush the hair away from her face.

Acknowledgments

I am indebted to Megan Lynch, Leigh Feldman, Elizabeth George, Robert Eversz, Hedgebrook and Amy Wheeler, PEN, Ron Rosenbaum, Dr. Loretta Kane, Shirin Galili, Dr. Haleh Massey, Christopher Massey, the elders of my family, my aunt, my husband, and above all, my mother, who teaches me courage by the way she lives.

About the Author

PARNAZ FOROUTAN lives in Los Angeles with her husband and two daughters.